I0741134

Also by Ross Cavins

Follow The Money
(a collection of interconnected short stories)

BARRY VS THE APOCALYPSE

by

Ross Cavins

For my family.

There is nothing more important.

Except maybe bacon.

Published by RCG Publishing – RCGPublishing.com

Trade Paperback ISBN-10: 0-9827720-6-8
Trade Paperback ISBN-13: 978-0-9827720-6-5
Hardcover ISBN-10: 0-9827720-5-X
Hardcover ISBN-13: 978-0-9827720-5-8

Special Thanks to ...

Christine Ryan … for believing in Barry from the very first words. You were the first to read Barry, and I'm glad you convinced me you shouldn't be the last.

Jennifer Pearce … for being my first-level editor and beta reader, and for being one of my bestest friends. You tell me like it is, whether I want to hear it or not. Everyone needs someone like you in their lives.

Steven Huntley … for being a long-time friend and supporter.

Andrew Busbee … for believing in my project beyond any of my expectations. What part of the country are you moving to next?

Bobby G, aka Chuck Craddock, aka Davenport Harrison Ridgley, III … for being my soundboard, my comic collaborator, my number one fan, and my best friend.

Beth (Jaden) Terrell … for being the best editor ever. You understand what I'm trying to do, and that's so awesome.

Ray Peden ... for providing frank editing and story advice. And lots of encouragement.

Killer Nashville ... for having the Claymore Awards so Barry could become a 2014 Finalist. That honor solidified my confidence.

And everyone else I've not mentioned because I've only got so much room before this starts looking ridiculous.

Chapter 1

Istrolled through the beer aisle of the Exxon down the street from my apartment, contemplating the tasty merits of Black Dog versus Dirty Monk. Gordon appeared at my side so quickly I almost dropped both bottles. "Damn it, Gordy. You've got to stop—"

"We have a problem up front," he snapped.

"I do too." I licked my lips and closed the store's cooler door, holding up the open beer in my left hand. "Black Dog has this fruity undercurrent, but"—I displayed the open beer in my right hand—"Dirty Monk tastes fuller, kinda like a pale ale, but with some hoppy attitude."

Gordon's face hardened. "I'm talking about a real problem."

"I am too. I mean, on one hand you got the fruity wheat theme—"

"Barry."

"What." I turned to him. "They out of Altoids again?"

"No, Barry, I'm serious. The place is getting held up."

I shrugged. "So? We can wait back here a bit. It'll give me time to make up my mind."

"Barry."

"Gordy." I mocked his seriousness with a whining tone. "You know how I get if my beer doesn't match my food just right. Besides, I'm retired. Remember?" I turned up the bottle of Dirty Monk and gulped a few swallows. Smacked my lips again.

"He's got a gun on Rafi." Rafi is the teenage kid of the owner.

I studied the logo of the Dirty Monk bottle—a twelfth-century monk with a goofy smile grasping a stein of sloshing beer—and said, "Is Rafi doing anything stupid, like not giving the guy money?"

"Barry." Gordon lowered his voice. "Go do something."

I stared down at him.

"Now," he urged.

If Gordon had a Superpower, it would be the Super-Stare. Every time he whips it out, his eyes get bulgy and weird behind those goldfish bowls he calls glasses. A hard look from Gordon has the power to make the recipient feel very, very uncomfortable.

"Fine," I sighed, raising my eyebrows. "Dirty Monk it is." I opened the cooler and plucked out the rest of the Dirty Monk six-pack, saying, "You know, that stare of yours would be more sinister if you got your left eye to twitch a little."

Gordon didn't say a word, just stared, twitchless.

"You know, I'm not really dressed for this," I said as I picked at the pizza stains on my shirt, and when I looked up again, Gordon's left eye was twitching.

Attaboy.

I took a deep breath and exhaled. "Alright, alright. Back off. I'm going." I shook my head and lumbered up front, saying to Gordon, "You know, if there was a union for guys like me, you'd be in trouble. I'd want benefits and a regular work-week. And I'd want actual pay."

Gordon didn't respond.

The gunman wore black jeans and a black shirt with a white pinstripe NY Yankees ball cap. He even wore a black ski mask. How cliché.

Ski-Mask waved his gun around while Rafi stuffed cash from the register into a brown paper bag. I moseyed up to the counter and set my five-pack of Dirty Monks down; the gunman jumped back in surprise.

And before you ask, no, I can't do invisible. But I can do stealthy, even for a guy my size.

Ski-Mask jerked his gun toward me and told me to back up. I ignored him and said to Rafi, "Your pops needs to get a better selection of pizzas. Get some with cheese in the crust. Or garlic."

Ski-Mask's eyes grew big, and he croaked at me to back up again. I noticed he'd taken a few steps back himself. I downed the rest of the open Black Dog in one swallow, then belched like only a three hundred pound man can. I waved at Rafi with the empty bottle and set it down. "How much I owe you? A six-pack of Dirty Monks plus this empty Black Dog."

Ski-Mask shook his gun hand again, saying, "Hey, I'm talking to you!"

I turned toward him like I'd just seen him for the first time. "Little hot for all that, ain't it?"

The guy looked from me to Rafi to me again. He waved the gun, wilder this time, as if it would put more force behind his hollow words. "I said get back! And put your hands up!"

I pursed my lips and shook my head, then took another gulp from the open Dirty Monk. I said to Rafi, "People getting ruder and ruder all the time, you know? Don't people have manners any more?" I finished the beer and snatched a new one from the carton, leveled a gaze at Ski-Mask, and said in the hardest voice in my arsenal, "You got three seconds to leave, pal."

The gunman steadied himself and flicked his gaze to Rafi, then back to me.

"One."

The gunman's eyes drew close together.

"Two."

He pointed his gun at my chest, still shaking a little.

"Three."

The guy braced himself, and I shrugged, saying, "Don't say I didn't warn you."

While I was talking I'd cocked my thumb under the cap of the beer I held in my hand. I moved my hand a tad left, then right, winked at the gunman, and with the speed of a jackal—I hear jackals are supposed to be fast—I flicked my thumb upward with a slight twist.

The cap dislodged from the top of the bottle with a loud pop and struck Ski-Mask's gun hand with such force the weapon flew out. It flipped and twisted over his head, then clattered to the floor behind him.

Ski-Mask backed up a step, shaking his hand in pain, his eyes wild and uneven. Two of his fingers had already started bleeding where the cap had sliced through his skin. I took a quick swig of the beer and grabbed another bottle from the carton.

"You want another?" I asked, pointing the bottle at him, my thumb cocked and ready.

The guy took another step back and bumped his foot against the gun. He hesitated, eyes skirting downward for a brief second.

I said, "One."

His eyes widened and when I flinched myself at him, he turned and flattened himself against the one double door that was still locked. He recovered and flew out the unlocked door without looking behind him.

Gordon materialized out of nowhere and scooted up beside me. "Little dramatic don't you think?" he muttered.

I took another swallow of beer, then shook my head. "Nah. You know what would've been cool? I've always wanted to stick my finger in the gun barrel, but he wasn't close enough." I drank some more beer.

"Besides, I missed my target. I was aiming for his forehead."

Turning to Rafi, I said, "How much for the beer?"

"And Cheez-Its," Gordon added, dropping the box he was holding on the counter.

Rafi, his eyes still bulging from their sockets, shook his head after a moment.

"Nothing?" I said with mild amazement.

Rafi shook his head again, still speechless.

I saluted him with my beer. "You're alright, kid." I grabbed the carton and nodded at the rolls of lottery tickets to his left. "Since you're buying, how about a few of those Lucky Leprechauns? Say ... three of them?"

"Barry." Gordon shot his Super-Stare at me as he plucked a twenty from his wallet.

"Fine. How about a Snickers? Can I get one of those?" I grabbed the king-size candy bar before Gordon could say anything, then nodded at Rafi and started for the door. I stopped and turned back. "Hey. I was serious about those pizzas, kid. Tell your old man he needs to get a better selection. Cheesy crust that rises or something."

We headed out, and as I opened the door of my beat-up Pontiac Aztek, Gordon asked, "So why not use your Super-Speed or something to disarm him?"

I wedged myself behind the steering wheel. "That's overdone, don't you think?"

"But you could have missed with that little bottle cap stunt. Rafi could have been shot."

I started the truck and turned toward him. "I've been practicing."

Gordon shook his head. "That's not what I mean. You know as well as I do that you're not perfect—"

"Gordy." I tsk-tsked and shifted into reverse. "Gimme some credit, buddy. I scanned his gun before we ever got up front. He had as many bullets in that thing as Barney Fife on a good day."

"Which episode?"

I didn't answer.

Gordon clicked his seatbelt together. "Even so, do you have to be such a show off?"

I shrugged. "I was bored." A pause. "And besides, I really have been practicing."

I pulled out of the parking lot toward home as Gordon flicked on the radio. He said, "One of these days, Barry, your boredom is going to get somebody hurt." He turned his head toward me. "Again."

I didn't dignify him with a retort.

Chapter 2

I stopped at the gate to my apartment complex and punched in my code: 0-0-7. I know what you're thinking: a Superhero who lives in an apartment? Why not a mansion or a fancy sky loft in the big city?

Let me tell you a little secret they never share in the comics or movies.

Superheroes can't create money out of thin air, and since I've never had a real job—they're too demanding and I don't take direction well—I think I'm doing pretty good. After all, it's a luxury apartment. We have a gate and everything.

I parked and nudged Gordon, nodding toward the pool. "Christine's lying out again."

Christine Ryan is a soccer mom who lives with her two kids on the third floor in my building, and she's as deserving of the MILF designation as any woman on the CW network.

Gordon acted as if he'd not heard me and started down the sidewalk.

I caught him. "You're just jealous I can see her naked and you can't."

Gordon inserted his key in my lock and stopped, turning toward me.

"But you're doing it without her permission. Don't you feel dirty every time you use your X-Ray-Vision on a woman?"

I thought about it. "Yeah, I feel dirty. That's why I do it. How much fun would it be if it didn't make me feel dirty? I might as well spy on my fridge."

He opened the door. "You've got a problem."

"I call it a gift." I followed him inside. "Come on. You can't tell me if you had X-Ray-Vision, you wouldn't use it to look at people naked."

Gordon threw his keys on the kitchen counter. "I wouldn't."

"Right," I said, plopping on the couch and reaching for the remote. "I call total bullshit on that one. I don't care how nerdy and righteous you are, you'd look at titties and dude's packages every chance you got." I opened another beer. "Hell, even gay dudes and straight chicks would look at titties. Titties rule the world."

Gordon shook his head. "You are so vulgar."

I tipped the beer up and found a rerun of *House* on TV. "Your point?"

Little Man chose this moment to traipse into the room, *mrow* in my general direction, and hop up on the opposite end of the couch. He threw one of his back legs high in the air and showed off his agility by licking his privates.

Gordon sat in the easy chair next to the couch with a Diet Mountain Dew in his hand. "My point is that you should be doing something important, not drinking beer and watching trashy TV shows all day."

I glanced at him. "*House* is not trashy TV."

"You know what I mean."

"I watch movies, too."

Gordon gave me the Super-Stare again. He's good at that.

"What?" I said. "You think I should camp out at some bank and foil robbers all day? They got guards for that. How are those guys gonna pay their rent if I put them out of a job?"

"You know what I mean. You're wasting all your—"

"Yeah, well, Gordy, they're mine to waste. We've been over this before and nothing's changed. If I don't feel like saving every damsel in distress, I don't have to. This ain't Hollywood, and my life's not a screenplay tied up in a pretty bundle with the heroes wearing white and the villains in black." I paused. "Okay, except for that guy today."

I swigged some beer and continued, "The world is a muddled mess, buddy, and I'm perfectly happy living in the gray areas with everyone else."

Little Man lowered his leg, mewed his agreement, then started licking his left front paw.

Gordon sipped on his Dew, and a commercial for insurance popped on the screen. I glanced at the wall to my left and scanned. "Ooh, Christine just stood up. She's toweling off. And now she's turning this way ..."

I sat up. "Dude, she's shaved. I mean, she's as smooth as—"

"Do you have to give me a play-by-play all the time?"

I threw my hands up, spilling some beer. "Fine. Whatever. First you accuse me of never sharing, and when I do, you get huffy."

Gordon's mobile rang.

"Who is it?" I asked.

"Kimberly."

Kimmy Moser is Gordon's twin sister. She's tall, sexy, and a true redhead—carpets, drapes, the whole shebang. She's also a Homeland Security spook and about the only other living soul who knows my Superhero secret. If there was one woman in this world I could have on a deserted island with me, it would be her.

I watched House bitch out an intern while I tuned my Super-Hearing into Gordon's conversation.

"Gordon," Kimmy said. "I need help."

"What is it?"

"Andrew's disappeared."

Andrew Busbee is Kimmy's Homeland spook partner. He's the field agent half of the duo.

"What do you mean, disappeared?" Gordon asked.

"He didn't check in at his designated time."

"How long's it been?"

Kimmy paused. "Eighteen hours."

"It may be nothing," Gordon said. Gordon always likes to smooth things over, keep everyone calm. That's what therapists like him get paid to do. "He's missed check-ins before."

"I'm worried."

Gordon paused. "What's the agency doing about it?"

Kimmy sniffled. "Nothing. They say it hasn't been long enough to try an extraction."

Now House was fighting with his hottie boss, the chick who played the call girl in West Wing. She showed as much cleavage playing a hospital administrator as she did playing a hooker. If only my X-Ray-Vision could work on the TV.

Gordon took a breath and continued, "So what makes you think this is more than just him being late? He's been late before. Like that time last year when he dropped his phone into the toilet. You know when you're undercover, things come up, and you can't always check in when you're supposed to."

"Gordon, Andrew's transmitter isn't active."

Gordon stiffened. "It could've run out of battery power."

"You know he wouldn't let that happen."

Gordon remained silent, his eyes flickering toward me. I stared at the TV, drinking my beer. House was berating a fat patient about his lifestyle choices.

Gordon finally said, "So ... you want me to ..."

"Could you please?"

Gordon paused. "You can ask him yourself; he's been listening the whole time."

I looked over at Gordon. "Have not."

"Have too."

He began the Super-Stare, and I said, "How'd you know?"

"You've been nursing your beer instead of guzzling."

I said to my beer, "Snitch." Then to Gordon and his phone, I said, "I'm retired. You guys always seem to forget that."

Gordon shook his head. "Retirement indicates an actual profession." He put his phone to his ear. "How soon can you be here?"

A knock came at the door, and I shook my head. "Stupid question."

Kimmy already had the door open before Gordon yelled for her to come in.

I turned back to the TV and said, "The answer's still no."

"Come on, Barry," Kimmy said. She waltzed in wearing a gray business skirt and white silk camisole.

"I already got plans."

"Please?" She stood in front of me now, blocking the TV screen. House was in the middle of telling off some police officers who thought they had a constitutional right to be in the emergency room.

"Can't," I said. "There an *NCIS* marathon on in half an hour."

"Pretty please?" She leaned over now, displaying her creamy cleavage for my perusal. All the X-Ray-Vision in the world can't compare with the seductive quality of professionally supported cleavage. My insides quivered.

Even Little Man sat up and looked at her.

"You think that'll work on me?" I said. "You're just using me, and I know it."

"And yet still," Kimmy continued, licking her lips. "You can't resist me."

I squirmed in place. "You remember I can see it all whenever I want, right?"

"Yes, but I know how to make you very uncomfortable." She squeezed her cleavage together.

I glanced at Gordon. "You're just going to let her do that to me?"

Gordon shrugged and pretended he wasn't enjoying my discomfort.

Kimmy ran a finger down her neck to the top of her half-exposed breasts.

"Stop!" I felt like I'd been holding my breath. It was bad enough she was Gordon's twin sister—that alone made her forbidden fruit—but to be that hot and seductive at the same time was cruel and unusual punishment. There's laws against that.

She sat beside me and slapped my knee. "I knew you'd see it my way."

Little Man curled up to her, and I grunted, positioning my hands to cover my lap. This was slightly embarrassing.

Gordon leaned forward in his chair. "So where is Andrew supposed to be?"

Kimmy turned toward Gordon, hesitating. "It's classified."

Gordon raised his eyebrows.

Kimmy exhaled. "Sorry, occupational hazard. He'd gone off-book investigating some kind of terrorist group based out of Burlington."

"Burlington? As in North Carolina?" I said. "Now you're messing with me."

Burlington is a little factory town just down the highway from Greensboro, where I currently live. Greensboro is known for very little other than hosting the ACC tournament. I like it that way. I've lived in big cities—New York, Chicago, and Los Angeles—and between you and me, it got real tiring, real quick. There was always someone who needed saving, and that's not my game any more. The hours of a Superhero are long and thankless, and the pay sucks.

"Yes, Burlington," Kimmy repeated.

"Burlington's barely got a Walmart," I said. "And you're telling me they've got terrorists? What are they against, outlet malls? They gonna blow up the J. Crew?"

"I'm serious," Kimmy said, her eyes tearing up. "He wouldn't tell me much yet, but from what I've been able to glean, it's a major terrorist organization with cells all over the nation, maybe the world. And Burlington's their hub."

"Does my smartphone even work there?" I said.

"Kimmy," Gordon broke in. "What kind of intel do you have on the group? There's got to be some kind of paper trail Andrew was following."

She said, "I've looked everywhere at the office."

"You look at home?" I said before I could stop myself. Having gotten their attention, I continued, "If he was doing this on the down-low, he probably kept his documentation at home. He would if it was a TV show."

Gordon tried the Super-Stare, but I was ready, deflecting it with my Air-Of-Indifference.

"What?" I said. "I'm helping. You wanted my help, didn't you? Even House knows you always search the home for clues, and he's not even a cop."

Kimmy said, "Andrew wondered how far up it went. He said there were some powerful players." She paused. "I got the feeling he didn't trust anyone at HQ. He said he couldn't report anything until he found out more."

"You think they got a mole in Homeland Security?" Gordon asked.

I erupted in a laugh. "Come on. This ain't Hollywood, Gordy. It's Burlington. They don't even have a good strip joint, and you think they got a terrorist organization big enough to have Homeland Security spies?"

"Barry—" Gordon began.

"I'm sorry." I threw my hands up. "I'm having trouble buying it."

Kimmy placed her hand on my knee. "Will you at least come help search his place?" She batted her dazzling green eyes at me, and my stomach fluttered.

Well, not exactly my stomach, but you get the idea.

Chapter 3

Andrew lived in a small house north of the airport. Three bedrooms, two baths, fenced-in back yard with a little goldfish pond. Azaleas out front, sidewalk to the front door, double garage. Multi-colored brick.

"He rent or own?" I asked.

"I don't know," Kimmy said. She frowned. "How would that help?"

I shrugged and trudged up the sidewalk. "It'd help me know how much he makes."

Kimmy unlocked the front door, and we walked inside. Andrew must have been raking in the bucks, because he wasn't home and the air conditioner was on full blast. It was the middle of summer, but this was ridiculous. I found the thermostat in the hall and raised it to seventy-six.

"What are you doing?" Kimmy asked.

"Saving your partner a little dough."

She gave me one of those nasty looks I've helped her perfect.

"What?" I said, giving my best nasty face back. "You want him to come home to a four hundred dollar electric bill, that's on you." I punched sixty-eight back in the thermostat. "He got a safe?"

Kimmy was looking at the calendar stuck on the fridge. "I don't know. Can't you do your little thing and see?" She wiggled her fingers at me.

"I'm not Barbara Eden." Which reminded me, Nick at Nite was supposed to run some sort of *I Dream of Jeannie* marathon next week. I didn't want to miss that.

Gordon patted my gut. "You're definitely not Barbara Eden. I'd hate to see you in a sheer halter." He ducked away before I could thump him in the ear.

"You know what I mean," Kimmy said. "Can't you X-Ray the place and see if he's got a safe?"

"Well, yeah. But it's generally a lot easier if somebody just tells me where it is."

I strolled into the living room and did my thing. I reached under the couch cushions. "These yours?" I twirled a pair of red thong panties and grinned at Kimmy.

She reached out, and I jerked them back. "Silky, stretchy. Same style as the black pair you're wearing right now." Kimmy jumped and snatched the panties from my outstretched arm, stuffed them in her pants, and shot me the evil eye.

"You see a safe or not?" she snapped.

I scooted down the hall to Andrew's bedroom. King-size bed set that looked like Rooms To Go had just moved it in. No clothes on the floor, not much personal junk on the furniture, a digital alarm clock with extra-large red numbers.

The room was disgustingly neat, just like everywhere else in the house.

I scanned the room. No safe.

Not even any porn hidden in a crumpled bag in the back of the closet. Maybe I could plant some gay porn and convince Kimmy the error of her ways?

She snapped me out of my thoughts by appearing at my side and asking if I'd found anything. I thought about mentioning the dresser drawer of panties and bras, but I doubted I'd get the rise out of her I wanted.

"No," I said.

I scanned the guest room next. It was even more sterile than the master bedroom. More semi-tasteful furniture, some mass-produced art on the walls, a neatly made-up bed. Nothing hidden anywhere.

This guy was no fun at all.

The office was next. Cheap desk with a Dell computer, pressboard credenza with a few books and knick-knacks, more bland art on the walls. Gordon was already sitting at the desk trying to work some magic on the computer.

Gordon was the smartest nerd I knew back in high school. I never failed when I cheated off him. X-Ray-Vision was the best Superpower a teenage boy could have. But amazingly, when people are asked what Superpower they'd choose over any other, they usually answer, "Flying."

Sure. I get that. It sounds cool. But people see you flying all over the place and a lot of questions have to be answered. Trust me. And if you're not careful, the government would cart you off somewhere remote and begin sticking probes in places you'd rather not have them.

No, sir. X-Ray-Vision is the way to go. That's the one power that's indispensable. Besides the obvious pro of seeing any chick naked, you can do all sorts of useful things: cheat on tests, win at cards, find lost keys, etc.

If knowledge is power, X-Ray-Vision is the key ring to knowledge. Or something like that.

I scanned the whole room and found nothing out of the ordinary. Paid bills, checkbook, office supplies. Normal stuff.

"What's the computer telling you?" I asked Gordon.

Gordon frowned. "I can't get beyond the password."

I glanced at Kimmy, and she shook her head no. Then she fidgeted. "Try 'poohbear.'"

I almost threw up a little in my mouth. "Pooh bear?" I asked.

She nodded. "One word, all lowercase."

Gordon typed it in and clucked. "It worked," he said, sitting up straighter.

I rolled my eyes and shot Kimmy a sideways glance she didn't return. She crowded behind her brother to look over his shoulder, and I left them with the boring geek work and trudged back to the kitchen. I pulled a Heineken out of the fridge, plopped onto the couch, and grabbed the remote. Andrew had HBO and one of my favorite movies of all time was on: *Back to the Future*.

Now there's a Superpower to have. Time Travel. What I wouldn't give for the ability to go back and forth through time. The stock market would be child's play. One leisurely day at the races and a man could retire in style.

I had just gotten to the part where Marty was being called Calvin Klein by his future mother—classic movie writing—when Kimmy strode into the living room.

"What are you doing?" she asked.

I was on my third beer and had demolished an entire bag of Cool Ranch Doritos. "Watching one of the best cinematic masterpieces ever made." I turned my beer up and gulped.

Kimmy looked like she'd just caught me watching *Debbie Does Dallas*. "Why aren't you still searching?" she barked, her arms rigid beside her.

I raised an eyebrow. "I take it Gordy's not getting much from the computer?"

She took my beer away, and I guessed the answer was "negatory."

"What?" I said. "I've scanned everywhere, but to be honest, there's not much here. You sure Andrew actually lives in this place? The dryer doesn't even have lint."

Kimmy threw her hands up. "There's got to be something." She slumped into the chair opposite me, eyes reddening.

I felt sorry for her. I really did. Andrew, I couldn't care less about. Just another spook on Uncle Sam's payroll bending laws for what he thought were the right reasons. But Kimmy really liked the guy—I still couldn't figure out why—and I hated to see her in anguish.

"Think hard," I told her. "He didn't mention anything out of the ordinary in the last few days?"

She shook her head.

"When's the last time you were together?"

"Tuesday night. We ate sushi at Asahi's, then watched a movie on TV."

"What did you watch?"

She frowned at me.

"Fine. When was the last time he said anything about the terrorist group?"

She thought for a second, her forehead crinkling into little creases. "That same night, right before the movie started. We'd just gotten back from dinner and changed clothes. We sat on the couch, and he told me he had a lead from one of his sources."

"He mention a name?"

"No."

"Not even a code name?" These government types love their code names.

She shook her head. "He did say it was a new source in Burlington."

"Hey." Something had just occurred to me. "Can't you dump his phone records or something? Maybe find out his last few calls? Trace the phone and see if it's on and where it's located?"

"Homeland can do that, but they won't yet. I already tried."

I scrunched my face and nodded at her. "Don't you know some guy in the nerd division you could shake those things at and get him to do it?"

Kimmy smiled. "He's by the book. And he's gay."

"So take him some pink curtains or something. Or better yet, take Gordy with you."

"I thought you were a little more progressive than that. Pink curtains?"

I shrugged. "You get my drift."

Gordon entered the living room. "You might be his type, Barry."

Kimmy laughed. "Yeah. Beer gut, mullet, and pizza breath. Lyle would never speak to me again." She glanced at me. "Sorry, I'm sure you're somebody's type, but no gay guy I know would go for you in a million years. Superpowers or not."

Now I got to say, that hurt. I mean, I brush my teeth regularly and take a shower every day. Some guys can't even say that.

I took the abuse while Gordon told Kimmy he couldn't find anything on the computer. Kimmy shrank in her chair with that lost puppy look, and I wanted to do something to inflate her back up.

I said, "What if I knew someone shady who could look up the phone stuff for you?"

Kimmy smiled and the twinkle returned to her eyes. She usually frowned on the gray areas of my life, but I guess when it benefited her, she was okay with it.

Chapter 4

Hannah Diggins was a chick I'd busted way back for stealing identities and the credit limits that accompanied them. I only cared because she'd hacked into my own accounts. I don't have any credit to speak of, but she'd gotten my internet shut off while I was enjoying a particularly brazen webcam show from a very bendy Russian with huge boobs and an accent right out of James Bond.

I took that personally.

Hannah could do things with computers Gordon only salivated about. The thing with Hannah was her caffeine and sugar intake. No matter when you called on her, she acted like she'd just downed a pot of coffee and a box of Twinkies. She's thin and short and pretty in a tomboy kick-your-ass kind of way.

Hannah's paranoid about talking on the phone so the three of us hopped in the Aztek and drove twenty minutes to Kernersville. She had a small home at the end of a cul-de-sac. She liked her privacy.

Thirty seconds after we knocked, the door opened and Hannah regarded us with an air of contempt. She wore a ratty t-shirt and running shorts too big for her.

"What do you want?" she said.

"That's a real friendly hello," I replied.

"You didn't call first."

"I figured you'd take off if I did." Did I say she was paranoid about phones? In actuality, she's paranoid about *me* on the phone.

"I would have." She turned and retreated into her house.

I followed her. Gordon and Kimmy trudged behind, unsure if they were welcome. Hannah hadn't acknowledged them. As we entered the dark hallway, I said, "You need to mow your lawn."

"There's a push mower out back. Help yourself."

Hannah's attitude almost made her sexy.

She disappeared into her office, what the builders of the house had meant to be the master bedroom. The office was filled with equipment from floor to ceiling. Racks of computers and monitors and lighted gadgets. I think Gordon got a boner.

Hannah asked what I wanted again.

"This any way to treat an old friend?" I threw my hands up.

"Friend? Friends tell you Happy Birthday. Friends send you Christmas cards. Friends hold your hand when you get sick, offer to make you chicken noodle soup, and run to the store for you when you're out of toilet paper." She glared up at me.

Did I mention when I busted Hannah and didn't turn her in to the cops, she developed a crush on me? Yep, she wanted her some Barry loving. But I have a few rules about women I date: they have to weigh more than my left leg, they need to be tall enough I don't pull a muscle going in for a kiss, and they need to be able to handle the Barry-Meister being on top.

These rules already assume the prerequisite of looking like a girl (and actually having girl parts—that incident in New Orleans will never be repeated again).

I sank into one of her rolly chairs. "Hannah, did I turn you in to the

Feds when I caught you?"

She did that glaring thing again.

"What?" I said. "I didn't rat you out, did I?"

"No," she finally admitted, swiveling in her chair to face one of her monitors. "So what do you need from me?"

"It's important," I told her.

"It always is. Like that time you wanted me to build a box so you'd get free porn over the satellite." She turned to me with an eyebrow cocked. "That one was so life-threatening you wouldn't let me pee until I finished it."

"And that was some quality work. Box is still going strong. There's an old-school Linda Lovelace marathon coming on later this week—"

"What do you want, Barry? I was kind of in the middle of something here." She motioned to the screen where a bunch of program windows were open, half of them displaying computer code, the other half showing numbers that were continuously updating. Every once in a while, the computer dinged and an entry highlighted itself.

I pointed to Kimmy and Gordon. "This is—"

"Don't care," Hannah interrupted without taking her eyes off me. "What do you want?"

I half-grinned and looked at Kimmy.

Kimmy cleared her throat, and Hannah slowly focused on her, face still impassive. "I'm looking for someone," Kimmy said. "He's disappeared, and I need you to trace his phone."

Hannah looked her up and down like she'd just noticed her for the first time. She scrunched her face up. "You smell like the government. You some type of agent?"

"I'm with—"

"Don't you have resources to do this yourself?"

Kimmy shifted on her feet. "Yes. But—"

"Why aren't you using your own geeks to do this already?" She paused, her eyes lighting up a little. "You off the grid or something? You gone rogue?"

"No, no, nothing like that." Kimmy took a breath. "They've tightened the rules, and everything gets logged now. No favors."

Hannah scanned her eyes over Kimmy. "And I bet you could get them too, huh?"

Kimmy started to speak, and Hannah held up her hand. "Name and phone number?"

Kimmy told her. Hannah's hands flew over the keyboard, clicking and clacking in rapid staccato. In a few seconds, she looked up with an amused look. "He's a spook, too?"

Kimmy's eyes widened. "He's undercover. You shouldn't be able—"

Hannah sighed. "He's an only child, he's got six hundred dollars in his savings account, he owns a burgundy Acura with seventy thousand miles, and his credit score's six-twenty." Hannah clicked twice more and whistled.

Before Kimmy could react, Hannah turned the monitor toward us. There was a picture of Andrew wearing a banana hammock on the beach, his body oily, tan, and taut.

"Now we all know what caliber gun Andrew has," I quipped. Nobody laughed. Tough audience.

Kimmy turned pink, and Gordon stood there transfixed.

Somebody like Andrew made us older Superheroes look bad.

I sucked in my gut a little and said, "Can you get us his last few phone calls?"

Hannah closed the window and clicked a couple of keys. A printer to my left revved up and spit out a sheet of paper: all the numbers Andrew had called for the last week, and all the numbers that had called him. Complete with names.

I held the paper up and told Hannah I owed her one.

"You owe me more than one."

"Well, technically," I said, "Kimmy here owes you for this one."

Kimmy smiled and told Hannah thanks, then snatched the paper from my hands.

Hannah waved it off and looked at me. "You know, you've really let yourself go in the last few years."

"Gee, thanks, Hannah. You've got me teary-eyed."

She shrugged, flicking her eyes toward my gut. "I'm just saying."

Chapter 5

After we'd merged onto the highway, I turned to Gordon and said, "You know, Hannah could probably benefit from a few sessions with you."

"She'd need more than a few."

"I'll bet you could do your little therapist mojo on her"—wiggling my fingers at him—"and make her normal again. Maybe even make her want to grow her hair out and put on make-up."

"Yeah," he said. "My mojo's worked so well on you."

"I have a strong resistance to change."

Kimmy sat in the back, circling names and numbers on her printout like she was a kid with a Sears Wish Book. Does that still exist?

I pulled into a gas station to fill up. "Anybody need anything?"

Gordon glanced at the lottery signs in the window and tried the Super-Stare on me. I was ready and deflected it with my inflated sense of self-worth and overbearing feeling of entitlement.

North Carolina is one of those states that voted to institute a government-sponsored lottery based on the insurmountable fact that every state around us already had one. Numbers didn't lie. The amount of money that left the state every week for the slim chance of winning *another* state's lottery was astronomical.

Even a red state this conservative couldn't ignore the facts.

So the good folks in the North Carolina legislature got together and figured out how to best sell the blasphemous idea of a government-sponsored lottery. In a state that still had dry counties and was home to Baptists and Methodists who ran bingo nights like they were a birthright, an official lottery was an affront to God.

And behold, the North Carolina Education Lottery was conceived. How could a person in good conscience vote against our children's education? How could a good Southern Christian want our kids to go without books? How could a God-fearing taxpayer not be for higher teachers' salaries without having to raise taxes?

The idea was hotly debated—on the pulpit as much as the legislature steps—and narrowly passed. The North Carolina government could now capture all that money that was bleeding out of the economy every week. Our children were saved.

What it meant to me was no more driving to the Virginia border for gas money.

I entered the convenience store, walked up to the counter, and scanned the selection of scratch-offs. I gave the clerk a hokey smile and told him I wanted four Triple Diamond cards.

I handed over four bucks, and he ripped off the tickets. Still standing there, I scratched off the fourth one and handed it back.

"A twenty dollar winner!" the kid said.

"Yep." I smiled, then told him I wanted eight Lucky Leprechauns, three Crazy Eights, and four Old Maids. While he busied himself with the tickets, I stepped to the back of the store, grabbed a diet Mountain Dew and a Fifth Avenue candy bar and returned to the counter.

I scratched off five of the fifteen tickets and gave them back, smiling in wonder at my amazing luck. The kid's eyes were big as headlights as he counted out my winnings of eighty-eight dollars.

I looked at two of the twenties, then at the kid. "You know you're passing funny money?" I asked him.

His face showed no trace of understanding.

"These two twenties?" I held them up. "They're counterfeit." I waved them at him, and he looked closer.

"No they're not," he said.

"Sure they are. The hologram doesn't move when you turn the bill."

"So?"

I could tell this was going to be an uphill battle, so I said, "Okay, whatever."

I gave him fifty-five bucks—paying with the two fake twenties—and told him I needed fifty in gas and to keep the rest.

Easy as pie.

I know what you're thinking. It's dishonest. It's underhanded. It's criminal.

Using my X-Ray-Vision to take advantage of a government-sponsored lottery is wrong.

Well, I don't see it that way.

Can you tell me what the take-home pay for a Superhero is? I'll give you a hint: the net amount is the same as the gross amount.

It's a big fat zero.

For years, I thwarted criminals and thieves for the good of the public. All I ever received as compensation for my hard work was an occasional roll in the hay from a thankful recipient of my services.

Not that I minded the attention, but I never received any actual money for my heroism. Not all of us Superheroes are trust fund babies. We have money issues just like everyone else.

Do you have any idea how much the material for a properly fitting

Superhero suit costs? Size sixteen boots? Masks that don't make you look like a gay S&M enthusiast?

And don't even get me started on how long it takes to hand-wash a suit. I sweat a lot.

Needless to say, I don't feel a bit guilty about scoring a few bucks from the government. I figure Uncle Sam owes me a whole hell of a lot more than I'll ever get.

I grabbed my snacks and went outside to pump gas into the Aztek. Gordon shot me the usual disapproving look through the passenger side window.

Gordon Moser, therapist to the rich, privileged, and mildly disturbed. He sets his own hours, charges phenomenal rates, and has the nerve to try and make me feel bad about a little lottery money.

It wasn't like I could predict numbers and win the big one. The tickets were already winners. I just insured the winnings would go to a good cause instead of booze and cigarettes.

Okay, maybe some of it goes to booze. But I have standards.

If one of Gordon's clients came to me saying his daddy spanked him as a child and his mother neglected him, and that's why he shoplifted granny panties, I'd tell him to grow some balls and get the hell out of my office before I kicked his ass myself. That's all it would take. One session—cured. Not three sessions a week for half a year.

Jeezus. Now there's a racket, am I right?

I wouldn't need to know what his feelings were, why he thought he couldn't achieve his goals, or why he wore pantyhose under his jeans.

I'd get in his face and tell him if he didn't straighten up and get his act together, I'd spread those photos I found on his computer all over the internet. I'd send them to his employer and that cute blonde he'd just met at the coffee shop last week.

That'd fix him quick and easy.

And I wouldn't charge him a hundred an hour to do it.

I finished pumping gas and hopped in the truck. Gordon was still firing the Super-Stare at me, but I responded with a huge smile and a wink.

Kimmy said, "There's a couple people here I'd like to check on," and handed the list to Gordon.

As Gordon skimmed it, I pulled into traffic determined not to get any more involved than I already had. But sometimes I don't get to make my own decisions.

Chapter 6

ordon read some of the names out loud as I drove us back to the apartment. Lanny Lancaster, Stewart Graves, Barbara Greene, Scott Thompson. They sounded innocuous enough, and I was becoming curious.

"You don't know who any of these people are?" I asked.

Kimmy said no.

"What about the others on the list?"

Kimmy bit her lip. "Let's start with these first."

When we walked through the front door, I grabbed a Newcastle out of the fridge and let Gordon do his thing on the computer. Hannah would have completed the searches quicker and more efficient, but Gordon wouldn't need his ego stroked. Plus, this was well within his abilities.

Hannah had tried to trace Andrew's phone before we left, but it wasn't on, and she said there was nothing else she could do unless he'd swallowed a homing beacon and we knew the frequency. I thought it was a joke at first, but when Kimmy answered that he wasn't tagged, I held the laugh in.

Sometimes it's hard to distinguish between the fictional world and the real one.

"Okay, I've got the addresses," Gordon said fifteen minutes later. "Let's go."

"Are you kidding?" I said. I'd just opened another beer and settled into the couch, my feet propped up. Little Man was curled and purring in my lap. "Why don't you call them first? See who they are."

Gordon huffed. "Then why did I just spend all this time getting their addresses?"

I shrugged and turned the beer up for a chug. "I thought you were looking up background checks and credit reports and stuff. I didn't know you were just getting their addresses. Hell. I could've done that."

I could feel Gordon's Super-Stare on the back of my head, but I didn't turn to acknowledge it, so it didn't work. I belched and scratched my leg, and realized I'd just answered the age-old question: If a Super-Stare fell in the forest ...

Kimmy said, "So are we calling them first or not?"

"Sure," I answered. "Here, gimme one. I'll show you how it's done."

Gordon strode to the couch and threw his notepad on my belly. Little Man jumped off me and curled himself into a ball on the floor. I sat up and grabbed my phone.

Lanny Lancaster. The first thing I'd ask the chick was what the hell was wrong with her parents, naming her that? It's like something out of a dirty limerick.

> *There once was a young girl named Lanny.*
> *Whose breasts were both huge and uncanny.*
> *The boys at the beach,*
> *Loved to grab and to reach.*
> *But they always went after her fanny.*

Okay, not my best work, but I was only on my second beer. I dialed the number and a guy answered.

"Lanny, please."

"This is him."

I brought the phone down. I mouthed, "It's a guy," then put the phone back to my ear.

This is the point where I realized I had no idea what I was going to say. I had been so gung-ho I hadn't thought it out. In my defense, I'm a Superhero, not an egghead. Thinking is not my specialty. I'm the guy who barrels in and busts the place up. So I can't be held completely responsible for my conversation with Lanny.

"You're a dude," I said.

A pause, then Lanny answered, "Yeah."

"Is that a family name?"

"Who is this?"

"Who is *this*?" I asked back.

A pause. "Is this Jeff?"

"Yeah, man." I was breaking into stride now. "Had you going for a second there."

"How's Christie?"

"We broke up," I said, running with it. "It's a long story, man. Caught her with another chick from work, a new girl, and when she wouldn't let me join in, that was it. I'll tell you all about it later. Hey, I've been looking for Andrew. You seen him lately?"

"Was she hot?"

"Huh?"

Lanny cleared his throat. "The new girl. Was she hot? A blonde? She have big ones?"

I sighed. "Yeah. Huge, but Lanny, you should've seen her fanny." See how I worked my new limerick in there? "I'll give you all the gory details later. Just picture leather, baby oil, and a car battery. But right now, I need to find Andrew."

"Andrew? I don't know any Andrew. What would they do with a car battery?"

I ignored his question. "Sure, you know Andy." I glanced at the paper. "You talked to him Saturday night."

A pause, then Lanny said, "Who is this?" The playfulness was gone from his voice.

I had reached the end of my cunning conversational tactics. "I'm the guy who's gonna come over there and help you remember what you said to Andrew Saturday night."

Click.

I pulled the phone away from my ear and looked at it.

"What happened?" Kimmy asked.

"He hung up."

Kimmy stared at me, then snatched the list out of my hand.

I stood and said, "Y'all call the rest of the names. I'm gonna take a quick ride over to Lanny's house."

Kimmy's eyes bulged. "You're not."

"Sure I am. I told him I was, so I am."

Like I said, I'm a straightforward kind of guy. I don't make simple things difficult.

Chapter 7

It took me about fifteen minutes to drive to Lanny's house, and I know what you're thinking: Why didn't I fly?

Do you know how popular Youtube is? It's that popular because every kid in America has a video camera on their phone. A video of me flying would be on the net before I landed. That wouldn't be good for the reasons I've already alluded to.

Plus, flying has gotten a little more difficult the older—and heavier—I've become. I'm not as aerodynamic as I used to be, and to be honest, there are things about flying that people don't think about.

You know that movie in the late seventies with Christopher Reeve? They weren't even close. Your hair is not perfect when you fly. Landing is not easy or soft or without a considerable amount of trouble. And there are bugs. Lots of bugs.

Now, you remember that eighties TV show, *The Greatest American Hero*? That's a lot more factual, with the flailing around and crashing into walls. The guy who created that show must have seen me flying in my heyday.

Oh, and did I mention the bugs? Think about how many bugs you see on a motorcycle helmet after he's gone a few miles in the summer. Can you imagine how many I'd get in my face if I flew ten to fifteen miles?

One time a mother goose attacked me. She was teaching her babies how to fly, and I guess she thought I was a predator or something. If you think geese are mean on the ground, try meeting them in mid-air.

I think "Kamikaze" is Japanese for "Goose."

And with the price of gas nowadays, you're probably wondering why I didn't use my Super-Speed either. Again, it's daytime so I'd be seen. Bugs are even worse on the ground. And despite what movies teach us about Superpowers, running very fast is extremely tiring.

Hollywood would have us all believe that a Superhero could run eighty miles an hour and not be out of breath afterward. That not only strains my lungs, but there's also a good chance of a heart attack. All that pumping of my legs and arms? You better believe my heart's running overtime.

I'm in my early forties now, and let me tell you, I don't have to consult a doctor about the wisdom of pushing my body like that for too long. Just because I can do it doesn't mean I need to.

I parked on the street in front of Lanny's little brick house. He had nice landscaping with little shrubs lining his sidewalk and a light blue Acura in the driveway. I strode up the front lawn and knocked on his door. A fluttery middle-aged man about Gordon's size opened it. He looked up at me and shrunk two inches. I never get tired of that.

"Yes?" he said.

"You Lanny?"

"Yeah."

"I'm the guy that called you on the phone a little while ago. You hung up on me." I gave him my best wrestler face.

Lanny's eyes widened. He slammed the door and bolted it.

Some people like to do things the hard way.

I knocked again.

Waited five seconds.

Knocked again.

I thought I showed a great deal of patience up to that point. Gordon would be proud of me taking control of my anger issues and not letting them rule me. I mean, I knocked twice before I ripped the door out of its frame. That's good, right?

When I say I ripped the door out of its frame, I'm not drawing you an accurate picture. I actually burst through the doorway like the door was never there. The entire inside of the doorframe exploded inward with the door, splintering and flinging wood shards everywhere. The door itself, surprisingly sturdy, held together and landed flat on the floor in front of a surprised Lanny Lancaster.

I stepped inside to find Lanny holding a gun. He was shaking and his eyes were big. He had the weapon pointed at me center mass.

"That thing's only gonna piss me off, Lanny." I told him, nodding at the gun.

I didn't move toward him. I looked him in the eyes and let him think he had some control of the situation.

"Get out," he said, a tremor in his high-pitched voice.

"Relax. I just wanna know how you know Andrew Busbee, Lanny. That's it. Once you tell me, I'll leave."

"Who are you?" he asked, his face crinkling in exasperation.

"Doesn't matter who I am." I paused. "I'm here because Andrew has disappeared and his girlfriend wants to know where he is."

"I told you I don't know any Andrew."

I shook my head. "Wrong answer, Lanny. You talked to him on the phone this past Saturday night. For thirteen minutes." I paused to let that sink in. "You trying to tell me you talked to someone you don't know for thirteen whole minutes?"

Lanny's eyes flickered.

"There you go. Now you're remembering." I walked to the right and into the kitchen, opened the fridge, and pulled out an Oregon Raspberry Wheat beer. Yummy, wheat beer with a touch of raspberry. It was almost healthy.

I turned to see that Lanny had followed me, the gun still leveled in front of him. He was shivering like it was the middle of winter and he'd locked himself out of the house in his boxers. Boxers with sailboats.

I sat at the rickety kitchen table and sized him up. He looked sort of like Gordon in an accounting kind of way, minus the thick glasses. Short hair parted in the middle. Thirty-something and probably still a virgin. He was slight, wearing a polo shirt and beige chinos. I checked his loafers for pennies. Yep.

I shook my head and took a sip of the beer. Light, airy, hints of the promised raspberry. Tasty. Reminded me of Abita's Purple Haze.

"So, Lanny," I began. "Where'd the name come from?"

He paused. "Family name."

I was doing my best to look non-threatening. Sitting down, crossing my legs, leaning back. It worked because Lanny's gun arm relaxed, and he stepped into the kitchen.

"He said his name was Jim," Lanny offered.

"The guy you talked to Saturday night?"

"Yeah. Jim Simpson or something like that."

Made sense. A spook probably never told anyone their real name. I should've thought of that.

"What did you talk about?" I asked, taking another sip of beer.

He squinted. "You said he disappeared?"

"Yeah. It's been a day now. What'd he ask you about?"

"He said he was from the FBI."

I downed some more beer. "Sounds right." I decided to take a different approach. "You call him or he call you?" I already knew the answer, but I got the feeling I needed to start Lanny off with simple questions and then work up to the good stuff.

"He called me."

I waited for more.

"He said he was investigating my company. We print the tickets for the state lottery. Sixteen other states too."

I raised my eyebrows. "The scratch-offs or numbered tickets?"

"The scratch-offs."

I sat up in my chair and uncrossed my legs. Now we were in my area of expertise. I can turn a computer on and use it to search for porn, but not much more. But state lottery tickets?

I know every lottery ticket the state offers, what it takes to win on each card, and what the possible winnings are. You have to when you depend on them for your only income.

"What exactly was he investigating?" I continued.

"He wanted me to check the computer programs we used to make the tickets. That's what I do; I design and program the algorithms that print out the correct percentage of winning tickets but make it look random."

Now this was interesting in a geeky sort of way.

"What exactly did he want you to check out?"

Lanny sat down across from me and laid the gun on the table.

"He wanted to make sure the payout percentages were correct."

"I knew it!" I stood up so quickly I startled Lanny and he reached for the gun. I pretended I didn't notice. "I knew those crooks were cheating us!" I turned toward Lanny. "What did you find out?"

He shrugged. "Nothing yet. I haven't had the chance." He set the gun down again.

I wanted to reach in my pocket and hand him my business card, but I didn't have one. What would it say? *Barry Glick, Superhero. Saving the world is my business.*

I said, "Lanny, you got something I can write on?" He nodded and fished a pen and pad out of a junk drawer. "Good. Do me a favor." I wrote my name and number down. "Call me as soon as you know something, alright?"

Lanny nodded again and got up to follow me out.

When we walked through the living room, he motioned to the floor. "What about my door?"

I picked it up and set it back in the frame. "Couple screws and some glue, it'll be good as new." I turned to him and gave him my best Superhero smile.

Lanny stared at me.

"What?" I said. "You shouldn't have closed it in my face. My therapist says I don't deal with conflict well." I shrugged. "It's not my fault."

Lanny still stared.

"Make you a deal," I said. "You call me with whatever you find out, and I'll put a new door in myself."

This seemed to satisfy Lanny, and he nodded. Didn't matter to me. It was all lottery money anyway. Easy come, easy buy-another-winning-ticket.

I skipped the part where I should have told him I've never put in a door before and didn't own any tools to do it with.

By the time I'd gotten situated in my Aztek, the front door had fallen back into the living room. Lanny stood there looking at me. I waved before I pulled away from the curb.

Chapter 8

Christine the red-headed MILF was still lying out at the pool when I got back home. Actually, she'd just taken a cooling dip and was emerging as I stepped out of the Aztek. It reminded me of that eighties flick where the chick exits the pool in slo-mo and turns toward the camera.

I admired her for the perfect specimen she was, and she waved. I smiled and waved back. She knew the effect she had on guys and wasn't afraid to shun the women's libbers to get her way. She relished in her power.

I know the feeling. My powers are so much a part of me that they help define my personality. At least that's what Gordon tells me.

He wants me to connect more with my inner Barry to figure out who the real Barry is—the Barry who can't bend a crowbar with his bare hands and run faster than a four-cylinder Chevy.

I didn't get my powers until puberty, and Gordon has known me my whole life. He says the powers changed me. I tell him they changed me for the better.

He keeps pushing me to remember the pre-pubescent Barry, the kid who used to get clobbered in dodge ball, couldn't get a girl's attention unless he sneezed on her, was happy to make a "C" on anything, and prided himself on his incomplete collection of comic books.

I tell Gordon that kid's dead and to send him flowers if he wants to remember him. Personally, I'm done with the old me. If the powers help define me, then so be it.

A man is, and will always be, defined by what he does in life. So why should me having my powers be any different?

I entered my apartment to find Kimmy and Gordon sitting on the couch talking, another episode of *House* playing on the TV. Little Man was in Kimmy's lap, purring as she rubbed his belly.

"Y'all make any calls while I was gone?" I asked, heading straight for the fridge and one of my Dirty Monks.

"What did you find out?" Gordon said.

"A-ha. Can't do that," I said. "I asked first."

"We called the other three names," Kimmy offered. "We were just talking about what we found out."

I sat down opposite them, popped the top on my beer, and propped my feet on the coffee table. "Shoot," I said.

Kimmy took a breath. "Stewart Graves is a fund manager for a big international hedge fund. Andrew called him posing as an FBI agent to find out if anything funny was going on with the fund. Were there outside or inside forces screwing with the values, possibly inflating them way beyond real values?"

"And?"

"He said he'd look into it. He didn't have any information yet. I told him I was Andrew's partner and to call me if he found anything."

"Barbara Greene," Gordon started in, "is a freelance financial reporter. Sells articles to Forbes, the New York Times, The Wall Street Journal ... you get the idea. Andrew posed as the same FBI agent—"

"Jim," I interrupted.

"Yeah. Jim." He paused. "Andrew was wanting to know if she'd run across anything odd, like if currencies were being manipulated. Artificially inflated and deflated to control monetary supply and demand, propping up conversion rates and then plummeting them."

I squinted my eyes at Gordon, then turned to Kimmy. "English, please."

She grinned. "Andrew wanted to know if the value of the dollar was being influenced while someone converted them to Euros or Yen, and back again."

I took a sip of beer. "That's the English version?"

"Making money illegally."

"Gotcha." I cheated my way through high school, but some concepts could be understood on any level.

"The other person we called?" Gordon continued. "Scott Thompson? He's a mortgage and credit specialist at Fannie Mae. He's one of the guys who runs their automatic loan qualification program. Brokers log in from all over the country, input the borrower's necessary information, and the program approves or denies them."

"Lemme guess," I said. "Andrew wanted to know if it had been tampered with?"

Gordon bobbed his little head.

I looked at Kimmy, "And Andrew said he was investigating terrorists? Sounds more like he was investigating the next Bernie Madoff."

Kimmy and Gordon regarded me with surprise.

"What? I watch the news every once in a while. I know what's going on out there." I waved my hands around. "Basically."

"When do you watch the news?" Gordon asked.

I brought my right hand to my chest. "That hurts, Gordy. That really hurts. You know I watch the Naked News."

"Of course you do." Kimmy rolled her eyes.

"There's a redhead on there, does the sports—"

"We get it, Barry."

"Sure, she's had surgery, but lemme tell you, it cost her a pretty penny because that doc's a god with a scalpel—"

"Barry. Shut up. Please." Kimmy shot me a half-lidded look full of disgust.

"What? You want a kid to eat oatmeal, you put sugar on top, right? Maybe mix a little peanut butter in, a few chocolate chips."

Gordon butted in. "Not the best metaphor, Barry."

I took another pull from my beer and turned toward the TV.

Actually, I've learned all kinds of things from the Naked News. For instance, did you know Kazikstan's a real country and not a place made up by Borat? Also, we have a national kickball league. And I've learned no matter what kind of news you have to share, if you have a naked woman tell you, it's very hard to get upset.

After a brief silence where Kimmy and Gordon exchanged knowing glances about me being me, Kimmy asked what I'd found on my trip.

"Lanny's a computer geek at a printer who makes lottery scratch-offs for seventeen states. Andrew wanted him to check the programing in the payoffs to see if they were off. Lanny's supposed to get back with me." I paused and glanced at Gordon. "Also, you know how to put up a door?"

Gordon frowned and said, "So Andrew has been investigating a whole slew of financial angles." He scratched his head. "I don't exactly see how they fit together."

"Maybe he was fishing?" I offered.

"Fishing for what?" Kimmy said.

I shrugged. "I don't know. Maybe he got wind of something and was trying to narrow it down."

Kimmy shook her head. "They've got to be related somehow. Andrew was too methodical to go shotgunning for answers. He always has reasons for every move he makes."

At this point, I was at a loss. You give me a target and tell me to hit it, I'll demolish the damn thing. But you give me a puzzle and tell me to figure it out, I'm the guy who ends up smashing the puzzle into a bunch of smaller pieces.

The extent of my detective knowledge has been learned from watching decades of police procedurals on TV. I know you check for DNA, fingerprints, footprints, carpet fibers, hair follicles, dirt samples, and handwriting analysis. You send it all to the lab, go take care of some personal stuff, and by the end of the show, you get all the information back with some guy's name typewritten at the top, his info already on file for some B&E he pulled when he was a teenager.

But even then, it's never him. You have to stumble across the real perp by accident when someone has a revelation, like the real guy being left-handed, or some file doesn't look right and you can tell it's been changed.

But real life is different. There's no structure or time frame, like knowing you'll get a great clue just before the first commercial.

Then I had a brilliant idea. "You canvass the neighborhood yet? See if the neighbors saw any suspicious characters or cars or cable trucks?"

Gordon stared at me. "Sometimes I can't tell if you're serious or not."

I gave him my best serious face.

He said, "There wasn't a struggle at Andrew's place. You saw it. It was still pristine, just the way he left it. And besides, his car was gone."

Oh yeah. I knew that.

Kimmy's eyes lit up. "That's it. Andrew's Cadillac has On-Star. I can call them with my badge number and get a GPS fix on it." She was already scrambling for her phone.

Little Man was not happy to be traded for a phone. He lumbered over to Gordon.

Fifteen minutes later, with the help of Kimmy's contact at On-Star, we had the GPS coordinates of Andrew's car. Gordon entered them into an app on his smartphone, and we waited for the map to pop up. Burlington. Right off Church Street.

We piled into the Aztek and took off.

Chapter 9

Andrew's Caddy was parked in the back lot of Fiesta Mexicana, a local restaurant known for their jumbo lime-mango margaritas. On-Star unlocked the car and Kimmy began searching it. I stood outside and did my own scanning on the car. It was hard to focus with Kimmy bent over like that, but I concentrated.

I didn't find anything, and as Kimmy popped out of the car to announce she got the same results, my stomach grumbled. Both Gordon and Kimmy looked at me. I guess it was loud.

"It might help to think on a full stomach," I suggested, heading for the restaurant before anyone could object.

We were seated almost immediately in a booth near the middle of the restaurant by a young Hispanic girl who spoke perfect unaccented English. In fact she spoke better English than most of the locals. The place was done up in stucco and red clay tiles, and colorful sombreros hung on the wall like art.

Chips and salsa appeared on our table as if by magic, along with three glasses of water. We munched away, perusing the menus as if we didn't already know what we wanted. The waiter who took our orders was struggling with facial hair and still producing pimples. He had a ponytail, and when I said, "Hola!" in my best Mexican accent, he regarded me with the contempt of an eighty-year-old man suffering from bowel issues.

Gordon ordered the shredded chicken burritos with ranch sauce, Kimmy ordered the steak fajitas, and I opted for the chicken in mole sauce with a healthy side of sour cream and guacamole. And a Dos Equis to top it off.

For good measure, I pronounced "mole" like the animal instead of *mo-lay*. The deadpan look the kid gave me made my day.

By the time our food arrived, a water girl came around to refill our glasses and bring more chips and salsa. Struck with an idea, I asked if she worked last night.

She nodded and smiled.

I told Kimmy to bring up a picture of Andrew on her phone. Her eyes lit up as she started clicking buttons, then showed the phone to the girl.

I asked if she'd seen this guy here during her shift.

She smiled and shrugged, nodded again.

I returned her smile. "Would you like to have a three-way with me and this beautiful woman tonight?" I motioned to Kimmy.

The water girl smiled and nodded a little.

I thought as much. She probably didn't speak English well, which is why she was a water girl and not a waitress. I told her *gracias* and grabbed the next waitress who passed.

She spoke English well, but she didn't work last night.

"Try him," Gordon said, pointing at a waiter.

I shook my head and gave him the *tsk, tsk*. "For a therapist, Gordy, you sure have a lot to learn about human nature. You see this mug?" I held up the phone. "Mr. GQ here would not only have been noticed by every female here, they'd have talked about him. They'll remember what he wore, what he smelled like, and most important, who he was with. To the senoritas, he would have been more than a table number; he would have been a topic of conversation."

Kimmy and Gordon raised their eyebrows at me.

I grinned. "I don't know a lot of book stuff, but I got a black belt in human nature."

I flagged down two more waitresses before I found one who lit up at seeing Andrew's picture. She yammered away in Spanish for another waitress to come over, then pointed. Both girls smiled at me, the kind of smile that said they'd not only noticed him, but they'd fantasized about him too.

I asked again if Andrew was here the night before. They both nodded and blushed. One pointed to another booth, indicating where he sat.

Now for the question of the day. "Was he with anyone?" I asked.

They both nodded again. The second girl said, "Very pretty. Long blonde hair." She raised a hand in the air, palm down. "Very tall."

"Do you remember who paid?"

The waitress pointed to the phone. "He did."

I figured that, but it was worth a shot. "Now, girls, this is very important," I continued. "Did you hear him call her by name?"

They both shook their heads no. I thanked them and they scurried off, chattering in clipped, giggly Spanish.

"Okay," I started. "Here's what we know. He ate dinner with a woman. Probably an informant or maybe even a suspect or someone directly related to a suspect."

Gordon was deep in thought, and Kimmy still wasn't speaking, so I continued. "But the most important thing we know is that when he left here, Andrew didn't leave in his car. That means he either left to be shown something or was grabbed."

I turned to Kimmy. "As a fellow spook, can you say whether or not

Andrew would have left his car behind willingly? Is there some regulation or something like that?"

Kimmy pursed her lips. "No, he wouldn't have. He would have followed her somewhere. We're trained to have an exit strategy for every situation we enter."

"Okay, so it's safe to assume he was snatched out of the parking lot. There's a chance someone saw it happen."

Our food arrived, and I was glad for the distraction. I'd run out of ideas and needed the time to think. Plus, my stomach had growled loud enough for the family in the next booth to turn and shoot me wide-eyed looks.

We ate for a few minutes in silence, and I ordered another Dos Equis. I stopped the waitress to get more chips and salsa.

Then Gordon spoke. "I think I know who she is. The blonde."

We waited for him to continue.

"When I was searching on Andrew's computer, I checked his browser history."

"Kinky," I said. If you looked at my browser history, it actually would be kinky.

What? The internet is for discovering new things without fear of some perv glaring at you from the next aisle while he fondles a leather vagina.

Ahem. Gotta remember to erase my browser history.

Gordon continued, "I think she's the chief financial officer at First Burlington Bank. Andrew had her profile page up on his computer two days ago."

Gordon pulled out his smartphone and started punching away. Then he went over to one of the giggly waitresses we'd snagged earlier, showed her the phone, and came back.

"That's who it was. Jennifer Pearce."

Way to go Gordon! I was so proud of my little buddy at that moment.

Kimmy brightened, and I said, "Alright. So that tells us he was hot on this financial angle he was looking at. And this Jennifer chick was the last person to talk with Andrew before he dropped off the grid."

I was talking like I knew what I was saying when in fact, all I was doing was repeating lines from movies and TV shows. Sounded good, though. Truth is, I wanted to get back to my chicken mole. A zesty sauce made with dark chocolate? Come on. Get serious, man. That stuff was amazing!

We finished dinner, and with On-Star's help, Kimmy drove Andrew's Caddy back to my apartment. I gave it another scan, looking for signs of struggle or other clues, but I didn't see anything special.

Kimmy and Gordon headed home, and we promised to meet for breakfast at eight the next morning so we could converge on First Burlington by the time they opened.

Chapter 10

We had asked for two extra baskets of chips and salsa during dinner, so I was pretty full. Okay, I'm the one who asked for the all the chips and salsa, and I'm the one who ate them. Hey, I have a high metabolism rate. You try lifting a Honda Accord without a hefty meal in your gut.

The point is, I was full and looked forward to collapsing on the couch with a cold beer and catching a cheesy crime show on the tube. Maybe I'd get some more great ideas.

I pulled my last Dirty Monk from the fridge and made a mental note to get more tomorrow.

The beer made it to the first commercial break, and I stared at the empty bottle. Turned it upside-down and watched the last drop gather itself and meander the length of the glass toward the opening. Held it over my mouth and waited for it to drippety-drip to my tongue.

It finally freed itself, splashing into my mouth, and I savored its tartness, its sweet subtle flavor of hops and malt and barley, and I realized at that point I had a problem. A major problem.

I was out of beer, and it wasn't even eight.

I grabbed my keys and drove to Shoffner's. Rafi was on duty, his iPod earbuds glued to his head. I said hey to the kid, and he nodded.

I tell you what. This young generation is something else. I saved his skinny little life, and not more than six hours later I barely got a nod of recognition. This same generation never used a rotary phone, never watched a thirteen inch black-and-white lo-def TV full of static, and never had to wear shoes without arch support. They're spoiled.

I strolled to the back cooler and picked out a large case of Corona— eating Mexican got me in the mood. Rafi was still quietly jamming to his music when I set the beer on the counter. Wonder if he knew what a Walkman was? Or even a cassette tape?

I scanned the scratch-offs and waved my hand to get Rafi's attention. I told him to peel me off ten Bingo Blasts and three Crazy Eights. I could've bought five Double Diamonds and racked up another fifty-two dollars. But hey, I'm not greedy.

I scratched off the winning tickets and turned them in, then paid for the beer and a huge bag of Cheetos.

Rafi handed me my change and the rest of my winnings in one clump. $224.36.

I may not be greedy, but I'm very practical.

I stuffed the money in my pocket, then pulled it back out, scrutinized the two hundreds, and handed them back to Rafi.

"This is funny money."

Rafi looked at me, iPod buds still shoved in his ears.

"I said this is funny money," I repeated.

He fumbled with the iPod and said, "What?"

I cleared my throat and tamped down the urge to crush his iPod, then told him again the money wasn't real.

He looked at it, saying, "I counted it out."

"No, Rafi," I said, holding the two hundreds up. "These bills right here? They're fake. No good. Counterfeit." I waved them in front of his blank face.

He took the hundreds and held them up to the light, then handed them back. "They're real."

I frowned. I knew what I was talking about, and I told him so. "No, Rafi, look. The hologram here, it's off. And the strip inside the linen is wrong; it's too thin. Here. Feel them." I gave them back.

He ran them between his fingers, then shrugged. "Feels fine."

I was losing patience. "Trust me. I know what real bills feel like." I'd busted more rings of counterfeiters in my heyday than I could count. I definitely knew what I was talking about. These bills were very good, but not perfect.

"Just do me a favor," I told him. "Gimme a bunch of twenties instead."

Rafi glared at me the way a teenager glares at anyone who tells him what to do, but he swapped the hundreds out for twenties. I thanked him and by the time I was out the door he'd turned up his iPod and was clicking away on his phone.

Two of the twenties he gave me were fake, but I was tired of messing with it.

I pulled into my parking spot at the apartment and stared at the man propped against my door. Sullen, unshaven, hunched over. He stared back at me with sad, hateful eyes.

The night had just gotten a whole lot longer.

The man pushed off the door as I trudged up, and I regarded his surly gaze with wariness. He was a head shorter than me and had to crane his neck to look me in the eye.

"What do you need?" I said.

He was blocking the door, and I made no motion to go around him.

"Do I have to need something to see my only son?"

"I live in a gated community for a reason."

He grinned, revealing a space in his smile where an incisor had once been. I'd knocked it out the night I left home. Now, some twenty-six years later, he still hadn't gotten a fake tooth in its place, like it was a badge of courage for him, a reminder of the ungrateful son he could blame everything on.

Or maybe he thought it would make me feel guilty.

He said, "You've never changed your password. Everywhere you live, you use the same one. 0-0-7? I'll bet you even use it as your ATM pin."

That's where he's wrong. They require four digits for the bank card so it's 0-0-0-7. Shows him.

"What are you doing here?" I asked.

He fidgeted. "You didn't call on my birthday."

"That was three months ago."

He sniffed and looked back up at me. "Why aren't you happy to see your old man?"

"Easy," I said. "I know you."

I stepped toward the door, and he moved aside. I unlocked it and he followed me in.

"I can't believe you're still renting," he said, closing the door behind him.

I plucked a beer out of one of the six-packs before I shoved them in the fridge.

"Oh yeah," he said. "You have to prove your income to buy a house. I forget."

I ignored him, popping the top on the Corona and grabbing the bag of Cheetos. I sat on the couch and propped my feet on the coffee table.

"You not going to offer me a beer?" he said.

"I was hoping you wouldn't be here long enough to drink one."

He strolled into the kitchen, and I heard him open the fridge. Then I heard drawers opening and closing. Then he said, "Where's a bottle opener?"

"Don't need one," I yelled back, smiling.

A pause. "That's okay. I'll use the counter."

I heard him pop it open, and he walked into the living room and sat in the chair opposite me.

He'd lost a little weight since the last time I saw him. Lost some more hair too, and was wearing it shorter. He looked wrinklier, almost feeble. God, he was getting old. He turned sixty-four this year but was looking more like seventy-four.

"You've shrunk," I told him.

He tipped his beer at me and took a swallow. "You've gotten fatter."

His eyes, as steely blue as ever, had a way of cutting into you like a dull machete. I turned my attention to the TV. One of those crappy acronym police shows was on; the cops had a guy in the interrogation room, giving him the once-over, yelling at him, then talking soft, then yelling again. I knew what that felt like.

Dad invented passive aggressive behavior. Cultivated it like a pro. Gordon explained it all to me in simpler terms, but in the end, that's what it was. Passive aggressive bullshit.

"You ever gonna cut your hair?" he asked. "You look like you should be stalking around a trailer park, beating up women and teaching kids how to smoke pot."

Okay. That was clever. I'll give him that one. He was always good with insults. He should be; he practiced all the time. It's about the only thing he was good at.

We watched TV another twenty minutes before he spoke again.

"What do you do nowadays?" he said. We were both on our second beers.

I tipped the beer at him. "You're looking at it."

"You still scratching off tickets for small potatoes?"

"That any of your business?"

Half a minute later, he said, "One trip to Vegas, you'd never have to worry about money again."

"You mean *we'd* never have to worry again."

He shrugged.

I said, "Because personally, I haven't worried about money in a very long time." I turned my beer up.

Another few minutes of silence.

"I'm gonna lose the house."

The perp was in the interrogation room again, and the big white cop was in his face, yelling so hard spit flew from his mouth.

"I'm four months behind."

I sipped my beer. Now the black cop was arguing with the white one, screaming about a character I'd missed earlier in the show.

"I'm getting letters. They've started the foreclosure process."

The black cop won the argument and the white cop left the interrogation room, grinning as he closed the door behind him.

I said, "Sell it."

"That was mine and your mother's only house. She planted that maple in the back yard the day we closed."

More silence.

"You grew up in that house."

"And I left it." I paused. "I hated that house."

"Your mother loved it."

I turned to him. "Correction. I hated *you* in that house."

I let that marinate as I turned back toward the TV. The perp was crying now, slobbering all over the table as he spilled his guts about who did it and how they did it.

"I need two grand," Dad said.

"Your latest scheme not work out?"

"You want me to beg? I'll beg. I'm begging you for money. That make you feel better? Me begging for money?"

I took another swallow of beer. "Yeah. It does. I do feel better now. Thanks." I smiled and turned to him. "It feels even better to say no again."

"Fuck you."

He stood and stomped out the door, slamming it as he left.

Hmm. Turns out the black cop was wrong; the wife didn't do it. But the white cop was wrong, too; the brother didn't do it either. All along, it was the father who'd shot the son in the heart. Just because he was different.

Chapter 11

First Burlington Bank was a red brick building with white Grecian columns and a pitched metal roof. Not too swanky, but not too shabby either. Exactly what you'd expect in a small hometown bank.

At breakfast, we had debated on who should approach Ms. Pearce. Kimmy, with her fake FBI badge and credentials, was a gimme. I, with my Superhero-ness and obvious intimidating nature, was another gimme. Gordon ... well, Gordon discovered her as a clue, so how could we ask him to wait in the truck?

I was personally for the idea that Kimmy and I pose as a couple, but Kimmy nixed that before I could point out all the movies it worked in.

At the bank, though, still parked outside, Gordon said, "All three of us can't walk in there and ask this woman where Andrew is. That won't work."

"Why not?" I said.

"I'm not a spy or anything," Gordon continued. "But don't you think this is one time we should come at the problem sideways instead of head-on?" He looked at me.

"Here's the deal," Gordon said, addressing both of us again. "If she had anything to do with Andrew's disappearance at all, we'd hit a dead end if we confronted her with accusations. And we'd let her know something very important—that we're onto her. If she's not connected to Andrew's disappearance, then there's no harm done. But if she is, there's no advantage in showing all our cards."

This went against most of my sensibilities. But Gordon just might have a point.

"Okay," I replied "So what's the plan?"

He said, "I think Barry's original idea isn't so bad."

If I had been drinking something, I might have done a spit-take.

Gordon pointed at us. "You two should go in as a couple who own a business. You're looking for a banking partner, somewhere to invest your money for maximum return and minimal capital gains taxes."

I looked at Kimmy. "I'll be Davenport Harrison Ridgley. You can be my wife, Millie." Kimmy frowned. "It's short for Millicent," I added.

"And I'll be your accountant," Gordon said, opening the door.

"Wait, what?" I said.

Before I could object, both Kimmy and Gordon had left the car. I caught up before they entered the bank, and as we walked in, I grabbed Kimmy's hand. She tried to shake it loose, but I held on tight. We had to look the part, right?

A chubby girl with big round cheeks and frumpy green dress sat at a desk to the right. She looked up from her computer, and I told her we were here to see Ms. Pearce. No, we didn't have an appointment, but she'd want to see us. We were big clients.

The receptionist hesitated and I shot her my Superhero smile. She glanced at her computer, clicked a few keys, and told us Ms. Pearce had a nine-thirty, but she could squeeze us in before that.

Four minutes later, we entered the bank executive's office. Jennifer

Pearce stood behind her desk and extended her arm.

"Davenport Harrison Ridgely," I said, meeting her hand. Then I added, "The third."

Kimmy opened her mouth, but I continued, "And this is my lovely wife, Millie. And our accountant ... Gordon"

Damn. I hadn't thought about an undercover name for Gordy yet.

Ms. Jennifer Pearce was indeed tall. Her long blonde hair was curled slightly, and she wore a smart, charcoal business suit. Underneath that she wore a sexy black bustier and garter set. *Va-va-voom.* And underneath that? Well, let's just say Ms. Pearce works out regularly.

There were only two guest chairs. I sat in one and before I could pull Kimmy to my lap, she took the second chair. How rude to make her brother stand.

"So how can I help you?" Ms. Pearce asked.

I took the lead. "Millie and I own a chain of stores, and we're looking for a good place to park our profits. We want a bank flexible enough to work with us, but also big enough to keep all avenues open."

I got that off a commercial I saw the night before. I added the part about the "chain of stores" myself to make us look more important.

"Oh really?" she responded. "What business are you in?"

"Lingerie."

It just came out. The ad after the bank commercial was for Victoria's Secret. Sometimes I think linearly. And truth be told, I was still mesmerized by the lacy bustier sitting in front of me. It would be on my mind for a while. I mean, who wore that stuff under their clothes during the day?

As soon as I said, "Lingerie," I heard Kimmy suck in her breath. I felt she had the urge to backhand me. Gordon surprised us all by stepping right in.

"We have stores in five different states, and we're looking at buying out another chain that will increase our revenue by more than forty percent."

I shot Gordy an appraising smile. He stood passive as always, as if he'd just told me I needed new gaskets and my brakes were going bad.

"I see," said Ms. Pearce. "Maybe I should summon one of my commercial loan originators and get you started on that process."

Gordon didn't hesitate. "Oh, we don't need a loan. We're buying them with cash and company stock. What we need is a way to generate capital from our cash reserves. You know, some fairly safe investments with decent, short-term returns so we stay liquid."

Jennifer smiled, revealing a set of perfect teeth. "I think that's something we may be able to accomplish." She pulled some papers from a folder on her desk, saying, "May I ask how you heard about us?"

Before I could open my big mouth and say, "Andrew," Kimmy slid forward and said, "Jim Simpson."

At the mention of Andrew's fake FBI alias, Jennifer Pearce, CFO of First Burlington, replaced her smile with a thin line. Not a puzzled or surprised expression, but one of emotionless disinterest. A look that said to me, "I'm guilty. I did it. I'm the one you're looking for."

All pretense flew out the window. I hadn't even had a chance to describe my plans for the new S&M product line I wanted to build out, how I wanted to combine Lycra and breathable rubber for a new kind of undergarment line.

Kimmy must have sensed the attitude change too because she said, "I believe he met with you Monday night?"

Jennifer straightened in her chair and set the pen in her hand down. "I don't know what you're talking about," she said.

Not *who*, but *what*.

I laughed. "Now that's a bullshit line if I've ever heard one."

"Who are you?" Jennifer asked, narrowing her eyes.

I was about to answer, "Your worst nightmare," or something equally cliché, but once again, Kimmy beat me to it. Damn it, either this "getting older" thing was slowing my reflexes, or I was severely out of practice.

Kimmy whipped out her fake FBI badge. "Katy Barwell, FBI."

Jennifer glanced at the badge but remained quiet.

Kimmy said, "So what did you two talk about over dinner?"

Jennifer paused, then said, "That's kind of personal, don't you think?"

My Super-Nose was smelling something fishy. Okay, so I don't have a real Super-Nose, but you know what I'm saying. "What do you mean by that, Jenny?" I asked. I felt we knew each other well enough for first names. After all, I'd seen her in lingerie already.

"It's Jennifer, and by personal, I mean we had a date."

"A date?" Kimmy exploded.

Jennifer slid back in her chair.

"You're saying you two went on a date?" Kimmy's voice rose.

Jennifer's left eyebrow raised and her mouth turned into a smirk. "Is that so surprising?"

Kimmy lunged forward, and I stood, extending my arm in front of Kimmy to hold her back. I said, "Okay, I think we should be going."

Kimmy stammered, "But, but—"

"Let's go." I turned to Jennifer. "We're so sorry to have disturbed you. You've just had the pleasure of meeting Jim's overzealous girlfriend of two years. I think this is a matter for Jim and her to discuss in private."

"But—"

I corralled Kimmy toward the door and said over my back, "Thank you again for your time."

Kimmy protested all the way down the hall and outside until I shoved her into the Aztek, Gordon bringing up the rear without a sound. I started the car and zipped out of the parking lot, drove down to a McDonalds, and parked.

The whole time, Kimmy was muttering, "Andrew would not be on a date with that Amazon whore. She is totally not his type. I'll bet her boobs are fake. Her nails were fake, even I could see that."

"Kimmy," I began. "Shut up for a minute. You almost screwed the pooch back there. First of all, let me assure you, her boobs are definitely not fake. You should see how well they—"

"Barry!" Kimmy smacked my arm.

I rubbed it like it hurt, but we know better than that, don't we? I laughed, then said, "Should you tell her, Gordy?"

"He used his alias."

Leave it to Gordon to keep it short. I was wanting to go into this big, long explanation of all the subtle cues in her actions and reactions to our questions. Then I'd lead into a step-by-step explanation about each of her answers, and if she was really on a date, she would have answered *this* instead of *that*. Then I'd reveal that parts of her flushed when "Jim" was mentioned—and not the right parts. And finally, I'd point out the whole alias thing.

But Gordon had boiled all the investigative fun down to four simple words. If my life were a movie, he would suck every bit of fun from it.

"I had suspicions before she claimed it was a date," I said. "But that was the clincher." I paused. "Think about it, Kimmy. He went on a date and left his car behind? You're not thinking clearly here."

She returned my gaze, eyes furious.

I continued, "Once you flashed your badge, she was a little too cool. She should have been freaked out that you were FBI, but instead, she claimed she was on a date, with someone she thought was named Jim."

"She knows what happened to Andrew," Gordon offered from the back seat.

I nodded and put the Aztek in reverse. "Let's go find out all we can about Ms. Pearce."

Chapter 12

Back at my place, beer in hand, Kimmy and I stood behind
Gordon while he worked his magic on the web. I don't have a
lot of gadgets and gizmos in my house, but one thing I do have
is a kick-ass computer—courtesy of the North Carolina Education
Lottery—and a super-fast internet connection.

Gordon googled Jennifer Pearce and pulled up a whole bunch of
stuff. Job promotions. A social networking page. Articles she'd written
for financial websites.

No naked pictures, though.

Google must be slipping.

Seems Jennifer was very knowledgeable about money and how it
worked. She had spoken at international conferences and even presented
a paper at the annual IMF meeting a few years ago.

Jennifer Pearce was big potatoes.

Yet, she was just the CFO of a podunk state bank with three small
branches.

I smelled fish again.

"You see anything funny about this?" I said aloud.

I explained what I meant.

Kimmy said, "You know what the IMF is?"

All my wonderful deduction and detectivery, and she zeroed in on my knowledge of a three-letter acronym? I tilted my head at her. I wanted to tell her the Naked News was as robust a news source as CNN. Just because all the women took their clothes off while they informed you about worldly happenings didn't discount the validity of what they said.

Ask any good teacher, and they'll verify the overwhelming benefits and power of visual aids in the classroom. But somehow I figured that wouldn't impress her very much, so I left it alone.

"Okay," I began, "what possible reasons would a woman of her credentials stay with such a small no-nothing bank?"

"To keep a low profile," Gordon said.

"Even though she's done all this other stuff?"

"That's to make contacts," Kimmy offered. "Powerful contacts."

"Okay," I said. "So she's working at this no-nothing bank, in a no-nothing town, while cultivating these high-level contacts? To what end?"

Gordon clicked away while Kimmy chewed her bottom lip.

"Come on guys," I said. "I'm not the brains here. I'm the brawn."

"I'm thinking, I'm thinking," Kimmy said.

I sipped on my beer and looked over Gordon's shoulder. He was reading some of Jennifer's published stuff. Kimmy continued to chew her lip—which I must say was distracting me quite a bit—and twirled her hair—which was also distracting me.

"I tell you what," I said after a few minutes. "You guys sit around here and do the thinking. I'm gonna do what I do best." I pulled my keys out of my pocket and said, "Call me if you find something."

Kimmy asked where I was going.

I scratched Little Man on the head as I walked to the door. "Jennifer

Pearce was the last person to see Andrew, right? So I'm going to go be her best buddy."

"What does that mean?"

"Relax. I'm gonna tail her and see if she leads me somewhere."

Sometimes you can overthink a problem, and all you really needed in the first place was some good old-fashioned luck.

I walked out just as Christine from the third floor was shuffling to the pool. She wore a tiny yellow bikini with thong bottoms, and I didn't need my X-Ray-Vision to appreciate the view.

Had she been working out? She had to be about my age, and I swear, as she sashayed across the parking lot, not one thing wiggled on her that didn't firm back into place immediately.

She stopped at the gate, and as she turned, she saw me and waved. I waved back and realized I was sucking in my gut.

Some things will never change.

I parked at the Sonic Drive-In beside the bank and ordered a cheeseburger combo from the freckled roller-skate waitress. The best thing about a stake-out is the food. It's like having a permission slip to eat the greasiest, fattiest diet known to man.

Not like I needed permission ...

I scanned the bank and found Jennifer in her office, typing away as she read from some forms. She'd probably be in there another five hours, but it's not like I had anything better to do.

In the old days, I didn't do stake-outs. Things were simpler. When Gordon and I lived in New York, we'd just camp out on a city block, and I'd scan the area for crimes being committed. It never took more than an hour for something bad to happen.

A mugging. A hold-up. A simple home robbery.

Of course, that's when I was young and dumb. I hadn't had my powers long and *Superman II* had just opened in theaters. I found it uncanny that he and I were so close in powers, but since Superman was actually created back in the thirties, I wrote it off to luck.

I mean, we had a lot of differences, too. I wasn't an alien from a dead planet. I developed my powers at adolescence instead of birth. And there was no such thing as Kryptonite that zapped me defenseless—if you didn't count redheads.

I was lean and mean back then, and yes, I wore a Superhero suit. Only I didn't depend on slicked-back hair and no glasses as a disguise from my normal self.

How lame.

I had an actual pull-over mask Gordon's mom made one Halloween. In fact, she made me an entire costume. We told her it was for a Superhero party, and she didn't bat an eye; just asked what colors I wanted it in.

Red, white, and blue was a little overdone. Superman. Wonder Woman. Captain America.

So I chose a respectable array of slate blues. And I looked bad as hell.

There was this bank robbery I lucked into once. Three guys inside with guns; one waiting in the getaway car.

They were so surprised at my appearance that none of them squeezed off a single shot. I took care of the getaway guy first, then used my Super-Speed to disarm all three of the inside guys in less than two seconds. They showed the footage from the bank's cameras on the news that night.

I was only a blur.

So that's what the tabloids started calling me. *The Blur*.

After that, I had Gordy's mom sew a cursive "B" on my chest. A little double meaning never hurt anyone.

The "legitimate" newspapers didn't print any photos, and they didn't spread my new nickname. They described me as an "unidentified person." They didn't even mention my Super-Speed; only printed that I'd disarmed the bank robbers, and the police wanted to interview me.

But the tabloids played it for everything it was. Every caper I foiled generated front-page headlines about *The Blur* in the *National Enquirer,* complete with fuzzy photographs and wild speculation about the real-life Superhero.

Eventually the real newspapers began to publish stories about me, too. Some were strictly factual, and some were purely opinionated, and they weren't always flattering. Still, I was a star.

Then came the posers and copycats. Guys dressed in slate blue who tried catching criminals. They patrolled the street at night looking for trouble.

But when a security camera caught *them*, they were never blurry. The tabloids came ablaze with new photos of *The Blur*, claiming a high-speed camera had finally caught me on tape. Even though the guy was maybe 5-8 and a little on the skinny side.

Less than a month after *The Blur* mania began, it ended. A fifteen-year-old kid with a makeshift costume and a police scanner finally beat the cops to a scene.

It was his first and last time.

A domestic disturbance call had come in around 10:30 one hot and humid summer night. It was less than a block away from the kid's apartment, where he lived with his single mom and six-year-old sister. It took him less than five minutes to get there.

I know because the news reports said when the cops arrived just under six minutes after getting the call, the back wheel of the kid's bike was still spinning from where he'd let it crash onto the sidewalk.

Inside the brownstone, Randy Hooper, high on coke, came home to find his girlfriend cheating on him. According to the new lover, Randy took one look at the wannabe Superhero charging toward him, laughed and threw the girl into the entertainment center. Then stuck a Bowie knife in the kid's gut.

Fifteen times.

The Blur ceased to be a hero the next day. He was labeled a vigilante who encouraged kids to emulate him. Something akin to tobacco companies using cartoons to sell cigarettes.

A month later, Gordon and I moved to Chicago.

The suit stayed in New York. In a dumpster.

The roller-skate waitress interrupted my thoughts to ask if I'd like something else. I looked toward the bank, then told her I could go for another milkshake. I took the last bite of my cheeseburger as I watched her skate away, her ponytail swaying back and forth like a teenage metronome. She twirled around a Dodge Charger with ease, laughing as she skidded to a stop at the driver's window, startling him.

It's amazing how kids get so much younger each year.

It was going to be a long afternoon.

Chapter 13

Around two o'clock, after my third chocolate shake, Jennifer Pearce gathered her briefcase and prepared to leave. I sat up in the driver's seat and waved to the roller-skate girl. I'd learned her name was Corey, and she was a freshman at Elon College studying Psychology. I handed her a twenty and told her to keep the change.

Her smile was wide and full of teeth. She wished me luck as she and her ponytail whisked off to another car. I'd been bored and told her I was on a stake-out.

I had to give her some reason for camping out in her spot during lunch rush hour. Might as well be the truth. Now she'd go back to her dorm and tell her friends she'd fed a guy while he was on a stake-out. I bet she'll tell her grandchildren one day.

Pearce's Lexus pulled onto Church Street five minutes later. I followed a ways behind, always keeping a few cars between us. I don't know where I expected her to go, but when she pulled into a Bed, Bath and Beyond, I remembered that thought about this being a long afternoon.

Next, she stopped by a used book store; then at three, she pulled into Burlington City Park. She stepped out of her car with her briefcase and looked around the parking lot. Twice.

I tried to duck down and hit my head on the steering wheel. Twice.

What's really sad is that she'd never had a chance to see me. I was using my X-Ray-Vision to scan through six cars to spy on her, but sometimes, human nature has a way of taking over before you can think. So I blame my quick reflexes and animal instinct for the shiny new goose egg over my left eyebrow.

I scanned Jennifer's briefcase and wouldn't you know it, it was filled with money. Lots of money. I couldn't tell the denomination from where I was, but let's just say, it was an assload. And if she was dropping it off to someone here, it was more than likely not a legal transaction. I hopped out of the Aztek to follow her.

She wound through the park, past the historical merry-go-round, past the see-saws and swing sets. I stayed at a safe distance, wandering slowly as if I were a guy on my day off with nothing to do but kill time.

A few minutes later she sat on an isolated bench and positioned the briefcase on the ground toward the middle. I wandered around, pretending to enjoy the landscaping and the squirrels.

I wore a faded blue t-shirt, a pair of dirty cargo shorts, and some beat-up tennis shoes. I looked like the type of guy who'd stroll around a park aimlessly, sniffing flowers and gawking at animals.

Hell, I looked like I'd be trying to talk to them, too, maybe trade recipes and gossip about the beavers down the creek. *Did you see the latest dam they built? Shoddy. Absolute horrid workmanship. I can't believe it holds water.*

Five minutes later, expensively-dressed Jennifer Pearce was joined by a man about my size. He had my height, my barrel chest, my good looks. He didn't have my gut or mullet, though.

I could take him.

I tried to use my Super-Hearing to home in on their conversation, but I only got static. Odd. That had never happened before. They were using some kind of device that interfered with my power, or at least garbled their voices into white noise.

I concentrated harder, zoning out everything around me, but still couldn't get anything from them but hollow static. They were definitely up to no good.

I was puzzling through what could be causing the interference when the guy hopped up and walked away. With the briefcase.

Jennifer stood and headed back in my direction.

I had a decision to make. Follow him, or follow her. It was a no-brainer. Every cop show always teaches you to *follow the money*.

Hmm ...

But to go after the goon, I had to get by her without her recognizing Davenport Harrison Ridgley, the Third.

My Super-Speed is pretty damn fast, but it's not like I could race by her without her seeing me, like Hollywood plays it up. I'm more like a car with a beer gut whizzing by.

I was called *The Blur* because twenty years ago, security cameras were slow and their resolution sucked. But in reality, my Super-Speed isn't crazy fast. Maybe about 80 mph. With the weight and shape I'm in now, I might max out around 60 or so.

And truthfully, I haven't tried flying much in the last ten years. It might be classified more as strong hovering now.

Either way, Jennifer was approaching at a fast pace, and I needed to find a way to hide. So I did what any disheveled Superhero would do—hide in plain sight.

I curled up on a bench with my back outward and pretended I was a homeless man catching up on my sleep. I looked the part, and as

Jennifer scurried by, I even squeezed out a rebellious fart.

I heard Jennifer gasp and increase her pace. Mission accomplished.

As I reveled in my ingenuity, another fart slipped out. Then another.

My stomach gurgled and shifted and gurgled some more as milkshake fought intestines for an exit strategy. I tightened my sphincter as hard as I could, but another fart erupted: a wet, pungent one that silenced the chirping birds.

At least I didn't hear any birds. But then again, my senses were being assaulted on a level they hadn't experienced since the Great Pickled Egg Eating Contest of 2004. Now that was an event anyone with an ounce of intelligence would have stayed away from.

But there I was with two dozen other contestants, gathered at The Tasty Pig, eating nothing but pickled eggs as five minutes ticked down to zero. Timmy Rentenbach, a scrawny kid with a crew cut and freckles, beat me out with twenty-two eggs to my twenty-one. To win, though, a participant had to keep their eggs down for thirty more minutes.

The top seven hung around, hawking each other as the time slowly evaporated. Eighteen minutes later, the first fart eked out. It wasn't me, but as the seal had been broken, I offered the second fart with a sly smile.

The other contestants quickly followed suit and when Susan Bowers lost her eggs all over the hardwood floor, the restaurant cleared except for us seven. Even the judges retreated to the kitchen to watch us through a window.

Those final twelve minutes were an eternity. Between the smell and the mess, it was a total disaster. In the end, Timmy held on to win, sporting a summer cold that I argued was an unfair advantage. My protests went unheard as the kid hoisted the trophy above his head and chanted his own name.

The Tasty Pig never held the contest again.

I stood from the bench, waving the air around me, and searched for the goon with the money. I finally found him, but it was too late to catch up—he was getting into a running car at the opposite end of the park. As the car took off, I zoomed in on the license plate and memorized it.

Hopefully it wasn't a rental, and Kimmy could run it through a national database to trace it. I made my way back to the Aztek. Jennifer was already gone, but I had a feeling I'd gotten the info I was looking for.

She was doing something dirty, and she wasn't doing it alone.

Chapter 14

I parked my Aztek in front of my apartment and slid out. Christine was still sunning by the pool. Did she ever work?

I opened my front door to find Kimmy napping on the couch, Little Man curled at her feet. The TV was on C-Span. That explained why Kimmy was napping.

When I turned the TV to USA for the marathon-du-jour, Kimmy sat up and swung her legs over the edge of the couch. "Well?"

"Gimme a sec," I said, heading for my room, stomach still gurgling.

I grabbed a clean pair of underwear and changed. Not much damage, just a few skid marks.

"Okay," I said when I returned to the living room. I looked around. "Where's Gordon?"

"He had a client emergency. Said he'd check back in."

I wanted to say something smart about what kind of an emergency one of his uber-rich clients could be having, but there were too many jokes to make. So instead, I slid Little Man over, sat, and told Kimmy about Jennifer dropping off the briefcase of money with the goon, and then I gave Kimmy the car's license plate.

Kimmy isn't what I call a real spook. She's more of an analyst specializing in crypto-algorithms. In short, she breaks codes. She's very smart, but this cloak-and-dagger stuff is a little beyond her capabilities and pay grade.

She did, however, have access to certain databases, one of which was DMV records. We went back to my computer room, and I stood beside her while she searched the entries for the plate number and got a hit: Argyle Industries.

Didn't sound very ominous. Maybe that was the point. If you're going to be a super evil corporation, it probably isn't a good idea to name yourself something like *Weapons R Us Inc.* or *International Villains Organization LLC*.

According to their website, Argyle Industries was located in Burlington and made all things argyle. Socks, table cloths, scarves, kilts, jacket linings.

You name it. If it was argyle, they made it.

And they were a worldwide corporation, sourcing and shipping their products to every continent on the globe. They had the perfect cover for a major terrorist organization. Who would search a shipment of argyle sweaters from America for weapons of mass destruction?

Kimmy stood and stretched.

I backed up and admired her.

"Stop that," she said.

My eyes moved up to hers. "What? I thought you were giving me a thank-you show. I was about to applaud."

She rolled her eyes. "You're impossible."

"You know," I told her. "Once you go Superhero ..."

She threw a stapler at me.

"Fine, fine," I said. "You don't know what you're missing."

"You mean like syphilis? No thanks."

I raised a hand to my heart. "That hurts. That really hurts."

"Actually, it should hurt a little lower than that. You should get that checked."

The fact is, Kimmy and I had gotten together once a long time ago. In high school, I tried forever to kiss her and get her to "go with me." She said it felt too weird. I told her I could work with that.

She said, "No. Like a *brother* kind of weird."

To be fair, I was over at Gordon and Kimmy's house so much of my childhood I *was* like a member of their family. I generally liked being anywhere as long as it wasn't my own home.

And we did have sort of a brother-sister type of a relationship growing up. We chided and teased each other and called each other stupid names like "brace face" and "zit head." We had arguments and told each other, "You're stupid." We celebrated milestones, pulled for the same teams, and hung out together after school.

Then we both hit puberty and two things changed.

I developed my Superpowers, and she developed boobs.

And that's when I reconsidered that whole *brother-sister* thing.

Then, at Kimmy's and Gordy's eighteenth birthday party, I snuck some beer in and schemed all night how to get Kimmy drunk and alone. I loved her bright red hair when it was banana-clipped and poofed out. It smelled like raspberries.

Sometime after midnight, somebody—I wonder who??—suggested playing seven-minutes-in-the-closet, a much more fun version of spin-the-bottle. In Seven Minutes, the mantra was "anything goes."

When it was my turn to spin, guess who the bottle pointed toward? I swear, I never used any special powers to make that happen. I could control my powers about as much as I could control my erection.

Everyone *oohed* and *ahhed* as they shoved us into a cramped coat closet that smelled like sweat, which clued me in to how well Eric Sapley's seven minutes with Michelle Buckingham had gone.

If I had a Kryptonite on this earth, it would be the combination of Kimmy's large green eyes and shimmering red hair. They made my knees shake and my toes quiver.

Kimmy and I fumbled around for a bit, giggling and whispering, until our drunk lips found each other. At that moment, I was ruined for life.

Every future kiss would forever be compared to the feeling from that first sloppy smooch of Kimmy's. My heart stopped. My blood heated. My mind blanked.

The only thing that existed right then were Kimmy's lips. Well, that and my raging hard-on.

I had imagined the kiss so many times I was afraid I might have built it up too much. Put it on a pedestal that could never be reached.

But that pedestal crumbled to a pile of dust the moment our lips locked. Nothing could have prepared me for that moment.

We groped and giggled and tongued for the entire seven minutes. The time stretched into hours, and then abruptly, into seconds. Just like that, it was over.

The closet door yanked open and everyone made kissing noises, waggling their tongues at us. We separated and stepped out, flushed and sweating.

Later that week, a rumor went around that I'd felt Kimmy up, got my hand somewhere special, and made her excited. The rumor said she'd put me in her mouth for "just a little bit," and that she'd mentioned something about "going all the way" when we got alone.

Kimmy heard the rumor and didn't speak to me for two weeks. I swore up and down I never started it. I tried to tell her how guys got in gym class, how they made stuff up and added to it and blew it out of proportion.

"Guys are like that," I told her.

I begged her to go on a real date with me, to give me a chance to make things right.

I found an old bike missing the front wheel abandoned in a ditch. I tore it to pieces and bent the frame into a heart within a heart and gave it to her.

No matter what I tried, she wouldn't give me another chance. I'd had my moment. And that was all I'd ever have.

I guess I never should have started that rumor after all. Live and learn.

"What are you looking at?" Kimmy barked.

"Huh?"

"Where were you?" she asked, calmer.

"Nowhere." I took a breath. "So what do you want to do next?"

She bit her lip. "I want to search the Homeland Security databases, but I'm afraid."

"Afraid you'll trip the same wires Andrew did?"

Kimmy frowned. "Yeah."

"It's alright to be afraid, Kimmy. You're not a field agent; you're an analyst." I wanted to put my arm around her and comfort her, but I was afraid she'd take it wrong.

"That's easy for you to say. Nothing can hurt you."

She was wrong there. I was looking at the only thing to ever truly hurt me. It had unruly red hair and sparkling eyes.

"Tell you what," I said. "Until we figure this out, you can stay here. Then you don't have to be afraid."

I could tell part of her wanted to say yes. The other part, the one I hurt so many years ago, held the line.

"Thank you, but no."

"Kimmy, that's just being stupid. You're afraid. I can protect you."

"I've got a gun, and I know how to use it."

"And yet you're still afraid. Otherwise you'd be doing an extensive search on Argyle Industries right now." I crossed my arms, defying her to disprove my logic.

She locked eyes on me. I saw a mixture of fear, hatred, and tears. I had called her cowardly and stupid, the worst things you could say to an independent woman. Kimmy was the type who fought a losing battle because she still had fight in her. She'd never be a damsel-in-distress.

It was the hardest thing in the world for her to accept help. It had taken everything inside her to come to me in the first place, and me being myself, I'd insulted her for her trouble. I knew exactly what would happen next.

"I'm leaving," she snapped. "I've got things to do."

"Kimmy, I'm sorry. How about I stay at your place tonight? I'll sleep on the couch, and you won't even know I'm there."

"No."

"Come on. I won't even look at you naked unless you're really standing in front of me naked."

She grabbed her purse without cracking the faintest of smiles. I could always get a chuckle out of Kimmy, but not that time.

"Thanks for your help," she said. Her wall was up. I'd lost her. "Tell Gordon to call me."

And before I could get another word in, she darted out the door. I wanted to go after her, but she'd just push me away harder. I knew Kimmy well enough to know what she'd do next. She'd go straight to her house, turn on her computer, and research the hell out of Argyle Industries. Damn the bad guys; Kimmy had her chin up, and it was her against the world.

I'm such a dumbass. What had I done?

Chapter 15

Not more than five minutes later, the doorbell rang. Kimmy had come to her senses. Thank God. I opened the door to a shock of red hair. It took me a second to realize it wasn't Kimmy, but rather a beautiful and shapely stranger instead. I must have won the redhead lottery.

"Well hel-lo," I said in my best seductive voice, elongating the word into two languid syllables. "What can I do for *you*?" I leaned against the door.

"Mr. Glick?"

Uh-oh. With her dress slacks, smart blouse, and formal demeanor, she was either a process server or an attorney. Take your pick; neither was good. My mood soured.

"Yeah?"

She smiled and said, "I've been looking for you a very long time."

"Oh yeah?" I appraised her again. "Well I've been looking for you my whole life."

She raised an eyebrow. "May I come in?"

I moved aside and flourished with my arm. "Entré."

I closed the door behind her. "Would you like a drink?" I asked. "I have Corona."

She stopped and turned. "Sure, why not."

I grabbed the beers and popped their tops behind the fridge door. "So, Miss ... I don't believe I caught your name?"

Stupid red hair. Always distracts me.

She sat her leather portfolio on the kitchen table and stuck out her hand. "Gerber. Samantha Gerber. But call me Sam, please."

As we shook hands, I got a funny feeling. Something wasn't right. I couldn't quite place it yet, but my intuition told me I'd made a mistake letting this woman in. Little Man had yet to make his appearance, and I wondered if he'd already sensed trouble.

I plopped down at the table and motioned for her to do the same. "What can I do for you, Sam? I must tell you, I already have a vacuum cleaner, and I don't do religion."

She pulled a glossy 8x10 out of her portfolio and tossed it onto the table in front of me. I took one look and felt my smile literally melt away. If I had a Spidey-Sense, it would have tingled the moment the doorbell rang.

There, lying on my kitchen table, was an enlarged full-color photo of me in mid-flight. *The Blur* twenty years ago. Only very much in focus and not at all blurry. At least I had my mask on in the photo.

Then I remembered Sam Gerber. A young coed at NYU majoring in photo journalism. NYU was where Gordon was working on his Bachelor's before the whole fiasco with the kid and angry boyfriend. I practically lived in Gordy's dorm room with him, never missing a chance to hit on cute college coeds.

She must have taken this one day when I "took off" from behind the dorm. I wasn't so careful back then. How's the saying go? Young, dumb and full of—

"Come now, Mr. Glick. That look familiar?" she said.

I tried to recapture my disintegrated smile. "What movie is this from? I don't recognize it."

She tossed another photo at me. *The Blur* masked and hovering outside a third-story dorm window. Gordon's window; Kimmy was visiting.

Another photo floated toward me. *The Blur* masked and picking up a car. That one was so cliché. I was showing off for a bunch of drunk sorority sisters that night.

Another photo. The Blur taking off his mask.

Fuck.

"You're a hard guy to find," Sam Gerber said.

"Excuse me?" My fake smile had melted away again. How do politicians do it?

"I followed you to Chicago, but by then you'd moved to Los Angeles. And by the time I tracked you there, you'd disappeared altogether." She paused for effect. "Vanished off the grid."

"I don't understand what you're getting at." I tried not to fidget.

"You don't have a social security number. You've never had a paying job as far as I can find. You don't even have a credit card and never had any type of loan."

I remained silent, waiting for the punch line.

"You're like the Invisible Man."

Hey, how about that. I *do* have the power of Invisibility.

"Only you're not," she continued. "You're *The Blur*."

"And you're crazy, lady." It was all I could think of to say. She had me off balance, and I wasn't used to that. First, the red hair and sexy body, then the revelations of hidden truths.

She continued. "The one thing you had that I could find ... you know what that was?"

I was holding my breath.

"A birth certificate. Your future and present may have been a mystery, but the past always stays the same. And how does the old adage go? You always return home."

And I had.

I was born in Wesley Long Hospital in Greensboro, North Carolina. I lived a couple of miles from that spot right now. I was always so careful not to leave a trace, each time Gordon and I moved. But we'd returned home after the disaster in Los Angeles.

"Mr. Glick, do you know how I found you after all this time?"

I already knew.

"Your father," she said. "You don't have much of a relationship do you? You know what I've learned about parents?" She paused. "They'll always be your parents, no matter what."

I'd learned the same lesson.

"Sounds like a great book," I told her. "Let me know when the movie comes out. I'll take a few friends."

Her mouth spread into a broad omniscient smile; the Cheshire cat would be jealous.

"Mr. Glick? May I call you Barry?" She didn't wait for an answer. "Barry, can we skip the charade?" She pulled out a pad and pen. "Let me get my interview, a few pictures, maybe one of you hovering with your suit on, and I'll be on my way."

Oh, that's all?

You want to expose me as the only guy in the world who can see through anything, fly without wings, lift a few tons without breaking a sweat, run as fast as a Toyota Prius ... I can see it now.

Government scientists dissecting me, trying to find out how I can do the things I do when even I don't know. Looking for answers I can't give.

"There's nothing special to flying," I'd tell them. "I just think of being there instead of here, and all the air particles move out of my way, practically pulling me in their wake." Then they'd cut out a biopsy of my brain, analyze it, and find nothing abnormal.

"Super-Speed?" I'd say. "You know how they make it look in *The Matrix*? The slo-mo stuff? It's something like that. Time slows down so I can slice through it while everyone else is barely moving, but here's the kicker—it's like I'm really moving at those high speeds because my lungs burn and my heart explodes if I do it for too long."

It would go like that for months, years, until finally I'd die in some stark white underground cell, electrodes plastered all over my body, an IV pumping sedative into my blood.

I'm a freak of nature. I know that. My dad reminded me every damn day of my adolescence until I broke his jaw and left for good.

I laughed at Samantha Gerber. It was the hearty laugh of an insane man, and she drew back in her chair. I laughed again, even harder, and took a swig of my beer.

"Lady," I said. "You are out of your fucking mind. You're chasing the wrong story for your Pulitzer." I took another swig and belched. "I think I'd rather you try to convert me to some half-assed prophet-oriented cult. At least then I could take you seriously before telling you you're crazier than the guy who decided changing Coke's recipe was a good idea."

I leaned back in my chair. Coke's recipe? It's amazing what you think about when you're losing your mind.

"If I give you an interview, will you put out?" I gave her the once-over. "I'm using my X-Ray-Vision on you right now, and you got a pretty hot body. What do you say? You want me to wear a mask when we do it?"

Sam Gerber stood, her eyes wide and her mouth wider. She was speechless.

"I know," I continued. "We could both wear masks and do it doggy style. I'd like that picture myself. I got a whip somewhere around here. Could we use that too?"

Sam grabbed her photos and shoved them into her portfolio. She was huffing, and I thought she might hyperventilate.

"I know what you want," I continued. "You want to join the mile-high club without using a plane. I gotta warn you, though, doing it like that is a lot harder than you think it would be."

She scurried to the door and shot outside, slamming it behind her.

I threw my beer against the wall and the bottle shattered into a million tiny pieces. I took a deep breath and closed my eyes.

The situation wasn't good. She'd come back once she calmed down and realized I'd been pushing her buttons. Gordon had always said I was a control freak, and I don't disagree.

I had to be.

Chapter 16

I knew Kimmy was going to research Argyle Industries, and I knew it would put her in danger. We were getting close to whatever Andrew had found, and he'd had the privilege of disappearing for his trouble.

The same would happen to Kimmy unless I protected her, with or without her permission. The night ahead of me was not going to be very comfortable. Because I was such an ass, I'd have to sleep outside her place in the Aztek instead of on her couch.

Ever since the Recession and gas crunch of 2009, Kimmy and most of her colleagues worked out of satellite offices. More specifically, their homes. They were outfitted with the latest computers and have access to all the country's most secret databases through some "pretty intense encryption"—Kimmy's words, not mine.

Being a spy isn't what it used to be in the cold war era.

Most spying nowadays can be done over the internet. Kimmy says everyone thinks nobody can see what they're doing, but the truth is, anyone can be a spy if they have the right software.

My phone rang. It was Gordon. I didn't want to talk to him because I knew the conversation already. But I'd hear it from him sooner or later, so I answered as I pulled another Corona from the fridge.

"What did you say to Kimmy?" he asked.

"Hey to you too, buddy. Good day so far?"

"What did you say?"

I collapsed on the couch and propped my feet up on the coffee table. This was going to take a minute.

"I told her to stay here. She said she was afraid, and I said she could stay the night."

Little Man hopped up on the couch and stretched.

"While you were undressing her with your eyes?"

"I did that first, but I was sincere about protecting her."

Gordon sighed. "Don't you know anything about women?"

"Gordy," I said. "I'm forty-three, and I've never had a serious relationship that didn't include a remote control or a mouse and keyboard. Are you being rhetorical or idiotic?"

I've never claimed to know a thing about women, and I never will.

"Well, whatever you said, Kimmy called me crying."

There was a pause where Gordon probably expected me to say something insightful or thoughtful. But since I'm me, I took a swig of beer and let the silence speak for itself. Little Man *mrow*ed.

"You don't have anything to say?" he asked.

"I'm sorry, okay? Whatever I did, I'm sorry. I was just trying to offer my protection."

Gordon sighed again, then said, "I'm about to finish up here. What's your night like?"

"I'm gonna go park outside Kimmy's."

"Why's that?"

I told him how I thought she was going to do something stupid and filled him in about Argyle Industries.

"Want some company?"

I thought about it. "Sure, why not? We can take turns napping."

He came by in thirty minutes, and I voted on Chinese as our stake-out food. Another half hour later, ignoring the warning signals from my stomach, we were parked down the block from Kimmy's, plowing into some eggrolls. We'd pull closer to the house once it got dark.

"So tell me about your appointment this afternoon," I said to Gordon.

He looked at me like I'd just asked him to show me his penis. "I can't do that," he said. "You know better."

"Come on. Tell me about somebody crazy."

"My clients are not crazy. They have problems, and I help them find solutions."

"Right," I said, shoveling some Kung Pao Chicken into my mouth. "What was his problem? Getting kicked in the balls excites him, and he doesn't understand why women freak out about it?"

Gordon leveled his gaze at me, then nibbled at his Pork Lo Mein.

"He likes wearing women's clothes and trying to pick up guys?"

Gordon chewed and drank some Diet Coke, looking straight ahead.

I snapped my fingers and said, "I know. He's one of those guys that likes to be choked right when he—"

"For God's sake, Barry," Gordon snapped, a noodle flipping from his mouth and slapping against his chin "Is sex all you ever think about?"

I took a bite of an eggroll. "Ninety ... ninety-five percent of the time. Sure. Don't you?"

Gordon shot me the Super-Stare.

"You got a ..." I motioned at my chin.

Gordon wiped the noodle off and sipped some more drink.

Getting under Gordon's skin was so easy. All you had to do was talk about sex.

"You gonna answer me?" I asked.

"Huh?"

"I asked if you thought about sex all the time, because the way I see it, you should think about it twice as much as I do, since you're ... you know ... playing for both teams."

Gordon bit the corner off a Crab Rangoon and shot me the Super-Stare again.

"I mean, Gordy, if you think about it logically, you should be sex-crazed. No one's off limits. You could go out on a date with a girl, then the next day, turn around and go out with a dude."

Gordon wasn't talking to me so I stuck an Elmore Leonard book-on-tape CD in and we listened to the exploits of Deputy Marshall Raylan Givens while we finished eating. The sun lowered in the horizon and we continued to sweat with the windows open.

"That truck that just passed by?" I said. "That's its third time."

"Yeah?" Gordon looked around. "You see who was in it?"

"Two goons my size. Navy blue Nissan SUV. My guess is they're scoping out the place, waiting for dark."

Gordon tensed.

When the threat of danger is just a possibility, there's a good chance it's only a false alarm. Pretend. It's not real yet. But when danger is imminent, the world takes on a whole new feeling.

To me, it meant I could save the day and still get to sleep in my bed tonight.

To Gordon, it meant conflict. And Gordon didn't care much for conflict.

When it got dark enough, we moved the Aztek in front of Kimmy's house. Her lights went out around ten. Shortly after midnight, the festivities began.

The dark blue Pathfinder crept by and turned at the end of the block.

I glanced at Gordon and said, "Showtime."

I left Gordon in the Aztek and jogged up to Kimmy's house, then shuffled around back. That's where they'd go—there was too much light around front.

I slid in behind a big bush beside her back door and crouched down. A few minutes later, using my X-Ray-Vision, I saw the two goons leap her fence with relative ease. For big guys, they seemed pretty agile.

I rubbed my hands together, barely holding in my glee. I hadn't beat the hell out of anyone in ages. This was going to be fun.

I wished I could see them better, but on that front I was going to be at a disadvantage. From what I could tell, both of them had on night vision goggles. Normally that would give them an advantage, but with me, it just meant they'd see what was coming right before it knocked them on their ass.

It wouldn't change the outcome, but it might be a fair fight for once.

As they neared the back door, I stood and stepped from behind the bush, saying, "Can I help you gentlemen find something?"

They jerked and straightened. Up close, one was my size and the other was slightly bigger.

Then something happened that I'll never forget for the rest of my life. The one on the left, the "smaller" of the two, leapt at me so fast I didn't have time to react.

His fist landed squarely on my jaw, and had I not used Super-Speed to at least roll with the punch, he would have taken it right off. As it was, I heard it crack—a sound completely foreign to me—and I was stunned as I stumbled backwards onto Kimmy's back stoop.

The bigger one came at me just as fast and landed a shot to my gut. I tensed just hard enough for him not to rupture my spleen, but for the first time in twenty years, I had the breath knocked out of me.

I rolled right and before I could stand, the first goon was on me. He grabbed my arm, and with speed I can only describe as equal to my own, flung me through the night air until I smacked into a huge oak tree and tumbled to the ground.

I stood, shaking my head, and the two goons spread out. I tried to catch my breath as I surveyed my surroundings.

The back yard was lit only by slivers of light from neighbors' homes and a moon partially hidden by clouds. I needed to even the odds a little more because these two were going to be more difficult than I thought.

I needed to get their goggles off. This fight was one-sided the wrong way.

Using my Super-Speed, I charged, juked left, then went for the goon on the right. He reacted immediately—keeping up with me—and side-stepped so I'd miss tackling him. Only he didn't know I was only going for his goggles.

My fingertips clamped onto the extended lenses, and I ripped the contraption from his head. Now he was as blind as me, even more so because his eyes needed time to adjust.

I twisted into a roundhouse kick á la Jackie Chan; my foot landed squarely on his chest. He yelped as he flailed and flew backwards.

I turned on his partner as I felt slight tinge in the back of my kicking leg—I'd just pulled a hamstring—but got tackled to the ground before I twisted all the way around. Damn, this guy was unbelievably strong. He squeezed me in a bear hug, and it felt like my dinner might come back up for an encore.

In fact, it did. For his trouble, Goon #2 got a face full of Kung Pao Chicken. But it wasn't enough for him to let go so I boxed both his ears. He loosened his grip, stunned, so I boxed them again, harder, and he let me go, groggily shaking his head. I took advantage of his momentary disorientation and snatched the goggles—and some Kung Pao—from his face and slammed them into his nose.

He cried out, and I pushed off of him. But the other goon was standing above me and kicked me in the ribs.

I heard a few bones snap and I screamed.

Then I yanked the goon's foot out from under him and twisted over, pushing myself to a standing position. The other goon—I forget which one now—dove at me with such speed I only had one way to go.

Up.

I jumped and hovered above them both as they gathered themselves. They exchanged a few words I couldn't hear because of the blood rushing in my ears. But more important, I noticed they weren't surprised by a 6'5" 310 lb. guy hovering over them.

Gordon came crashing around the corner of the house with a three wood in his hands, and I yelled for him to stay back. I could barely take care of myself with these two; there was no way I could protect him also.

At that same moment, the house lights flickered on, followed by the outside lights. The back yard exploded in bright yellow light.

The goons exchanged looks, then disappeared in a blur.

Yes, a *blur*.

I lowered myself to the ground as Kimmy burst out the back door, gun in hand.

"What the hell are you two doing?"

I looked at Gordon and said, "I'm not sure I know any more."

Then I collapsed to my knees.

Chapter 17

I ran my eyes up and down Kimmy's body. Even in the harsh light, she looked sexy. She wore baggy boxers and a t-shirt with a big, triangle-diamond box in the middle. Inside the box was a giant "S."

I said to Kimmy, pointing at her shirt, "That's just plain insulting."

She ignored me. "I asked what you two were doing in my back yard."

"You're welcome," I said. I held my hands up. "But really, no need to thank me."

"You're not answering me!"

"What were you going to do with that?" I said, looking at Gordon and his golf club. "Shank one in the woods?" I laughed and cried out in pain. I doubled over and grabbed my ribs. It felt like one was broken. Maybe two or three. I winced as I struggled to stand.

Kimmy and Gordon stared at me wide-eyed.

"You're really hurt?" Kimmy asked.

"Let's get you inside, right now," Gordon said.

I made my way up the back stoop and through the kitchen to the living room sofa.

"How are you hurt?" Kimmy asked.

She hadn't seen me hurt since my powers manifested themselves around age fifteen. Don't get me wrong; I'm still mortal like everyone else. I can't stop bullets, but I can move out of their way and react faster than the shooters can. I keep from getting hurt by doing that time-bending thing.

Except for tonight.

Kimmy brought me some water, and I asked, "You got any beer?"

She shook her head without comment, then said, "Wine."

"Liquor?"

"Just wine."

I almost asked what kind, but the truth was, I didn't care. I nodded and she padded to the kitchen. Gordon pulled up the ottoman and sat in front of me.

"What happened?"

His eyes showed genuine concern. Gordon and Kimmy weren't used to me being on the losing side of a fight. Hell, *I* wasn't used to being on the losing side.

Kimmy returned with a glass of red wine. I took a gulp, made a face, then took another gulp. It tasted unnatural, but as it spread down my throat, my nerves calmed.

Nerves? That's when I realized I was shaking. No wonder they were looking at me as if I was naked and painted blue. This was as foreign to them as a menu in Swahili.

When Gordon and I left New York after the incident with the kid getting stabbed, we moved to Chicago. We went there because Gordon could transfer his credits to DePaul University.

Gordon attended college while I played vigilante on the streets. But in Chicago, I went after gangs, figuring I'd stay incognito and still do the world some good.

I put a hurting on some big guys back then, and most important, none of my deeds made the front page of the paper or the evening news.

Gangs liked their privacy, especially when the news was a single guy coming into their den and kicking the living shit out of them. I wore a ski mask as a disguise and everything went copacetic for a year or so.

But word eventually traveled among the gangs that they had a common enemy. There was a threat to their very existence, and they literally "ganged up" on me.

One day I broke into the 23rd Street Gang's headquarters, a chop shop that fronted as an auto repair shop. I was only going at half my Super-Speed because I'd gotten lazy after a year of kicking their wussy asses. They were waiting for me.

I knew a couple of them were inside because I'd staked out the place earlier that morning. I busted in the back door and made it ten feet into the building before a well-placed muffler planted itself into my face.

My feet shot out from under me, and I did a backwards flip while still moving forward, like you see in Kung Fu flicks. Only I didn't need wires.

I landed on my back, stunned, and like hornets swarming over a hapless intruder, the gang jumped me. Simultaneous punches to my thighs, gut, chest, and face. Then kicks and punches landed everywhere, including the boys. That dazed me for long enough they got in another few seconds of beating until I cleared a few away.

Then, with the slo-mo aspect of my Super-Speed in full gear, I escaped with my parts still intact. I had to ice my nuggets down for a week, and my body was a deep color of black and blue for a while, but I lived.

However, the damage was done because I never attacked another gang. I convinced Gordon to move once the semester was over. Chicago was too damn cold to be a good crime-fighting city anyway. If I was going to foil crooks, I wanted to do it somewhere warm with hot chicks.

So we packed our stuff and moved to L.A.

Kimmy brought my vision back to the present as she sat beside Gordon, and her big green eyes regarded me like they never had before.

"Explain," she said, shooting me a hard look.

"Me and Gordon," I said, nodding at my sidekick, "figured you were going to do something stupid like run a search on Argyle Industries, so we decided a stake-out was in order."

Kimmy's eyes hardened a little.

"I had Kung Pao Chicken in case you were wondering." She wasn't. I could tell by the way her eyebrows drew together. I continued. "So I noticed this SUV had driven by a few times and figured they weren't out checking resale values."

I paused for the inevitable chuckles. Nothing. Tough crowd.

"I went around back 'cause I figured they'd come that way since you don't have much lighting back there." I jutted my chin out. "I was right."

I drank some more wine.

"So these two goons hopped the fence and started toward the house. They had night-vision goggles, and they were as big as me, but I still didn't see a problem yet, you know? Because I'm me, and they're not."

I tried to sit up a little more and winced. Definitely some broken ribs in there.

"I figured I'd take their goggles so they'd be blind for a bit so ... I used my Super-Speed ... at least I think I used it ... no, wait ... one of them hit me first ... on the jaw ..."

I went to touch it and pain shot through my skull. I must have shown the agony because Kimmy and Gordon both made the same sour-lemon face. You know which one I'm talking about. The one everybody makes when they watch a video of a guy getting knocked in the nuts with an errant wiffle bat or piñata stick.

I looked at Gordon. "They had my speed."

He nodded. He'd seen them split when Kimmy flooded the yard with light.

I shook my head several times. "They had my Super-Speed and my Super-Strength." I kept repeating it over and over to no one in particular because that part still baffled me.

I looked up. "I got a few broken ribs, a pulled hamstring, and something's wrong with my jaw. It's clicking when I talk."

Kimmy stood and said she'd get some bandages and ice. I was still shaking my head, repeating things as if I couldn't believe them. Because I couldn't. The ramifications were too big to consider.

All this time I thought I was one of a kind, the only person in the world with actual Superpowers. I had what everyone else fantasized about, what comic books and movies had glorified for decades.

But now, I wasn't alone.

I wasn't one of a kind. There were at least two other guys out there who could do what I could do. I wasn't the only freak of nature, which meant there were probably others. More than us three.

"They beat the shit out of me," I said.

Gordon and Kimmy nodded, neither knowing what to say.

"No, I mean, they really beat the shit out of me." They nodded in unison again, and I said, "No, really, I think I shit my pants. Help me get to the bathroom."

Kimmy covered her mouth and backed up.

Gordy frowned at me. "I wondered what that was."

I shook my head and held out a hand. Damned milkshakes.

Chapter 18

When I woke up on Kimmy's couch in the morning, Kimmy was leaning over me checking out my jaw.

"You're a sight for sore eyes," I said.

Kimmy sucked in and jumped back, startled.

The cool thing about X-Ray-Vision is that I can see through anything, including my own eyelids. I can have my eyes closed and see the world as if everything was colored in sepia.

It comes in handy.

Kimmy would normally smack me in the arm after I did something like that, but she didn't this time, probably afraid she'd hurt me. I wasn't sure if I liked this new Kimmy better or not. But it's nice to be nursed by a gorgeous woman; I can see the appeal in that whole Munchausen thing.

"You know," I said, opening my eyes. "I really do find that t-shirt offensive."

Kimmy still had on the red, white, and blue "S" shirt. She cracked a smile.

"I demand you remove it right now."

"I'll bet you do." She sat on the ottoman. "How do your ribs feel?"

I propped myself up, wincing, Kimmy mimicking my face. "That answer your question?" I asked. Before I'd passed out last night, she'd made me take my shirt off so she could wrap my chest in ACE bandages.

She told me to lean forward, and she unwrapped me. My ribs were black and blue where I was kicked. I popped some more Ibuprofen.

"You hurt worse this morning?" Kimmy asked.

I nodded, then said, "The pain's moved. It's down in my groin area now. How about you make sure everything's okay down there, too?"

She squinted her eyes at me, then shoved the ice bag she was holding into the boys. I flinched.

"How's that?" she asked.

I leaned back. "Could you move it a little to the left?"

Kimmy huffed. "You need antibiotics for what you got down there."

"Aw, Kimmy. You know I've been saving myself for you."

"Sure you have. Did that bimbo last week know that?" She raised an eyebrow.

Kimmy had seen me with a woman I'd picked up at a biker bar downtown. Kimmy was walking with a few of her friends when I came waltzing out of the bar with Nameless Redhead With Piercings.

Nameless Redhead was drunk, dressed in leather, and up for calling a friend of hers to join us. I was drunk, up for a threesome—figuratively and literally—and had my hands all over her.

Actually, my hand was inside Nameless's leather vest when my eyes met Kimmy's.

Kimmy pretended she didn't know who I was, which was fine by me; I didn't need her screwing up my chance at a threesome. But it turns out Nameless Redhead With Piercings had way more piercings than I was comfortable with, and her friend didn't have a Tramp Stamp ... she had a

Tramp Season Pass.

But hey, it was a threesome, so, you know ...

"She was just a placeholder," I said.

"Yeah, I could tell by the way you were holding all her places."

Ouch.

"Okay you two," Gordon said, appearing from the hallway. "If you don't play pretty, I'll have to take away your Xbox."

We looked at Gordon, and I said, "Gordy, was that a joke?"

He ignored me and continued to the kitchen. Gordon couldn't function until he'd had at least two cups of coffee every morning.

"Bring me a cup," I yelled to him. What I really wanted this morning was a fifth of vodka, but I'd settle for a steaming cup of Colombian.

Until I got home.

Gordon brought two mugs into the living room, took one look at me and said, "So last night really happened, huh?"

I smiled and my jaw ached. "Yeah, it did."

He handed me a mug and sat down, crossing one leg over the other. "So, how do you feel?" he asked.

"Like I look," I answered.

Gordon was in therapist mode now. He knew how big this was for me. It wasn't the physical pain that had me screwed up. It was the knowledge that I was no longer the only show in town.

On one hand, I wasn't the only freak any more. On the other hand, the other freaks were bad guys and probably wouldn't care to go out for a beer and swap Superhero stories.

Gordon let the silence hang in the air until it filled the room.

"They weren't surprised," I finally said. "I mean, they were at first, but then it didn't seem like a big deal to them. That I could keep up with them."

"And you're still surprised," Gordon said.

"Yeah, aren't you?"

Gordon shrugged as if to say, "This is your session, not mine."

"There's something else," I said. "When I hovered above them, one of them said something to the other."

Gordon and Kimmy waited for me to continue.

"I've been trying to figure it out, and I know what he said now." I paused. "Half-breed."

"Half-breed?" Kimmy repeated.

"Yeah, half-breed. But it's not just that. It's the way he said it that stuck with me. He spit it out with an attitude." I watched my coffee swirl in small eddies, then looked up. "Like it was a cuss word."

Chapter 19

I wasn't just a freak. According to the goons that beat the hell out of me, I was a *half-breed* freak. I had no idea what that meant, but it made me feel dirty. And not the good kind of dirty.

I knew what I was going to have to do now. And it was the last thing in the world I wanted to do. There was only one person who could shed some light on my lineage.

Dad.

I didn't want to see him, especially in this vulnerable condition, but he could hold the answers to the biggest question of my life.

Why am I the way I am?

It's the ultimate question every person eventually asks. In many aspects, I felt like I was an adopted child. Because in no way whatsoever did I feel like I was my parents' offspring.

At least not my dad's.

I knew nothing of my mother other than what he'd told me. And that wasn't very much.

Growing up, I used to stare at pictures of her and wonder how her voice sounded. What she smelled like. How tight her hug would be.

I had never met any of my grandparents. According to my dad, they were all dead. I once found a picture of his parents buried in his sock drawer. It was an old black-and-white. My grandfather's arm was around my grandmother's shoulder and neither was smiling, like they were angry about the invention of cameras.

Kimmy made us a proper Southern breakfast: bacon, eggs, sliced tomatoes, biscuits, and gravy, served with orange juice and coffee.

"I'm impressed," I said. "Smart, pretty, *and* domestic."

She cut her eyes at me as she spooned gravy over my biscuit.

"Don't get used to it," she said.

I was about to say something like, "I could get used to this," but now I couldn't. Just more proof we should be together—we had the same thoughts.

Only opposite.

I ate some eggs and told Kimmy, "You realize you're not staying here again until this is all over, right?"

She looked up from her plate, her chin stuck out. "I've got a gun."

"They've got Super-Speed, Kimmy. They could take your gun, empty it, and give it back before you even had a chance to raise it. You're not staying here, even if me and my six good ribs have to drag you out ourselves."

"He's right, Kimmy," Gordon said. "You can't stay here."

She set her fork down. "It's not like either of you could protect me."

That jab was meant mainly for me.

"I know what to expect now," I said.

"They know what to expect, too."

She had me there. I didn't have a good comeback, so I ate instead. I finished everything on my plate and grabbed the rest of the bacon, then made myself an apple jelly biscuit. I had to keep my strength up. And I was also putting off visiting my dad. I needed answers, but I didn't have to look forward to getting them.

Gordon had a client to see that morning, so I figured that was as good a time as any to find my dad. I'd probably have to wake him from a drunken stupor.

"What are you doing today?" Gordon asked Kimmy.

"My job."

"From here?"

"Where else would I do it? Besides, it's been over forty-eight hours since Andrew was supposed to check in, so now I can get my bosses to do something."

"You still can't do it from here," I said. "The bad guys know where you live."

Kimmy stood up, saying, "I'll do whatever I want to do."

"And you can do it where I can look after you. No more arguments."

She glared at me as I stood up and took my plate to the sink. She tried to maintain her stony front, but I could see she'd already caved. She was too scared not to.

The breakfast had helped me; I was feeling better already. I almost felt strong enough to confront my dad.

Gordon washed his plate out in the sink, and we waited on Kimmy to change clothes. She drove us over to my place to drop Gordon off for his car, then the two of us went to my dad's.

The situation was working out in more ways than one. Kimmy and I could spend some quality time together, and with Kimmy there, maybe my dad wouldn't be such an ass. I might actually get something out of him besides insults.

We pulled up to the house I'd spent my childhood years in. I'd only been back a few times since the night I moved out.

And boy was that a night to remember. My dad came home drunk after a binge session at a local dive. I was a senior in high school and already counting the days before I could leave.

He started in as soon as he walked through the front door.

"Hey Barry! Where the hell are you?" he yelled.

I was in my room playing video games. I'd been using my X-Ray-Vision to win at cards and had recently won a Nintendo. I was on one of the secret Super Mario levels when Dad burst into my room and started yelling at me, calling me a no-good thief and a freak of nature.

I did like I normally did and ignored him. That night for some reason, it infuriated him so much he ripped my Nintendo from the shelf and threw it at me.

I ducked and jumped up, my blood beginning to warm as it coursed through me. If there's anything my dad and I have in common, it's a short fuse. I've gotten better about it through the years, but back then, I would fly off the handle if you looked at me wrong. Around him, I generally kept it in check, but that night I got right up in his face.

He snarled at me, then laughed. "What are you gonna do, freak boy? See through me? Fly away?"

My X-Ray-Vision and Flying were the only powers I had at that time. At least, that's what I thought.

He pushed me back, and I held my ground.

"Sit back down, boy, before I make you."

I stood there, defiant, my chest rigid, my eyes burning with hate. I refused to back down any more to that son of a bitch. I wouldn't let him treat me like a second-class person ever again, drunk or not.

He spit in my face and laughed again, then said, "Think you're a big boy now, don't you?"

I *was* big. I had two inches and fifty pounds on him, and if you looked at us side by side, you'd wonder why I was so timid. But he'd bullied me my whole life, and to me, he was bigger than I'd ever be.

He took a swing at me, and I reacted on instinct. It was the first time I used Super-Speed.

I ducked his shot and watched, wide-eyed, as the world slowed to a crawl. Before I could think about the consequences, I struck back with a roundhouse right that lifted him from his feet and slammed him into my dresser, minus a front tooth.

Three others were loosened, but it was that one tooth I remembered most, because after I'd hit him, the world continued in slo-mo, and that tooth flipped over and over through the air. The world didn't speed back up to normal until the tooth hit the bare wooden floor.

Dad slid off the dresser and lay there on the floor beside his tooth, mouth bleeding, staring at me, stunned beyond words. He literally had no idea what hit him. One moment he was swinging at me; the next he was crumpled on the floor minus an incisor.

I gathered up some clothes as he watched, rubbing his jaw. And as I left the house to walk to Gordon's, I could hear him yelling at the top of his lungs, "Fucking Freak!" Even through the slurring, I could sense his hatred.

I sat there now outside his place, in Kimmy's car, the air conditioning blasting, rubbing my own jaw. This must have been how he felt. Angry, surprised, humiliated, helpless. No wonder he hated me; I threatened his very manhood. I had single-handedly emasculated my dad.

"Let's go back to my place," I said to Kimmy.

"What? Why?"

"He's not here."

"His car's here." She nodded toward his Chevy in the drive.

"You forget," I said. "I can see in the house. He's not here."

She put the car in gear and pulled away from the curb. As we rounded the corner, I looked back and saw the living room curtains move.

I couldn't face him. Not yet.

Chapter 20

We drove back to my place, and I told Kimmy to make herself at home. She declined my offer to walk around in her underwear eating ice cream, and then shot down my invitation to a group bath. So I took a long hot shower by myself.

When I finished, she was relaxing on the couch watching CNN.

Bor-ing.

I grabbed a Corona from the fridge, sat on the couch beside her, and clicked the remote to a rerun of *Psych*. I smiled and said to her, "Little Man likes Sean's crazy antics."

Besides, news without nudity seems downright useless.

"What?" she said. "No beer for me?"

I looked at her out of the side of my eyes, then got up and went to the fridge. "What you want?"

"What you got?"

"Good point." I snatched another Corona and joined her on the couch. She'd switched the TV back to CNN.

Sneaky.

I wasn't wearing a shirt, and she said, "Your ribs are looking better. Are they still hurting?"

I touched them and noticed they did hurt a little less. They also weren't as black and blue as they were the previous night.

"Wow," I said. "Maybe I have Super-Healing, too?"

Kimmy humphed. "It appears you do."

"It's been so long since I've gotten hurt."

I ran my hand over my jaw, and it didn't ache as much either. Now, *this* was cool! A new Superpower.

I remember when I first learned I had the ability to see through objects. I had just sprouted my first pubes and underarm hair. I was fifteen and the guys in gym class who had already hit puberty were ruthless. They teased everyone without curlies down below, asking if we were in the right locker room and what color panties we were wearing that day.

Some of us were a little chubby, and we had boobie nubs that would get pinched on our way back from the shower. It was a traumatic experience for every teenage boy who went through it.

Then one day, after I'd gotten two towel snaps and a nipple pinch, I struggled into my clothes and sat on the bench in front of my locker cubby. The wall behind it separated us from the girls' locker room, and I used to fantasize all the time that there would be a little hole in the wall where my basket sat. I could spy on the girls just like in all those classic eighties movies.

I stared at the cubby space, imagining how big the peep hole would be and how I'd have to shove my head in to get a good look. Useless. Stuff never worked like it did in the movies.

Then I thought about how much easier it would be to have X-Ray-Vision like Superman. Suddenly, the entire wall of locker baskets began to dissolve. The wall behind them appeared and melted away. The backs of more locker baskets appeared, then dissolved, and sitting in front of me was none other than Kimmy Moser herself.

It was like looking into one of those fairy tale mirrors. Kimmy sat there, brushing her magnificent shock of red hair, wearing only her panties and bra. A matching pink set with little roses.

I don't know how long I sat there and stared, but Gordon poked me.

"You alright?" he asked.

"Huh?" I turned to him, blinking, bringing myself back into the boys' locker room.

"I said are you alright?"

"Yeah." I considered telling him what had just happened, but he'd think I was bonkers. Or lying. What would I say? *Hey Gordy, old buddy, I can see through walls and your sister looks pretty damn hot in her pink underwear.*

That would go over well.

I thought about the incident all that day. I had to tell someone, or I'd lose my mind. Gordon was the only person I could share secrets with. He was my best friend, and once I proved I could see through stuff, he'd have no choice but to believe me.

We were sitting on his race car bed playing computer games when I laid it on him. "I got X-Ray-Vision."

"Excuse me?" His basilisk challenged my unicorn to a duel.

"You heard me. I can see through things."

"Okay." He turned back to the game, acting as though I'd just announced I was an alien.

Obviously I was going to have to convince him, and I had just the way. I grabbed a deck of cards from his desk—allowing him to kill my unicorn—and pulled them from their sleeve.

I handed them to Gordon, saying, "Go ahead. Pick one. I'll tell you what it is."

His eyes narrowed, but he went for it, if only to prove me nuts.

He chose a card from the middle of the deck and held it up, checking behind him for mirrors or reflective surfaces.

I relaxed and took a breath, focusing like I did in the locker room. Nothing.

I focused for ten whole seconds until Gordon said, "You're a regular magician alright."

"Just gimme a second. I haven't practiced much."

In truth, I'd spent most of the school day doing just that very thing. Trying to look through girl's shirts and dresses. Maybe what I should have said was that I hadn't gotten good at it yet.

Another few seconds and Gordon put the cards down, saying, "You're just trying to get out of this beating I'm giving you." He picked his joystick back up.

"Wait. I was almost there." I wasn't, but I really wanted to get a handle on it.

Gordon looked at me with skepticism.

"Just give me another minute or so."

He huffed and sat the joystick down, then grabbed another card from the deck.

I stared at the back of it, focusing, willing myself to see through it. Wishing I could just like I had in the locker room earlier that day. A few seconds later, the card and Gordon's hand dissolved! I had literally looked through the card, but I couldn't tell what was on the other side.

I explained the problem to Gordon, and he nodded slowly, giving me the early version of his "understanding-therapist" face.

"Look, just do this," I said. I threw a book at him and told him to hold it up with the card behind it, facing me.

"Sure thing." More therapist face.

"Gimme a break, man. I just learned how to do this today."

He nodded again, and I could feel my anger building. I just needed him to humor me for another moment. Then he'd be a believer.

He held up the book and card, and I stared. It was a thick Biology text book. I willed myself to look through it, and it dissolved into a transparent outline. The card behind revealed itself.

"Three of clubs," I announced, smiling.

"You saw it first."

I shrugged. "Change the card."

He did.

"Five of diamonds."

"You saw it somehow." He glanced around the room looking for an accomplice to my magic trick. A small mirror. A shiny surface. Anything.

I stood and turned around. "Hold up a couple cards behind it," I said.

"Alright. I'm ready."

I twisted around and scanned through the book. "Queen of hearts, jack of diamonds, four of spades."

Gordon's mouth dropped open. "How are you doing that?" He glanced around the room again.

I grinned. "I don't know how. I just concentrate on seeing through something, and all of a sudden, I can."

"Can you see through anything?"

"I guess. I know I can see through cinder blocks."

Gordon drew his eyebrows together. "Huh?"

I started to tell him about the locker room, but he beat me to it.

"That's what you were doing in the locker room today?"

"Yep." I didn't dare tell him it was his sister I was spying on.

"You could really see into the girls' locker room?"

"Yep."

I was grinning from ear to ear. I somehow possessed every boy's dream come true. X-Ray-Vision. If I could sell X-Ray-Vision to teenagers, I'd be a gazillionaire.

For the next hour, we tried my new power with different objects. We couldn't find a single thing that hampered my abilities. Then a thought hit me.

"You got anything lead?"

"Lead? The metal?"

"Yeah. To see if I can look through it."

He knew what I meant then. It was the only substance the guy with the "S" couldn't see through. Villains always shielded their doomsday weapons with lead so Superman wouldn't see it coming.

I rifled through Gordon's desk and plucked out a handful of pencils. I held them out and they dissolved before my eyes.

I turned to Gordon, smiling. "No problem."

"That's not lead. It's graphite."

I glanced at the pencils. "Says Number Two lead on here."

"Yeah. But they're graphite, not lead."

"Then why do they call them lead pencils?"

Gordon smarty-pants didn't have an answer for that, but I let it go. Even back then I knew to trust whatever he told me. Didn't mean I listened to him all the time, but I always heard him.

Turns out, we finally discovered I could see through lead too.

Suck it, Clark Kent.

I took a swig of my beer and looked at Kimmy sitting beside me. Twenty-five years later, she was still the most stunning creature I'd ever seen. With or without clothes.

"What are you looking at?" she said.

I jerked my eyes away. "Sorry."

"Don't you ever get tired of looking at my junk?"

I laughed. "I wasn't looking at your junk. But since you're asking, the answer to that question is 'No.' I think when you're eighty and your boobs hang halfway to your belly button, I'll still want to look at your junk over a twenty-year-old's any day."

"Stop. I'm getting all misty-eyed."

I took a swallow of beer, then said, "You know you were my first?"

"What?"

"My first ... you know ... X-Ray subject."

"Perv."

"No, really. It was innocent at first. The pervy stuff didn't come until later."

"Whatever." She turned back toward the TV.

Little Man jumped down and trodded toward the kitchen.

I drank some more beer, then said, "Your gym locker was on the exact opposite side of the wall as mine."

She looked at me, her eyes squinting. "What do you mean?"

I explained how it happened that first day, how the baskets and the wall dissolved, and then, as if by magic, there she sat before me in her underwear, detangling her hair.

She grinned. "I loved that bra and panties set."

"I know. You wore them a lot."

"Perv." She hit me in the chest.

"Ow." My ribs reminded me they were still broken.

Kimmy sucked a breath in. "Sorry." Then, "Serves you right."

I flexed a man-boob and made it jump. "Kiss it and make it better?" I asked.

She answered me with an eye-roll and shook her head. So I grabbed the remote and changed the channel back to *Psych*.

Chapter 21

Sitting there watching *Psych* with Kimmy, sipping beers and chatting, was as close to perfect as I imagined life could get. Of course, "perfect" would be Kimmy in a black corset and garter set, possibly with a whip and black stiletto heels, standing in front of me and ordering me to strip and get in the bedroom. Now.

"Stop that," Kimmy said.

"Huh?"

"Stop fantasizing about me."

"What do you mean?"

She cut her eyes at me. "You've got that look on your face. You're thinking of me in lingerie ordering you around."

My eyes widened. "How did you know that?"

She laughed. "I've got powers too."

I humphed. "Right. Remind me to kick Gordy's ass."

"The only thing I don't know," she said, "is the color of the lingerie."

I raised an eyebrow. "Black."

"Why black?"

I shrugged. "White's okay too, I guess. White's innocent, you know?

Red and pink are kind of tacky. But black ... black is elegant. That's why formal wear is black."

We were on our fourth beers at that point.

"So, why me?" she asked. "Why are you always after me?"

I turned my beer up while I thought about my answer. It was quite simple, actually.

"You were my first crush."

"What about Michelle Buckingham?"

Michelle Buckingham was pretty with long, wavy blonde hair, and she had that Loretta Swit thing going for her back when Loretta Swit was everybody's "Hot Lips Houlihan."

"She was alright," I said.

"You made out with her, didn't you?"

I ran my hand through my mullet. Talking about other girls with Kimmy was kind of uncomfortable, and in my mind, unproductive. But girls love that don't they? Talking about other girls and running comparisons.

"Sure, yeah, we made out a few times."

"She told me."

"Yeah?" I perked up. "What did she say?"

"She said you were sweet. Kissed her neck a lot."

I took a swig. "She had a soft neck."

"She also said you bought her flowers once, and when you went to Kepley's Field, all you wanted to do was hold her."

Kepley's Field was our version of Lover's Lane. Sometimes there'd be as many as twenty steamed-up cars and trucks parked out in that field, each rocking to its own beat.

I finished my beer and stood with some effort. "Well, it looks like Michelle Buckingham had a big mouth."

I grabbed us more Coronas and returned to the couch.

"You know what else she said?" Kimmy continued.

"Enlighten me."

"She said it seemed like you were holding back, like you were saving yourself for someone."

My face warmed. "Yeah, but Loni Anderson wouldn't return my phone calls."

Kimmy stared at me while I tried to watch *Psych*.

"Stop it," I said.

"Why? You always look at me."

"No. I always look at your boobs. Sometimes your ass."

"I've seen you look at me." She slid her feet up under herself and turned her body toward me. "And I know the difference between lust and—"

"Yeah, well, I got a thing for redheads, and you're a redhead." I fidgeted and scratched my knee.

"And why do you have a thing for redheads? Isn't that the magic question here? Why are you attracted to every redhead you see?"

"You sound like Gordon with his therapist mumbo-jumbo, always trying to attach reasons to things that just *are*."

She sipped her beer and said, "But isn't everything the way it is because of reasons? External stimuli?"

"Did you read some Cosmo article or something?"

"Am I making you uncomfortable?" she asked, grinning.

"You're killing my hard-on if that's what you're getting at."

Kimmy stood and scooted over in front of me. She took her shirt off. She had on a lacy white bra. She said, "Just tell me, Barry. Tell me how you feel. Right now. Tell me and we'll go straight into your bedroom."

I was stunned. I didn't know what to say. One thing I knew was that I wanted to give a solid shout-out to the monks that invented beer. They knew what the hell they were doing when they came up with that one.

"Come on, Barry," Kimmy said, slurring a little. "Just tell me how you really feel." She shook her breasts like a coochicoo dancer. "And you'll finally have what you've only been able to see through clothes."

Not completely true. I've watched Kimmy in the shower hundreds if not thousands of times throughout the years. As a matter of fact, just last month—

"Come on!" Kimmy yelled at me and threw her shirt at my chest. "Just say it out loud and you can finally have me."

I wanted Kimmy more than anything in this world. But not like this. Not as a drunken mistake she'd regret thirty minutes later. She'd hate me the rest of her life and never be able to look me in the eyes again.

"Come on, big boy! You all talk and no action? You afraid to show me that Super Penis you're always bragging about? What do I have to do to get me a piece of Super Barry?"

She reached back to unhook her bra, and like a complete dumbass, I leapt to my feet and grabbed her arms. I reached around her, clamped her hands before she could do anything, and pulled her close. She tensed at first, struggling with anger, then became jelly.

She sobbed, and I felt the tears run down my chest. I held her, not saying a word because honestly, I had no idea what I was doing. All I knew was it felt good and right. After she calmed down, I picked her up and carried her back to my bedroom. She was shaking.

I slid her under my covers and tucked her in. I laid on the bed and draped an arm across her. She was drunk and scared, and she was my Kimmy.

And at that moment, all I wanted to do was protect her.

Chapter 22

I slid off the bed thirty minutes later, found Kimmy's shirt in the living room and spread it out on the chair beside the bed. Whenever she woke up, maybe she'd be able to preserve a little bit of dignity.

It was almost five in the afternoon, and I don't think she'd eaten lunch. I know I hadn't. So it wasn't a surprise to me how fast the beers had gone to her head. How many had we had?

The answer: All of them.

I scratched Little Man on the head, hopped in the Aztek, and took a short ride to Shoffner's to pick up some Blue Moon Lager, a pepperoni lover's pizza, Diet Coke, tortilla chips, and salsa ... courtesy the North Carolina Education Lottery.

By the time I returned, Kimmy was up and dressed from her nap. She was sitting on the couch, remote in hand, flipping channels. To be honest, I figured she would take off when she awoke, but this showed me how scared she really was.

We sat and watched some bad sitcoms, each willing the shows to take our minds off things. It did. We talked about how bad most sitcoms were.

We snacked on chips and salsa and talked about everything else in the world, everything except what happened earlier that afternoon. I drank Blue Moon, and Kimmy drank Diet Coke.

Gordon called and stopped by, and I stuck the pizza in the oven.

"Who'd you see today?" I asked.

"You know I can't tell you that."

"Can't you at least tell me some stuff without names? Come on, you probably hear stuff they can't make up on TV."

He sat and crossed one leg over the other. He took one look at Kimmy and must have seen how her day went, because he said, "I saw Devil Lady today."

I raised my eyebrows, and Kimmy swiveled toward him.

"Devil Lady?" I said.

"That's my nickname for her. She wears red and carries a doll dressed in red. She's sixty-three years old."

I whistled low. I couldn't believe Gordon made up nicknames for his clients. That was so un-Gordon of him.

I said, "So what's wrong with her, other than the obvious?"

"I think she was abused as a child."

I turned my beer up and stood. "Who wasn't."

Gordon let that go and nodded at Kimmy. "How are you doing?"

I sorted through a drawer looking for a clean pizza cutter. I had a dozen of them; were they all dirty? I finally grabbed a butcher's knife and set it on the counter as Kimmy responded to him, "I'm hanging in there."

"What'd you do today?"

I returned from the kitchen and said, "We watched bad TV all day."

Kimmy flicked her eyes at me, but I pretended not to notice.

"And how are you?" Gordon nodded at my chest.

"Oh yeah," I said, brightening up. "Look at this." I raised my shirt.

"I'm almost healed. Looks like I've got Super-Healing, too."

Gordon's eyes widened. "Impressive."

"Yep." I felt like a middle-class kid on Christmas morning.

My own Christmas mornings weren't filled with candy, toys, and festive activities. Half the years, we didn't have a tree, and the years we did, Charlie Brown would've made fun of it.

I can't complain, though; my stocking usually had something in it: a stick of deodorant, stale candy canes, a pair of boxers (wrong size). Never anything good.

The highlight every year was Dad bitching about how stores weren't open to sell beer. The only family I had left was my dad. And soon enough, Christmas just became another day to navigate empty beer bottles while I scrounged for food.

"Stewart Graves called me back today about the hedge fund," Gordon said. "He said he still couldn't tell much. I asked him if Argyle Industries was a client, and he hesitated, telling me he couldn't give out clients' information."

I smiled. "And?"

"And I reminded him it was a federal investigation. He said Argyle was a huge client."

I nodded. "Good job, buddy. That verifies what we already knew. Argyle is where the bad guys are. Now how do we go about finding Andrew?"

"We go to Argyle tomorrow," Kimmy said, coming out of a daze. "And we push some buttons."

I shook my head. "I don't know if that's such a good—"

"I'm going," she said. "You can tag along if you want." She sniffed and looked over her shoulder. "That pizza ready yet?"

We ate and watched TV and chatted about nothing important. I tossed Little Man a pepperoni and got yelled at by Kimmy. Gordon left to go home around ten, and Kimmy stayed without discussion. She went to sleep in the spare bedroom, and I stayed up trying to figure out a game plan for the next day.

Shortly after eleven someone knocked at the door. I scanned the front walkway and saw a cowled figure. *Huh*? Well, I figured a bad guy wouldn't have knocked first, so I answered the door.

The guy stood over six feet tall, a hood pulled over his face, shadows hiding his features. One thing my X-Ray-Vision can't do is add light to what I see. So if the object is dark, what I see is dark.

"This is too big for you, Barry," the person said. It was a woman's voice.

"You have a cowl? Really, a cowl? Is M. Night Shyamalan out there somewhere?" I looked past her.

"Are you listening to me?"

"Who are you, and how did you get in here?" To no one, I said, "Is there a reason I live in a gated community?"

"You don't need to know who I am."

I crossed my arms. "Yeah, I do. I'd like to know who I'm not going to listen to."

She removed her cowl, and I was captivated by her electric blue eyes. She was older than me with graying hair pulled back in a bun. She said, "My name is Connie."

"Connie?" I almost laughed out loud. "Really? A cloaked figure appears at my door warning me I'm in over my head, and her name is Connie? This is unbelievable. You want a drink, Connie? 'Cause I think I'm gonna have one."

"I shouldn't be here," she said, looking around as if it were a cloak-and-dagger situation. Maybe it was. She did have a cloak.

"Who exactly are you, Connie?"

She thought for a second, then said, "I'm somebody who knows what's going on, and I also know you can't stop it." She took a breath, her eyes pleading with me. "Please, Barry. Leave it alone. Forget about Argyle."

So she knew about Argyle?

"Connie, I got a girl who's missing her partner, and until he's found, I'm in this up to my ears."

"It's too late for him."

I frowned and moved toward Connie. "It better not be."

"Even if you can find him, he knows too much." She glanced around again.

I paused for a second. "Connie, answer me one thing. How did you know where I was?"

She sighed. "Until yesterday, I was the only one who knew you existed. But now everyone knows about the half-breed."

Half-breed? She'd said that word, but without the disgust the goons attached to it.

"What does that mean? Half-breed? Someone called me that yesterday and—"

I heard the bedroom door creak open behind me, and I turned to see Kimmy slinking out, yawning. "Who are you talking to?" she asked.

I turned back to the front door and no one was there. Really?

I closed the door and said, "Wrong number."

"Huh?"

"Go back to sleep. Everything's fine."

And it was. I'd just had a confirmation that Argyle was the place to be. And I had a guardian angel of sorts. A guardian angel who didn't hate whatever I was. A guardian angel who one day might actually shed some light on *what* I was.

Chapter 23

The next morning, I tried to persuade Kimmy to stay behind while I went to Argyle. I didn't try too hard because truthfully, I liked her company, and I wanted her where I could keep an eye on her.

"You're going like that?" she said.

"What's wrong with it?" It was summer and I had on a t-shirt and shorts. That's what you wear in the summer, right?

"Do you have any shirts without holes?"

"Yeah." That was insulting. She should have mentioned she wanted me to dress up.

"Shirts other than t-shirts?"

I had to think for a second. "The kind you hang up?"

Kimmy blew out an exasperated sigh and headed for my room. By the time I got there, she had three shirts laid out on my bed. Little Man had just curled up for a nap on my pillow and he watched with simultaneous amusement and disdain at Kimmy's antics.

"Not that one," I said, pointing to the gray one on the right. "It shows my sweat too easily."

She threw it back in the bottom of my closet where it was before she dug it out.

"And not that one." I pointed to the red shirt. "It makes me look fat."

She cut her eyes and threw me the blue one I hadn't had a chance to complain about yet. It was a shirt Gordon gave me for Christmas last year. Figures.

"You have any khakis?" she asked.

"You mean like Dockers or something?" Her look made me point to a drawer.

She yanked it open and rifled through it, finally pulling out a pair of tan khakis. She took one look at them and said, "Do you not believe in hanging clothes up?"

"What's the point?"

She shook her head. "Where's your iron?"

I frowned and she threw up her hands. I squeezed into the blue shirt and held the pants in my hand.

"Put 'em on," she said, getting impatient.

I hesitated. "I'm commando today."

She rolled her eyes and turned her head. It was either commando or dirty underwear. I made a mental note to do laundry later. I got both legs in the pants and pulled them up, doing the one-leg-at-a-time pants dance. I couldn't get them buttoned.

"Got a problem here," I said.

She turned and laughed, covering her mouth.

"I feel like a sausage."

"You look like a sausage. Can you breathe?"

"Not very well."

"Well, you can't go out in public like that." She nodded at my cramped package. "You'll scare all the women and children."

I looked down. "My camel's foot not doing it for you?"

She laughed again, said to put on the best thing I could find, and left the room. I peeled the pants off and found a pair of decent-looking cargo shorts. I changed the shirt to a plain blue t-shirt and slipped into some hiking shoes. It was as dressy as I got.

I asked Little Man what he thought. He yawned and laid his head on his paws.

When I walked into the living room, Kimmy took one look and said, "Remind me to take you shopping later."

"Only if we go to Victoria's Secret."

Kimmy rolled her eyes and went outside. We piled into the Aztek, and she asked, "How are your injuries?"

I took a second to assess myself. "Fine, almost perfect." I tested my ribs. "They don't really hurt at all."

We picked up biscuits and coffee at a Hardees drive-thru, and by the time we arrived at Argyle Industries, we'd had all the grease, caffeine, and calories one needed to fight crime.

"The CEO is a guy named Rex Ruther," Kimmy told me as I parked the Aztek.

"Wait. Rex Ruther? Are you kidding me?" I shook my head. "When I sell the movie rights to my life, you've got to handle the copyright lawyers. They won't believe me."

We walked in the front door of Argyle, Kimmy in the lead, and I asked the receptionist for Rex Ruther. I snickered.

"Do you have an appointment?" she asked, wrinkling her nose at me.

"He'll want to see us," I said.

She regarded me and my "dress clothes" for a second before turning to Kimmy in her business suit and saying, "And whom may I say is calling?"

I stepped in front of Kimmy before she answered, leaned over the desk, and said, "Tell him the *half-breed* is here." I almost said to tell him

Clark Kent was here, but I wasn't sure she'd appreciate the humor.

She picked up the phone, puzzled, and spoke softly into it.

Argyle Industries was a huge textile plant with offices up front. The campus looked like it held several buildings that each performed separate automated tasks. The entryway was done in early nineties silver and blue. On the wall behind the receptionist desk was a huge Argyle logo—a diagonal tartan patch with "Argyle Industries" over it in block letters.

A guy my size dressed in dark suit appeared at a hallway to our right. He had black and blue ears. I smiled and stuck out my hand. "We haven't properly met."

Eyes half-lidded, he mumbled to follow him, then turned and led us through a maze of halls. He opened a set of double doors, and we entered after him. We were in some kind of outer office. Another goon closed the doors behind us, and just like that, we were inside the belly of the beast. Only now that we were here, I wished I'd sent Kimmy on a time-consuming errand, like buying me decent clothes that fit.

The only thing we had going for us was all the supposedly "innocent" bystanders in the adjacent offices. Surely Mr. Rex Ruther didn't want a lot of noise where he had a legitimate business, right?

I knew one thing for sure. If he was bald, I was going to lose it on the spot. Milk out the nose, soiled pants, the works.

Chapter 24

Kimmy and I walked into the inner office and a man with a fully-coifed head of jet-black hair sat behind an oak desk, smiling. We stopped about six feet in front of the desk.

The office wasn't decorated in gold or silver or platinum. It didn't have LCD monitors suspended from the ceiling displaying world maps with countries changing colors. It didn't even have expensive art on the walls or funky statues illuminated by bright columns of light.

The room looked like a normal office. Desk, credenza, modest computer display, desk calendar, matching visitor chairs. What kind of Supervillain headquarters was this? Things were definitely going to have to change for the movie.

The man behind the desk said, "So this is the *half-breed* I have been hearing so much about."

"Please, just call me Barry," I said. "All the bad guys do."

I paused, noting his European-style accent, and a thought occurred to me: All Supervillains have European accents. Was that too cliché to keep for the movie?

I cracked a smile. "And you must be the infamous Rex Ruther?"

"What is so funny?" he asked.

I looked around. "You're kidding, right? Your name is Rex Ruther, and you don't see the humor in that?"

He shook his head. "I do not get it."

His goons had straight faces also.

"Really?" I looked at Kimmy. "Really?"

She frowned at me.

I turned back to Rex. "Okay, let me ask you this. If I'd told the receptionist my name was Clark Kent, would you think that was funny?"

"I thought your name was Barry."

"It is. What I'm saying is ..."

Rex had looked off to the left, his face puckered in concentration.

I sighed. "Never mind. I guess I'm alone in this."

Rex resumed his creepy smile and nodded at Kimmy, "And who is this lovely specimen beside you?"

"This is the woman you sent your goons to visit the other night."

Rex laughed. "Ah yes. It slipped my mind that all of you have met. I feel as though I was not invited to the party." He looked at Kimmy. "It is nice to finally meet you, Kimberly."

Rex stood and came out from behind the desk. I doubled over in laughter. He stopped and stared at me.

"Come on," I said, straightening but unable to stop grinning. "You're ... you're ..."

"I am what?"

"You're short. I mean really short. Like midget short."

Rex scowled. "What is your point?"

"It's funny."

Rex drew his eyes together. "That is not funny. Did you poke fun at the smart kids in gym class too?"

I hesitated. "Actually, yeah, I did."

Rex shook his head.

I looked around. "Does no one think a five-foot tall Supervillain is funny but me? You're your own Mini-me for God's sake. You can't write this stuff."

"Stop being mean, Barry," Kimmy chided.

I threw my hands up. Whose side was she on? "You might as well be Danny Devito in a penguin costume."

"I am five-foot-three," Rex said, his expression dark.

"Five, five-three ... what's the difference? The point is, my sidekick could take you. And he's the kind of guy who keeps the pocket protector people in business."

"Do not let my size fool you, Mr. Glick."

"Yeah, yeah," I said. "Women the world over have heard that line since the beginning of time. They didn't buy it either."

Rex Ruther huffed and walked back around his desk. He sat in his chair and said, "Is there a particular reason you two are here?"

Kimmy stepped forward. "We're looking for my partner, Andrew."

"I do not know him."

"He was investigating your company before he disappeared the other day."

"Are you implying I did something to this Andrew?"

Kimmy and I said "Yes" in unison.

"I see." Rex steepled his fingers. "What if I told you I did not have him. Would you believe me?"

"No," Kimmy said.

"Okay. What if I told you I had him, and I would return him at the end of next week? Next Monday at the latest."

"This Monday?" I said. "Or next Monday meaning the one after this one?"

"The next one."

"So like, two Mondays away. About a week and a half?"

"Yes. That Monday."

I counted on my fingers. "The twenty-third?"

Rex stared at me, glanced at his desk calendar, then said, "Yes, the twenty-third."

I nodded. "What time?"

Rex lowered his hands to his desk, his eyes betraying his mood. His lips straightened as he said, "By the close of business."

"Are you feeding him well?" I asked. "Fresh change of clothes and all that? I mean, he's not handcuffed to some medieval wall and stretched out so far he can't feel his arms, is he?"

"No. He is fine. Comfortable. Three squares a day."

"Cable?"

"Satellite."

"Pay channels?"

"No pay channels, but I have the advanced package with SyFy, USA, and all the ESPNs."

I nodded and turned to Kimmy. "You ready to go?"

"What?"

"You heard the man. Andrew's in good hands; he's eating well and got a better TV package than at his own place. It's like he's on vacation, and he'll be back by the twenty-third." I turned and said, "My job here is done."

"Not so fast," Rex Ruther said.

I turned back around, bracing myself for the goons.

"I was hoping to get to know you a little better, Mr. Glick."

I checked my watch. "I got a minute or two."

"Surely, as a *half-breed*, you must know how much you interest us?"

"How do you mean?" I could tell Kimmy wanted to strangle me, but Rex had my attention now.

"Well, I know from my colleagues"—he nodded at the goons who hadn't moved since we'd entered the room—"that you have strength and speed equal to us. *And* you have the power of flight. That one is rare, very rare indeed. Tell me, what else is it you can do?" He leaned forward, eyebrows arched.

I tapped my watch, saying, "Minute's up."

I grabbed Kimmy and dragged her out of the office, through the maze of halls—only getting lost once—then shoved her into the Aztek.

"What the hell are you doing?" she said during our trip back outside.

I didn't answer her, just continued to drag her along. If she'd resisted me, I would have picked her up and carried her out.

"We can't leave! He's got Andrew," she protested as I pulled out of the parking lot.

"Do you really think me taking another beating will help us find Andrew?" I responded as I made a left turn. "The main thing is, we know more now. Whatever Andrew was investigating is going to come to fruition sometime next week. That's what we need to focus on. We also need Gordon to find out everything Argyle Industries owns, and we can start looking for Andrew that way. They gotta be holding him somewhere."

Kimmy fiddled with her seatbelt and relaxed.

"And we've got an ace in the hole they don't have."

"What?"

I smiled. "Me."

Chapter 25

I pulled into the Hibachi Express parking lot and turned the car off.

"What are we doing here?" Kimmy asked.

"I'm hungry. You in the mood for Japanese?"

"Do I have a choice?"

"Come on. A Superhero has to eat to keep his strength up."

She patted my stomach. "And his gut."

We ordered two plates of hibachi chicken with rice and veggies and sat to wait. I called Gordon on my mobile and told him to search for every house, business, and warehouse Argyle Industries owned. He wanted a blow-by-blow of our outing at Argyle, and I told him about Rex Ruther.

He didn't laugh either.

I hung up and said to Kimmy, "Why am I the only one to find this funny?"

"Because the rest of us aren't as warped as you."

"Well, I'm all you've got, honey."

Kimmy rolled her eyes. "Don't remind me."

Our food arrived, and we dug in. By the time we finished and got back to my place, Gordon had a list two pages long of Argyle Industries' holdings. He added another page of places owned by Rex Ruther personally.

"You still don't get it?" I asked Gordon. "Rex Ruther?"

Gordon handed me the three sheets of paper, saying, "I get it. I just don't think it's funny."

"Remind me again how we're best friends?"

I read down the lists and looked at Gordon. "Is there no way we can shorten this list at all? This will take forever."

"You could start with the places in and around Burlington."

I wondered if Gordon was making a joke there or being his usual dry self. I told him and Kimmy I was going hunting, and they needed to scour the net to figure out what big thing was supposed to happen this coming week. Peace Summit? OPEC meeting? Naked News IPO?

I hopped in the Aztek and drove to Burlington again.

The first two places I stopped at were rental houses. At least, that's what they looked like to me. The yards had patches of grass missing, the landscaping was minimal, and kids' toys were scattered everywhere. I scanned each house; no one was home.

The next place was a printing business named Speedy Print. I scanned the storefront and the warehouse floor and only saw people working. They were all busy and nothing looked odd. And none of them were Andrew.

It was beginning to get dark, and my X-Ray-Vision was getting tougher to use unless his hiding place was lit with artificial light. I grabbed some drive-thru and checked out a few more places on the list—a dry cleaner, another rental house, and a half-empty warehouse— before calling it quits for the day.

The whole time, I had one thing bugging me: *half-breed*. What made me a *half-breed*? The way Rex had talked, I was part whatever he was and part something else.

Was he some kind of "pure race" abstract like Hitler tried to make the world believe he was making? Some kind of "super race" genetically modified for speed and strength? It still didn't make sense.

To get answers, I was going to have to do something I'd vowed never to do. I had to call a truce with my dad. The prospect made me sick inside.

Like all visiting heads of state, I would come bearing gifts. There were two things in this world that spoke to that man: money and beer. Probably strippers too, but that would have distracted both of us.

I stopped by the first store I found with a neon "Lottery Tickets" sign: a small Texaco with two gas pumps. I walked to the back where the coolers were, snatched a six-pack of Steamboat Ale and a six-pack of Bud Lite—the man only drank mass-produced swill.

While I was checking out, I smiled at the woman behind the counter. She smiled back. "Kathy" had stringy, greasy hair pulled back into a sloppy ponytail and held together with a thick rubber band. She wore a striped Texaco shirt adorned with the logo, her name, and what looked like week-old chili stains. She didn't have a dental plan.

I scanned the ticket rolls, nodded, and asked for five Blackbeard's Treasures, one Perfect Pick, eight Old Maids, and four of the five-dollar Stock Market Stacks.

I paid for the tickets and beer with money I already had, then on a whim, flicked the Perfect Pick ticket at Kathy, telling her it was her lucky day. She looked at me as if I'd offered her a modeling job, then showed me her piano teeth again. When she scratched it off later to find a $75 winner, she'd probably pee herself.

I drove up to my dad's place, the house where I grew up and used to call home. It was hard imagining a woman living here. When my mom was alive, the place probably had flowers and fresh paint and a back yard with a wooden bench.

But the house I'd grown up in was as far from a Norman Rockwell painting as a Salvador Dali creation. It wasn't even a cheap imitation print you bought at a tourist trap. My childhood home was more of a yard sale painting: rained-on and sun-bleached and faded to the point that people wouldn't even pay a quarter for the rotting frame.

The house hadn't changed in twenty-five years.

I grabbed the beer and tickets and knocked on the front door. I could scan the house to see where he was, but I didn't feel like it. Who knew what I'd find? There are some things a son should never know about a father.

I knocked again, and he answered the door half a minute later after checking through the peephole.

"That for me?" He nodded at the Bud Lite and took it before I could answer.

I followed him in.

He sat on the couch and unscrewed the lid on one of the Bud Lite bottles. A paternity testing talk show was on TV, and he didn't mute it. He knew he was in control—I'd come to him—and he'd play it for all it was worth.

I was in for the ultimate pissing contest.

I sat in the chair opposite him and popped open a beer. The woman on TV claimed the guy she dragged there was the deadbeat father of her twin boys. The couple yelled at each other so hard I thought his gold tooth might fall out. He said she was a whore who slept with so many guys she didn't have a clue who the daddy was, she'd be back next week claiming somebody else was responsible. Then she said he was a no-good bleep who slept with her sister and mother and couldn't hold down a job.

Maury Povich announced the test results, and as it turns out, the mom had gotten lucky on the first try. Congratulations, another match created by Hollywood.

"I brought you something," I said. When Dad looked up at me, I tossed him the scratch-offs.

He stared at them a few seconds before reaching into his pocket for a quarter. I left the losing tickets connected so he'd at least have to work for it a little.

He smiled, frowned, smiled, frowned, frowned, grimaced, smiled ...

"This is just a little over a grand."

I nodded. "It'll stop foreclosure."

He stared at me another second before shoving the winners into his pocket, scowling. Not even one thank-you. Like I had come up $5 short on a debt payment, and he was still considering breaking a pinkie on principle.

We watched more TV, drinking beer, not talking.

"Tell me about Mom," I said over a feel-good State Farm commercial.

A pause. "Why?"

He had never wanted to talk about Mom when I was growing up. Not even before my powers began to develop and I became the freak son.

I said, "I don't know anything about her."

He sipped his beer. "What's there to know? We were happy, then you came along."

And there it was. The resentment. The hatred. The impasse that had always separated us.

"Do I have her eyes? Her hair? Her skin?" *Her powers?*

Dad never had pictures of him and Mom on display around the house. I'd snuck into an old trunk in the attic one time—searching for porn— and found some black-and-whites of them at the beach, arms around each other, smiling so hard the love jumped off the celluloid. The idea of

Dad and happiness occupying the same place in time were alien to me.

He looked up, contemplating his words. "You have her eyes and nose."

I let that sit for a while as we drank and another woman claimed some no-good bleep was the father of her little girl. The girl's picture was plastered next to his on a large LCD screen to the couple's left. She had pigtails and a sweet smile. He had dreads and a menacing glare.

"Could Mom do the things I do?"

There, I'd finally asked. Was I my mother's son? Was she special like me? Was she a freak too?

Dad opened another beer and took a swig. "No."

"Nothing?"

He looked me square in the face, his eyes burning into mine. "No."

Despite the overwhelming photographic resemblance, the guy with the dreads wasn't the father of the ponytail girl. The mother wailed and ran off stage. The guy jumped around, pointing at the crowd, yelling, "I told you so! I bleeping told you so!"

"What was she like?"

"Before you killed her or after?"

I stood and grabbed my beer, holding myself in check, and left. It took every ounce of my inner strength not the rip the door off its hinges when I opened it. As I drove home, I kept repeating the mantra Gordon had drilled into me.

Forgive him. Forgive him. Forgive him.

Of all the questions I had in my life, the question I truly I wanted answered after all these years was: When was it my turn for forgiveness?

Chapter 26

Saturday morning. I woke to the aroma of coffee. When I got in the night before, Kimmy was conked out in the guest bedroom , and I'd stayed up a little while watching her sleep.

Was I holding too much of my dad's hatred to make someone like her happy?

I drug myself to the kitchen. "Morning," I said to Kimmy, grabbing a coffee mug and filling it.

"Morning. When did you get in?"

"Don't remember."

"I guess you didn't find anything?" Kimmy sat across from me at the kitchen table.

I shook my head and told her about the places I'd checked, not mentioning the detour by my dad's house. Gordon stopped by with sausage and egg biscuits. We ate as he told us about calling Scott Thompson back yesterday.

Thompson said he could verify that the programming for Fannie Mae's mortgage approval process had been tampered with, but he'd need more time to see exactly what had been done. The code was much more complex than it should have been. If anyone happened upon it, they couldn't easily tell what it was doing.

Kimmy said Barbara Greene had called her last night, excited. The amount of FOREX trading in the last few months had been more than triple its normal volume. Somebody was moving a lot of money back and forth between countries, generating a lot of cash out of thin air. Barbara said it was feasible that if someone knew certain announcements ahead of time, headlines that affected the dollar or euro, they could make a killing by leveraging and converting to one type of currency, then back again once another set of headlines reversed the market's fears.

It was free money, she said, if you knew what was going to happen a few hours before anyone else did.

"Can she tell who's making the money?" I asked.

"No, only the volumes being traded."

So something big was coming, and Rex Ruther had probably been gearing up for a few months, maybe even longer. Interesting. Gordon and Kimmy had no more idea than I did about what was being planned. None of the pieces fit into a nice neat puzzle.

I called Hannah the hacker and woke her up.

"What time is it?" she asked.

"It's ten-thirty or something."

She groaned.

"The sun's been up for hours, Hannah."

"I had a late night."

"Doing what?"

"Fragging."

I raised my eyebrows. "Do I know him?"

A pause. "No. I said, 'fragging.' On the computer."

"Hey, you won't get any judgment from me. I do that all the time."

"No, you thickheaded mountain of hunk. Fragging is when you play computer games against other people and kill their characters."

"Sounds violent."

"It is when you lose. Then you respawn, and it begins all over again."

"Fascinating," I said. It wasn't. "Listen, I need a favor when you finally wake up."

"Surprise."

"Relax. This will be fun. I need you for your special hacking skills."

Hannah's voice perked up. "Oh yeah?"

"Yeah. And it'll be dangerous so you'll need to take every precaution you can. You can't get caught or be traced."

"What are you getting me into?"

"You don't want to know. Trust me. Let's just say I'll need you at your geekiest."

"Wow. You sure know how to flatter a woman. Let me go change my panties."

I paused as a visual ran through my mind, then I shook it out.

I continued, "I need you to find out everything a company named Argyle Industries is into. Stocks they own, businesses they run, everything. Break into their computers and find anything they're trying to hide. Think you can do that?"

"I can penetrate anything."

"Geez. Maybe you need to frag a little more first."

"You offering?"

"Hannah," I said. "If this is you first waking up, I'd hate to see you with a pot of coffee in you."

"I'm pretty much the same as I am now, but with the urge to pee."

I briefly thought about how much fun Hannah would be in the sack. Might be worth it to give Hannah a ticket for the Barry train. Just once. She might surprise me.

"You're thinking about it, aren't you?" she said.

"What?"

"Admit it. I'm getting through to you."

"Like a rash," I said.

She laughed. "Okay, I'll hop on your stuff in a minute, and I'll let you know something later."

"Thanks, Hannah." I paused. "And please be careful. I'm serious."

"Honey, I always wear protection."

I hung up, shaking my head. Hannah was a crotch rocket in a world full of mopeds. She was always at top speed and sometimes after I talked to her, I felt tired.

"I'm gonna visit Ms. Jennifer Pearce again," Kimmy said. "Maybe shake her up and see what she does."

"Be careful with that." I said. "Don't push her buttons too hard."

"I just want her to feel some heat. Make her do something stupid. If you don't play off the base some, the pitcher doesn't have a reason to throw the ball."

I looked at Kimmy. "Was that a baseball reference?"

She smirked at me, and I wanted to lay her across the table right then and there.

After a second, I asked Gordon what his plans were.

"I was thinking of going to help out Hannah."

"Oh?"

"She might benefit from some focused direction since she doesn't know exactly what she's looking for."

"You sure you don't want to give her a little Gordon sandwich?"

Gordon pinked up brighter than a ballerina's tutu. "That is the farthest thing from my mind."

"Sure, Gordy. Just take it one step at a time. Hannah would eat you alive."

"I can assure you—"

"You can assure me all you'd like, Gordy old boy. I'm just saying you got needs like the rest of us. You know what? I say go for it." I slapped him on the back.

Gordon adjusted his glasses and excused himself from the table.

"Stop doing that to him," Kimmy said.

"Stop what? Stop treating him like a guy?"

She smiled. "You know what I mean."

"You'd rather I set him up with the UPS man?"

Kimmy replied with a blank stare.

"It's just too easy, Kimmy."

"You're cruel sometimes."

"Would you like to punish me?"

She stood. "See you tonight."

Chapter 27

I got underway a little while later, after first catching up on the Naked News. Some scientist was arguing about re-including Pluto as a planet while the field reporter was busy exposing her own twin planets. And they weren't man-made.

The scientist did a great job of keeping his pocket protector on straight, but his glasses got a little steamed. Things began orbiting out of control as he fumbled his speech while trying to keep eye contact. The camera cut back to the studio anchor whose planets were large and definitely man-made.

I drove to Burlington and started back investigating the property list. First stop was another rental house—nicer than the day before—with a double garage and paved driveway. Then came a Biscuitville—I double-checked the address. Maybe Andrew was chained to a table in the back making biscuits.

I pulled out of Biscuitville and got the distinct impression I was being followed. Not many cars will pull into a Biscuitville and leave empty-handed like I did. But the car behind me did just that.

I drove for a ways, changing lanes a few times, watching as the Saab kept up with me. It was difficult to use my Super-Vision to zoom in through a rear-view mirror while I was driving, so I didn't try.

Instead, I pulled into Sir Pizza, steered the Aztek around back, parked, and walked to the corner of the building. Sure enough, the Saab followed, and when the driver saw my empty Aztek, he braked hard. But by then, I'd already seen who was driving.

I stepped from behind the building and waved.

The tinted driver's side window slid down and super-reporter, Sam Gerber, smiled back. I figured she was going to follow me all day unless I gave her some quality face time, so I strolled up to the car.

"Now what's a fine-looking woman like you following a loser like me?" I said.

"Oh, I don't think you're a loser. I think you're great at pretending to be a loser." She nodded at me. "The stained shirt is a good touch."

I looked down. This was one of my better shirts; what was she saying? I had thought the stain was an abstract design, but now that I was analyzing it, I could see where it might have once been spaghetti sauce.

It made me hungry.

"Wanna do lunch?" I nodded at Sir Pizza's side door.

Sam shrugged. "Sure."

She parked and started organizing a bunch of papers into a leather briefcase. I told her she wouldn't need all that stuff. She squinted her eyes at me, and I said, "Really. Let's just have a nice stress-free lunch. Okay?"

She hesitated, then left the briefcase in the passenger's seat, stepped out of the car, and snapped her fingers. "Up here."

"Sorry." I looked up. "Were your legs that long the other day?" Sam Gerber wore a short skirt that exposed long, lean legs.

She shot me a toothy grin, then leaned back into her car to pull something out of her briefcase. She straightened and waved. "Up here again."

"Huh?" I shook my head. "If you're trying to distract me, you're winning." I swept my right arm toward the building and half-bowed. "After you."

She squinted at me and took the lead.

We ordered sweet teas—they didn't serve beer—from the teenage girl waiting on us, and for the first time since meeting Samantha Gerber, I looked at her. Really looked at her.

She had that auburn red hair that drove me crazy, lightly curled with the volume of a bouncy shampoo commercial. Her features were what crappy novelists called *classic*. I think that's just the way their editors make them say *hot*. I could spend five minutes talking about her button nose or the spacing between her eyes or some other worthless detail, but I won't.

Sam Gerber was a Fox with a capital F, and she knew it. A veritable walking Revlon ad, she used her looks to her advantage, and it made me sad she was the enemy.

While Sam studied the menu, I studied her.

She was a very determined woman to follow me for more than twenty years. I was her big story. The story that would bring her international fame and perhaps a Pulitzer. She wasn't going to just leave me alone.

Ever.

I reached out and lowered her menu. "Wanna just split a pizza?"

"Sure. Meat Lover's?"

My heart skipped. "Sounds great." I waved the waitress down and told her to bring us a large Meat Lover's. "And you got any of that crust with the cheese or garlic in it?"

The kid stared at me like I'd asked her in Italian.

"Regular crust would be fine," I said.

She showed her braces and left.

Sam interlocked her fingers and rested her arms on the table. "So what were you up to this morning?" she asked.

"Just driving around."

"In Burlington?"

"Yep."

She paused. "Like yesterday?"

Damn. Stupid beer must have dulled my Super-Sixth-Sense yesterday. I never saw her. This woman was good. Maybe she let me catch her today on purpose.

Like all great politicians, I'd had my practice in handling situations just like this. "I don't know what you're talking about," I said.

"Uh-huh."

She wasn't buying it, so I went on the offensive. "Why were you following me?"

"I'm a reporter. I investigate things."

Now that I think of it, that was a pretty stupid question. I was using up my best stuff, and I was still on my first glass of tea. It was going to be a long lunch. I decided to take another tactic.

I nodded at her modest cleavage and said, "You know, I've always wondered what the deal with bra makers is. Why do they put little black bows between the cups like that?"

Her eyes flickered, and she adjusted her shirt.

"You ever investigate that?" I asked. "That's something I'd really like to see make the front page one day."

"I'll make a note of it," she said. "You know, I can run a check on all the addresses you've been to and figure out how they're connected."

Damn, she was persistent. This was going to call for a more offensive comment.

"So are those real?" I said, nodding at her chest. "Because they look real. What are they, D cups?"

Sam's gaze never left mine. "Very real." She paused. "And they're spectacular."

I laughed. "I saw that episode of Seinfeld. Teri Hatcher was on—"

"And Elaine tripped in the spa."

I pursed my lips and nodded. She was a worthy adversary. How could I make her my friend and not my enemy? The simple answer was that it would never happen.

She was a reporter. I was a Superhero trying to keep his identity and very existence a secret. We were natural enemies. Like cats and dogs. Republicans and Democrats. Rocky and Clubber Lang.

Sam cleared her throat. "So are you going to tell me what you're into, or do I have to do the work myself?"

If this woman could find me after the disappearing act I'd pulled in Los Angeles, she could look up a few addresses to find out their coincidental owner. And then she'd be in danger too ... and then I'd have to save her as well as Andrew.

"Do me a favor and leave it alone," I said with the straightest face I had.

She nodded, and I sensed she'd back off if I gave her something else in return. Namely, me. Maybe I could drag her out for a while, just until we had this Argyle Industries thing in the bag.

We sat in silence, sipping tea. Our pizza came and we dug in, eager for the distraction. I knew Sam wanted to pepper me with questions, but she was holding back, trying to loosen me up with "friendship."

We chit-chatted while we ate, covering innocuous topics like the weather, gas prices, TV shows with one-word titles. Finally, she unfolded a sheet of paper that looked like a printout of a newspaper article. It appeared our tentative truce was already over.

She slid the paper across the checkerboard table cloth, and I prepared myself for an article on *The Blur*. There was a picture and a story, alright. But it wasn't what I expected. It showed a car smashed beyond all recognition, wrapped around a bridge support. The headline read, "Pregnant Woman Saves Husband in Fiery Crash."

The pregnant woman was Catherine Glick; the husband, Farley Glick.

My parents.

I wiped the grease from my hands and picked the paper up. According to the article, Catherine was seven months pregnant. Farley was driving and reported to have had "a few beers" at a party earlier in the night.

Right. A few beers to my dad was eight or nine with a whiskey chaser.

Witnesses said the couple's Buick Riviera careened out of control and smashed into the bridge support at Asheboro Street and Highway 85. It burst into flames immediately.

Onlookers described the heroism of the pregnant woman as she busted out her door and dragged her semi-conscious husband to safety. One woman said, "One second the door was there, the next it was gone."

I hung on that last paragraph and reread it three times.

The door was there one instant, and gone the next.

I glanced at the picture with the article. It was grainy and splotchy from age. And copying didn't help the resolution either.

But I could still see the door. Torn off, lying up the hill in the grass, twenty feet away from the charred remains of the Buick.

I realized I had been staring at the article for a while, and I looked up. Sam didn't have a triumphant expression as I'd expected. She didn't even have an I-told-you face ready. Instead, her eyes were soft and her face downturned.

"You didn't know," she said.

I shook my head.

"Your dad never told you." It was a question framed as a statement.

"No." I took a breath, realizing I'd been holding it. "It doesn't surprise me though."

"Maybe he was embarrassed."

"My dad?" I snorted, then laughed, loudly. "Nothing embarrasses that man. He could make Jerry Springer blush."

"Maybe he was a different man back then. Before ... you know."

I raised my eyebrows. "Yeah, right. The only difference between now and then is that now he gets so wasted he can't find his keys to drive."

I read some more of the article. Charges weren't going to be filed, because no other cars were involved. 1970 seemed like a world away. Cops probably felt bad for the sap, his pregnant wife having to save his sorry, drunk ass.

I looked back up. "Why are you showing me this?" I already knew why.

"You mom must have been pretty strong."

I shrugged. "Adrenaline's a powerful drug."

"You think adrenaline can rip a metal door off like that ... without her turning green first?"

Touché.

"People do it all the time," I countered.

"Car doors back then weren't like the flimsy doors we have today. They were real metal. Heavy. Solid. Steel." She paused. "It was a Buick, for God's sake."

I had no comeback. She was right. Barring green skin or irradiated bites or magical hammers, there was no way my mom should have been able to do what she did. But she had.

"What are you getting at?" I asked, taking a bite of pizza.

"You know what I'm getting at."

"Say it. Out loud. I want you to hear how crazy you sound."

The insanity misdirection. I had her now.

She took the bait. "Your mother had more strength than humanly possible. And you can fly."

She didn't sound as crazy as I'd hoped. I couldn't bluff her any more, not like my previous bluffing had dented her resolve anyway. She'd seen me fly once with her own eyes and captured a photo to prove it. A photo from before Photoshop existed. A photo with a real negative.

She knew my secret; she just couldn't prove it.

Wait. Damn it. I'd been so distracted by her "assets," I'd forgotten the most important tool a reporter has.

"Turn it off," I said.

"Huh?"

"Turn it off, now." My voice took on an edge.

She smirked, reached inside her purse, and pulled out a small digital recorder. She clicked a button and set it down.

I relaxed. Took a sip of tea. Popped a pepperoni in my mouth.

"You can't do a story on me."

"Why not?"

"Because I'll have to move and hide again, and eventually they'll find me."

"They?"

"You know who 'they' is. The government. Scientists. Anyone and everyone who thinks it's in the public's best interest to dissect the freak and find out what makes him tick."

I let that sit for a moment.

"You know I'm right," I said.

I could see it forming in her eyes. The conflict. Doing what's morally right versus her lifelong quest of exposing the Superhero's real existence.

"I can see it if I was a bad guy," I said, straightening. "You'd be totally justified, exposing the threat to society. But I'm not. You'd be screwing one of the good guys ... and you know what that would make you?"

"I wouldn't have to reveal your identity."

I tilted my head at her. "Without confirmation, you'd be the laughing stock of the media world. You'd only get the story in the tabloids, sandwiched between the talking goat-boy and Emperor of the Planet Schizoid."

She knew I was right, and she had a decision to make she hadn't thought of before. She'd been so focused on getting the story, she'd not thought beyond it to the consequences and collateral damage.

"What is it you actually want?" I asked.

"What do you mean?"

"What are you looking for? Confirmation? Okay, you got me. I can fly. I have Super-Speed, and can look through your shirt, too. And you're right. Real *and* spectacular."

She raised her arms in front of herself. "You can really see through my clothes?"

I looked down, then back into her eyes. "Black thong. And a very classy ladybug tattoo just above your—"

"Okay. Okay. I get the picture."

Silence.

I said, "So is that what you needed? What you wanted? Or do you have to receive the worldwide recognition before you're truly happy?"

Sam sighed. "I don't know."

"Overwhelming isn't it?"

She grinned. "Yeah. I didn't expect ... I mean, I just ..."

"I know. You chase after something for half your life and once you get it, you don't know what to do with it. I know how you feel. It's like your life has revolved around this one thing. You've let it define you."

She nodded.

"And now, you're feeling kind of lost."

Just like me. I'm like I am *because my mom was*. I'm a half-breed, a result of a union between my dad and my mom, whatever she was. She was one of *them*. One of Rex Ruther's kind.

Rex Ruther.

"What are you grinning at?" Sam asked.

"Huh? Nothing."

We looked at each other in silence.

Sexy. Redhead. Legs that wouldn't quit.

"So," I said, raising my left eyebrow. "Are you one of those women unbelievably attracted to powerful men?"

She smirked. "Don't count on it."

"You could join the real mile-high club."

"Nope."

"I've got the stamina of a—"

"No way."

"You should see the size of—"

"You can stop now."

I brought a hand to my heart. "That really stings."

"I'm sure."

I paid for lunch and walked Sam to her car. She gave me her business card and wrote her mobile on the back. I asked her what that was for.

She opened her door and turned to me. "In case you ever want to talk."

"Off the record or on?"

She slid into the front seat and flicked her bedroom eyes at me.

"Either."

Chapter 28

This was becoming a frustrating situation, being surrounded by sexy redheads without getting any action. What good was being a Superhero if you never got the girl?

I stopped by Food Lion and picked up some chicken breasts, broccoli, onions, squash, and garlic bread. On my way to the checkout line, I grabbed a bouquet of pink and purple flowers, and a bottle of wine. Real wine.

It was almost seven bucks.

When I got home, I stuck the food in the fridge and arranged the flowers in a huge beer stein—I didn't own a vase—and positioned it in the middle of the kitchen table.

Neither Gordon nor Kimmy were there, so I grabbed a cold beer, spread out on the couch, and clicked away at the remote like I was playing Galaga.

After a few hours of watching seventy different shows, Gordon called. He and Hannah were making headway on Argyle. He said some computer mumbo jumbo about firewalls and protocol and brute force. Then he said something I understood.

"I'm going to stay until we get in. We're close."

Best thing I'd heard that day. Little did Gordon know, I was going to kick him out that night anyway. I wanted some prime alone time with Kimmy to try and seal the deal the right way. "Sounds good, Gordy. You keep at it."

Then the thought struck me that maybe Gordon *wanted* to stay for his own reasons.

"Bam!" I heard Hannah yell through the phone. "Take that!"

I heard Gordon ask what had happened.

"Alright, buddy," I said. "You have fun there and don't forget to wear protection."

He talked back into the phone. "Is Kimmy back yet?"

"No. Not yet."

And then someone knocked at the door. I scanned. It was Kimmy. What's that thing about twins been psychically linked?

I yelled for her to come in and told Gordon she'd just arrived. I told him goodbye and hung up. Kimmy was sweating and her hair was pulled to one side. She went straight to the fridge, popped a beer open, and downed half before saying hello. I sat up on the couch and turned the TV down.

"How'd everything go with Jennifer?"

"Horrible."

I patted the seat beside me on the couch. "Tell me about it."

She sat in the chair opposite me and threw a leg over the side. "Well, first of all, the air's out in my car." She wiped her forehead with her shirt sleeve. "Second, that bitch Jennifer didn't do anything all day but work." She paused. "In her air conditioned office."

I wanted to laugh. I wasn't used to Kimmy being so flustered.

"I tried to get in to see her so I could mess with her, and her secretary told me her day was full. I flashed my badge, and she didn't even blink."

Kimmy was getting excited, her hair coming loose from where she had it pinned. She was animated as she talked, waving the beer around so much I wondered if it would fizz over.

"I could see right in her office, and she didn't have anyone in there at all. All day!" she shrieked. "What good is having a fake FBI badge if it doesn't get anyone's attention?"

I laughed out loud and let Kimmy carry on for a few more minutes before I asked if she was hungry.

"Yeah. What you want to order?"

"I was going to make dinner."

In the resulting silence of my announcement, I could hear the sweat dripping from her forehead.

"Cook?" she finally replied. "You?"

"Yeah," I said. "I know how to cook."

"On the stove?"

"Yeah."

"You have pots and pans?"

Of course I did. Those were the metal things you couldn't put in the microwave. Learned that one the hard way.

I said, "You want to eat or not?"

Kimmy grinned. "What are we having?"

"Stir fry."

She said, "Great," then jumped up and announced she was getting a quick shower. Before I could say a word, she added, "And no, I don't want any company."

She disappeared down the hall, and I started on dinner. Little Man came to the kitchen to watch, probably thinking he was going to get some food too. A lot of people don't know this about me, but I like to watch the Food Network quite a bit. I don't watch for the new techniques or recipes, I watch to figure out what to eat that night.

Of course, I'm usually too lazy to find fancy restaurants that deliver, so I end up popping something frozen in the microwave or oven. But sometimes, I accidentally learn something about cooking.

I was glad Kimmy wasn't there to watch me find the skillet. It took a few minutes. Why would it be behind the cereal?

Anyway, I peeled the stickers off it and pulled the food out of the fridge. The great thing about stir fry is that it's super easy to make.

Cut up the food, dump it in the skillet, and cook until it looks like it does on the TV shows. Occasionally add some salt and pepper and anything else you've got in the spice rack, and voila: stir fry.

I cut up the chicken, onions, broccoli, and squash, and threw them in the pan with some butter; sprinkled some salt and pepper and some stuff from my spice rack.

Easy Peasy.

Gordon gave me the spice rack a few years ago for Christmas. I gave him a winning lottery ticket. He never cashed it.

Kimmy shuffled into the kitchen wearing some shorts and a t-shirt, her hair up in one of those towel turbans. *Grrrr.*

"That smells wonderful," she said, eyeing the flowers without commenting.

"You sound surprised."

She raised her eyebrows and saw the frozen bag of garlic bread. "You want me to stick that in the oven?"

Crap. I forgot about the bread. The stir fry was taking all my concentration. "Sure," I answered.

She rooted around in my cupboards for a while, then said, "You don't have a bread pan?"

Uhh ... "Get a pizza pan. Under the oven."

Kimmy opened the door and froze. "How many of these do you have?"

I turned my attention from my stirring and frying to see her standing there, mouth locked in a smirk.

"What?"

"You've got like a dozen pizza pans here."

I shrugged. "They're different sizes. And some have holes."

"Why on earth do you have so many?"

I stirred and fried, then said, "You cook all your pizzas the same way? What if you get one of those rising crust pizzas? If you don't use a pan with holes, it won't rise evenly. And if you're baking a twelve-inch pizza on an eighteen-inch pan, the crust isn't gonna cook fast enough."

She stared at me.

"You know how many kinds of pizza crust there are?" I continued. "You got those Totinos pizzas where you want extra crispy crust, so you got to use the holy pans. But you take your DiGiornos and your Freschettas, and those are best on a pizza stone or thick double-layer pan."

"You have a pizza stone?"

I pointed. "There's three of them under the sink. But I'd use a holy pan with the garlic bread." I paused, never having made garlic bread before. "What do you think?"

"I think your stir fry is burning."

Crap. I stirred and turned down the heat while Kimmy made the garlic bread. You can't distract a man while he's cooking. She may as well have come out of the bathroom in a small towel asking me if I could come wash her back.

When the garlic bread was ready, I served the stir fry and broke out the bottle of wine.

"What's that?"

"It says it's a Cabernet. The lady at the store said it was spicy."

"Do you have a corkscrew?"

Double crap. Then I remembered something. God bless Swiss Army Knives. I ran to my bedroom and returned with my trusty little buddy opened to the corkscrew.

Kimmy snatched it from me and told me to find two wine glasses while she opened the bottle. I chose two glasses from the cupboard.

Grown-up stuff was harder than I thought.

"Those aren't wine glasses," Kimmy said, holding up the one I'd given her. It had a picture of Yosemite Sam.

I looked at her and said, "Did you really expect me to have wine glasses?" She didn't answer. "At least they match."

My glass was Daffy Duck.

She didn't find my Looney Tunes glasses impressive, but let me assure you, they were. I've had those fast-food freebies ever since I can remember. They're classics.

We sat and began eating.

"What do you think?" I asked.

Kimmy nodded, chewing, and said, "What's that flavor? Mint?"

Okay, so maybe you can't add *anything* in the spice rack to stir fry. Who's bright idea was it to include mint in a spice rack anyway?

"Is it bad?"

She took another bite. "No ... just different." She added salt and pepper.

After dinner Kimmy cleared the dishes and said from the kitchen, "You have five more pizza trays in the dishwasher?"

"What? You expect me to wash one every time I use it?"

I poured the rest of the wine into our glasses, and we settled to the couch to watch a movie. Little Man followed and stretched out on the couch between us. Judas.

Kimmy chose the movie: "Green Lantern."

I'd seen it before, but it was a fun movie and everybody loves a movie where the hero wins. Although, if you ask me, the whole premise of Green Lantern is pretty fake. An alien crashes and hands a ring to a guy, and suddenly, he can do anything? Even fly in space?

Sorry. I don't buy it.

During the movie, I tried my best to slide closer to Kimmy without being too obvious. That's not an easy thing to do for a guy my size, and if I was any good at planning a date, I'd have bought two bottles of wine instead of one.

The movie ended, and I'd gotten a foot closer to Kimmy, although Little Man was still wedged between us.

Kimmy yawned, kissed me on the cheek, and said she was "all tuckered out." I watched as she pulled herself up and headed toward the hall.

"Thanks for dinner," she said, turning to me. "It was nice to get my mind off things."

She smiled, then added, "And I loved the flowers."

I rubbed Little Man under his chin and watched as she disappeared into the guest bedroom. I didn't know at the time, but that would be the last moment I saw Kimmy for a while.

Chapter 29

I heard the noise before I woke up, and by then it was too late. It was one of Little Man's favorite toys—a hacky sack filled with catnip, a single bell sewn into the top. It jingled but didn't jangle. When Little Man attacks that thing, it won't stop jingling and jangling for ten minutes. But this time, it jingled only once.

I came awake just as a freight train the size of a dumbbell rammed into my gut. It knocked the breath out of me, and I struggled to roll out of bed.

I rolled the wrong way.

Within seconds, I was pummeled more times than I could count.

I kicked out with all the Super-Strength and Super-Speed I had at my disposal, which wasn't much in my half-awake state. I struck something and even though it was a glancing blow, it knocked the intruder far enough away from me that I could sit up.

That was when the other one pounced on me from behind. I stood and shook him off, but not before he got in a few quick punches to my kidneys.

There was just enough light in my room to see who I was dealing with as I turned. Goon Number 1 and Goon Number 2.

So they came back for more?

I dashed for Goon 1 and immediately stubbed my toe on the bed. As I was hopping up and down shaking my left foot, Number 2 tackled me from behind like I was a ninety-pound quarterback. We went flying through the air until we crashed—or should I say, *my face crashed*—into the opposite wall.

All the Superpowers in the world can't stop the fact I have a very normal skull. My nose is a little big and my ears stick out a tad, but despite Gordon's constant comments, my head isn't very hard.

After the violent introduction of my forehead to the drywall, things became a little woozy. I remember swinging back with my elbow and hearing something crunch.

Could have been somebody's face, could have been my elbow.

At one point I got someone in the nads; I heard him groan. I didn't have time to celebrate or taunt him because my nads were next.

I doubled over and passed out for a bit. I must have, because I woke up sideways with somebody's ankles in my face. Ankles?

Something primeval took over, and I leaned forward, biting his exposed ankle with everything I had. My teeth sunk through flesh, and he screamed like a teeny bopper at a Bieber concert. That was when I got kicked in the ribs a couple times. Hard.

I let go of the ankle and tried to roll out of the way, but the wall blocked me. Having nowhere to go, I took a couple more shots until I grabbed the ankle again and bit into it.

More kicks to my gut and ribs until I relinquished my hold. I couldn't breathe, I couldn't see, and I couldn't think.

Somebody across the room said, "Back away from him."

I knew the voice. Rex Ruther.

I struggled to sit up, but I hurt too much.

He said, "Go get the girl."

No! I tried to pull myself to the door, but my body wasn't listening to the commands my brain was sending it.

"You should have left well enough alone, Mr. Glick," he said. "You will get Ms. Moser back in a week if you quit snooping around." The voice moved closer. "If I see your *half-breed* face at all this week, I will kill her. Do you understand me?"

He poked me in the forehead. "Do you?" he repeated.

I nodded, still unable to breathe enough to grunt.

"And after her," he said, his face so close I could smell the Cheetos he had earlier. "I'll kill you and the nerd next."

Then came the tasing.

And the blacking out.

Chapter 30

My dad hovered over me on a flying carpet, eating Cheetos, calling me *freak* and *half-breed*. He threw Cheetos at me, one at a time, aiming for my face.

"This is what you get," he said, "for being a freak."

I asked him what he meant.

He threw more Cheetos at me. I tried to catch them in my mouth. I was hungry.

Rex Ruther flew into the scene on his own rug. He was eating Cheetos the size of those sausages you see hanging in deli windows. I wanted one. Bad.

He pointed, and I followed his gaze with my eyes. There was Kimmy, a thick rope wrapped around her. She looked like a trussed Christmas tree, and she was also floating on a carpet. She looked at me without saying anything. She was sad.

Rex waved and said, "Over here."

I looked toward him.

He said, "I could have killed you, but I didn't. You won't get another pass."

Then he pelted me with one of his giant Cheetos. It hit my chest and it hurt. He threw another at me, and another.

A siren wailed and someone yelled, "He's coding."

The next Cheeto that hit me exploded into lightning that engulfed my entire body. I screamed, but no noise escaped my mouth.

Sam Gerber flew by on a rug. She wore a lacy black bra and a black thong. She waved and another electric Cheeto slammed into my chest, sending a jolt from head to toe.

White. Light Gray. Gray. Graying. Darkening.

Blackness.

Chapter 31

I opened my eyes. Mouth dry. Beeping all around me. Blinked a few times. Blurry. Chilly. Disinfectant. White ceiling tiles. Wires. Pain. Steady breathing. Pain. Beeping.

Move fingers. Toes. Chest tight.

Mouth dry.

TV. Hugh Laurie's voice. *House*. Appropriate.

I tried to laugh, but it came out as a dry cough.

"Barry?" a soft voice said.

I grunted. Couldn't close mouth. Throat blocked, but still breathing.

Beep, beep, beep.

"Don't try to talk," the voice said.

Reached up. Pulled. Scratchy throat. Wanted to throw up.

"Don't do that. Let me call someone."

Tube. Pulling tube. Long tube. Out. Free.

Deep breath. Another. Dry throat. Cough.

"Water," I murmured.

Something touched my lips a second later. A straw. I sucked on it, and it produced water. Cold, wet. I swallowed, choking.

"Slowly," she said.

Her red hair came into view. Kimmy. It was all a dream.

Blurriness sharpening.

Her face. No. Not Kimmy. Samantha. Samantha Gerber.

Confusion.

I took another sip of water. It traveled down my throat without choking me, its iciness tracing a path deep into my gut.

"I found you," Sam said. "You were half dead."

I nodded. At least I think I did. It felt like it.

"You were lying on the floor in your bedroom, barely breathing. You were unconscious."

"Kimmy?" I croaked.

Sam frowned. "Who?"

"Guest bedroom."

She shook her head. "Nobody else was there. The whole place was torn apart. The door was wide open."

I nodded. The stuff before the weird Cheetos dream had really happened. The events flooded through my brain. Rex Ruther had Kimmy, and he wanted me to believe he'd give her back in a week as long as I stayed out of his way.

"The doctors said you went into a mini-coma," Sam continued. "They said your body has been fighting hard. You even died once."

I nodded toward the water, and she stuck the straw back in my mouth. Three swallows. Smoother.

"Not much of a Superhero, huh?" I tried to laugh.

Sam frown-smiled and touched my hand. "You're still human."

"I guess."

Was I? I used to feel invincible. Maybe this was what "being human" felt like. Fragile. Vincible. Was that a word?

My brain hurt.

Sam backed up as a nurse popped in to adjust my machines. "I see you're still with us," the nurse said through thin lips.

"Yeah."

"It was touch-and-go most of yesterday, but this morning we felt pretty good about your chances." *Yesterday?* "You stabilized about eight this morning, but you're not out of the woods yet." *This morning? Yesterday?* "I'll be back in a little while to check on you."

And she left.

Sam returned to my side.

I asked her, "What day is it?"

"Monday."

"And you found me—"

"Yesterday morning." Then she came closer and held my hand. "Who did this to you?"

What she really wanted to ask was who *could have* done this to me.

"You wouldn't believe me if I told you," I said.

"Try me."

"No, really. You'd think I had a speech impediment."

She scrunched her brow, and the doctor walked in. I knew he was a doctor by the wizened face, confident posture, and white smock he wore. He also said, "Hello, Mr. Glick. I'm Doctor Schmidt."

I smiled at him as much as my face would let me.

"The nurse told me you'd woken up. I thought I'd come look in on you. How are you feeling?"

"Sad."

He looked confused. "Sad?"

"I've been here two days, and I've not gotten any lime Jello yet. Have I at least gotten a sponge bath from a hot little nurse?"

Dr. Schmidt laughed. "That answers my next question of how clearly you're thinking."

"Really, doc, who I gotta tip to get a sponge bath around here?"

He went into to a long list of things that were wrong with me. Couple of shattered ribs. Collapsed lung. Contusions on my chest and abdomen. Blah, blah, blah.

Would have been quicker just to say, "Mr. Glick, my diagnosis is that you got the utter shit beat out of you. As a remedy, I'd suggest you not piss off whoever you just pissed off."

Dr. Schmidt fiddled with some of the machines, hesitated, then stood beside me and said, "Mr. Glick, frankly, I'm puzzled about a few things. Your right lung, for instance"—he creased his brow and looked to the side, then back at me—"has healed remarkably. It had collapsed and by the time we got to it, it was fine. And your other injuries ... well, they're all healing at an amazing rate."

Oh boy.

"I'd like, with your permission, of course, to take some more blood, and try to figure out what your white blood cells are doing in there. My research is in Immunology and your ... recovery has me intrigued. Would you mind if I used you in a study?"

I showed as many teeth as possible. "Sure. No problem."

"Great, great!" He looked like he wanted to hop in place and clap his hands. He left the room in a rush, practically giggling the whole way.

I turned to Sam. Her face was a mixture of confusion and worry. "You gotta get me out of here."

"I can't do that!"

"Sure you can. They do it all the time on TV. Just go get a wheelchair and one of those small nurse's uniforms."

She raised an eyebrow. "Small nurse's uniforms?"

"Yeah, the smaller the better."

She tilted her head at me, eyes half-lidded, then left the room. I tried to sit up. It felt like somebody's Aunt Hazel was sitting on my chest. I started to rip out all the wires and tubes attached to me, but figured that would alert the staff. I pulled out the IVs—no alarms hooked up to them.

Then I yanked the catheter out. Oh. My. God. Talk about your uncomfortable situations. I thought I was going to throw up right then.

Sam opened the door and pulled a wheelchair in behind her. She was wearing a doctor's coat.

"That's not a small nurse's uniform."

No answer. She pushed the wheelchair over by the bed and stopped, looking down. "There's something wet on the floor."

"Don't worry about that," I said. "Look for my clothes."

She found a plastic hospital bag in the little closet-thing. I told her she was going to have to help me put them on. She looked like I'd just asked her to hold the bedpan for me while I squeezed one out.

"Look," I said. "It'll be way easier than you're thinking. Get my underwear."

She found them and held them up. "Leopard-print bikinis?"

"What? I'm a Superhero. You think Batman wears boxers under that skin-tight suit of his? Robin maybe, but Batman? Come on."

"Batman's fictional."

"So are all Superheros, but they got movie deals anyway."

She rolled her eyes at me.

"Just slip them on me before someone comes in."

Sam got both my feet in and said, "I can't get these on you."

"Sure you can. You forgot something." I hovered off the bed about six inches. "I can do cool shit."

She smirked and worked the underwear up my legs.

"Be careful around the python there."

"Python? Looks more like a garter snake to me."

"Hey. It's cold in here."

"Not that cold." Sam snapped the underwear into place, and I flinched. She slid my shorts on the same way. No shoes, socks, or shirt.

"Okay," I said. "Get the chair ready. I'm gonna pull these wires off, and then we gotta move fast."

I ripped the wires from the various parts of my body, and the machines immediately began beeping in tandem. Sam brought the chair under me as I hovered over to it. The whole process was relatively painless until I let myself relax in the chair.

My body wasn't prepared for the weight shift, and I yelped in pain. Then, we got the hell out of there.

Chapter 32

I was sure the hospital was going to be pissed I'd skipped out without giving them my insurance information. They'd be even more pissed to learn I didn't have insurance. Maybe I'd send the doc a lottery ticket.

We pulled up outside the apartment, and Sam helped me out of her car. We'd left the wheelchair at the hospital, so I had to make the trek to the apartment myself—without hovering.

If I said it was painful, I'd be grossly under-exaggerating. It took me ten minutes to walk the fifty feet to my front door, leaning on Sam as much as she could take.

We were accosted by Christine in a bright pink bikini. She'd just come down the steps and was headed back to the pool.

"Barry! What happened?" she cooed, placing her hand on my arm.

"Oh, I just got into a little altercation."

She gave Sam a sideways glance but didn't acknowledge her existence. "You tell me if you need something. Just call, and I'll be right there." She ran a hand through my chest hair. "Any time, day or night."

It gave me chills. I smiled at Sam. Sam didn't smile back.

"I'll do just that, Christine."

I watched as she walked away. Turns out the bikini was much smaller in the back. Sam punched me in the arm.

"What?" I said, looking up. "If she's gonna advertise, I might as well enjoy it."

Sam let out an exasperated huff and shook her head.

I busted out a little stained-glass window next to the door and started to reach inside to turn the knob. Sam pulled my keys out of her pocketbook.

"A little late now," I said.

"You didn't ask."

"You didn't offer."

"I was concentrating on keeping your heavy ass from hitting the sidewalk. How much do you weigh, anyhow?" She slid the key into the lock.

I could have hovered in by myself at this point, but I was enjoying her body being pressed against mine. She was soft in all the right places.

"Wait," I said. "So you grabbed my keys after calling an ambulance, but you didn't think to grab a shirt, a pair of shoes, or my phone?"

She shrugged and manhandled me back to my bedroom. The place was destroyed. Walls had caved-in holes the size of a human head. My dresser was turned over and splintered into a bazillion pieces. Clothes were everywhere.

I collapsed onto the bed, trying not to think about it. I tried to get Sam to undress me and give me a sponge bath. She declined, even when I told her it wasn't as cold in my place as it was in the hospital.

"It's room temperature," she said. "You still don't have a chance."

I was worn out. My body definitely needed more rest, and I was fading fast. I grabbed Sam's hand and squeezed until I had her full attention.

"Thank you," I said.

She patted my hand. "It was nothing."

But it *was* something. It was everything. If she hadn't come by, I'd more than likely be dead.

I needed to call Gordon. He didn't know about Kimmy. He had probably stopped by here in the last day or so and was freaking out at this very moment wondering what had happened. I asked Sam for my mobile phone, but it came out as a low mumble.

She patted my hand again, and I tried again to ask for my phone.

But I was tired, and the world soon quietened and faded to black.

Chapter 33

I woke up seven hours later. Nine at night. My mouth was dry, but at least I could breathe easier. The room was dark. Light spilled in from the hallway. I could hear the TV in the living room. It was a chick flick by the way the woman was talking; all giggly and young and Julia Roberts-ish.

I sat up. A lot less painful. Bearable. Had to pee. Went to the bathroom.

I tossed the hospital gown on the floor and found different clothes, but not necessarily clean ones. My floor was full of shirts and shorts and underwear, but to be fair, it was like that before the goon party.

I found my phone, plugged it in, and turned it on. Eight voice mails from Gordon.

I'd been dreading this call, but it had to be made. Gordon answered on the second ring.

"Where the hell have you been?" he said, his voice taking an edge. "What happened to your apartment?"

"Hello to you, too."

He waited for my answer, so I told him. "Hospital."

"The hospital?" He paused. "What happened? Where's Kimmy? Neither one of you have been answering my calls. This may excuse you but—"

"Gordy, they got Kimmy."

"They what?" His voice shot up.

"They took Kimmy last night. Or the night before ... I'm still a little hazy on that. I'm sorry—"

"You let them come into your home and take my sister?"

I felt my face heating up. "I didn't *let* them do anything. They almost killed me."

He breathed into the phone. "Was it the same men?" he said. "The ones we scared off at Kimmy's house?"

"We? While I was busy getting my ass kicked all over the yard that night, you were sitting in the car listening to America's Top Forty stroking your three wood." I was yelling now. "*We* didn't do a damn thing. *I* saved her that night, not you."

"And I see you did a great job saving her a second time."

"Fuck you, Gordon."

"Fuck you back, Barry."

I had never seen Gordon angry a single day of my life. But more than that, I'd never heard him utter anything remotely close to a cuss word.

My mouth opened to retort, but nothing came out. I was literally thrown off my train of thought. I floundered, then struck back the only way I knew how.

"Let me ask you something," I said in a calm tone. "How much do you think those naughty nurse uniforms in the Victoria's Secret catalogs cost?"

Silence.

I continued. "You know, the ones with the garters and fishnet stockings and little hat? What, thirty or forty bucks?"

Gordon found his voice. "You're one hell of a Superhero, you know that?"

"No, Gordon, I'm not. That's what I keep trying to tell you. I haven't been one in a very long time. And I don't want to be one."

"But you have an obligation—"

"Don't talk to me about obligations, Gordon. My first obligation is to live to a ripe old age where I forget which pills to take and shit myself occasionally. That's my only obligation in this world, and I've been very careful to assure that."

"Well, aren't you a chip off the old block?"

"Gordy, your psychobabble mumbo jumbo bullshit won't work on me. Yeah, I got PTSD, and you know what? I'm rolling with it. That's just the way it is. You want me to lie down and tell you all about my mother?" I laughed. "Well, guess what. She's dead. I'm alive. End of story."

"You're being a coward."

"You know what, Gordon? You're right. I've been a coward for the last twenty years, and I'm happy. Cowards live a very long time."

"Barry, the last twenty years, you've lived a miserable existence with no purpose. You've got nothing to show for it, and if you dropped off the face of the earth tomorrow, no one would notice." He paused, his voice quiet again. "You used to stand for something."

I scoffed. "You're getting me mixed up with a comic book character who wears tights and never goes to the bathroom."

"No, Barry. I just remember what you were like in the beginning. I remember those days well. It's sad to see what you've become."

I shook my head and gripped the phone tighter. "You don't understand, Gordon. All that stuff back then was you pushing me to be like that. I never wanted it. Never. I actually enjoy apathy. It's fun. I eat what I want, and do what I want, when I want to." I paused. "Do me a favor, pal. Just leave me alone and let me be."

I hung up before Gordon could say another word. Turned the phone off.

I'd just cheated death, again. The last time was when the gang trapped and surprised me in Chicago. I'd told Gordon then I needed to get away, go somewhere nice. The land of surf and sand and busty starlets.

The city of Los Angeles ...

Chapter 34

We arrived in L.A. in June of 1991. Bikinis were everywhere, and I was in heaven. All you had to do to get some nookie was say you were a producer or director.

I even had cards made up.

During the days, I strolled the beach. Nights, I clubbed and screwed and occasionally listened to the police scanner.

B&Es were the most fun. I'd get there while the alarm was still going off, knock the dudes senseless and let the cops find them. I got all the fun while they had to do the heavy lifting. The headlines and articles the next day were my favorite part.

Thieves Found Napping in Nordstroms

Robbers Robbed of Consciousness

Looters Left Loopy in LA

Bel-Air Bomber Strikes Again

New city, new nickname. The Bel-Air Bomber. I saved every article. It was fun. A game. Could I hit two places in one night? Three? Think of the headlines ...

The papers described me as a vigilante who did what the police couldn't. But even better, I was a vigilante who didn't break any laws. It was the best of both worlds.

The public wrote in and supported me. The police department had a dismal record of corruption, still reeling from the Rodney King debacle. No one respected the boys in blue.

But they loved the Bel-Air Bomber. Cartoonists drew caricatures of a muscular guy with a "raccoon mask" wearing a pair of boxing gloves. I was the people's champion, a real Superhero. I could do no wrong.

Then one night I heard a call around ten for an address in the posh neighborhoods above Beverly Hills, where the mansions were gated and the owners dripping with money. The roads to get up there were winding and long, so I flew.

I knew exactly where I was going because just the week before, Gordon and I had gone sight-seeing to get an idea how the other half lived.

I flew there in record time, wearing my "Bel-Air Bomber Mask" I'd bought off a street vendor in Chinatown. The back door was broken at the casing, and I entered, keeping an eye out for thieves. It was a large house and unless I was lucky, I thought it might take me a minute to find the bad guys.

I found one in the downstairs office, emptying the safe of papers and cash. I ran up on him and slammed his head into the wall. Down for the count.

I found the second guy in an upstairs bedroom. He held a gun on a family of four. Mom and Dad, middle-aged and reeking of money. Son around twelve, Beverly Hills 90210 air about him. Daughter around eighteen, movie star beauty with tears streaking down her face.

The guy looked up and saw the mask, then turned the gun on me. He said, "You're the Bomber."

A statement, not a question.

I nodded. "You picked the wrong house tonight, pal."

"No, you did," he said.

He fired, but I'd already sped right. The bullet floated by me as I charged him and delivered a crushing shoulder to his gut. He exhaled with force and slammed into the dresser behind him. There was a crack as his head connected with the expensive wood, and he slumped to the floor.

I smiled to the family and asked the dad if he wanted my autograph. But he was looking behind me.

I turned and saw the third guy with what I learned later was a Tec-9. A Tec-9 is a handheld semi-automatic arsenal that can deliver up to five rounds a second. And they're legal.

He opened fire, and I immediately juked left, crouched low, and flew at his feet. Including reaction time, it took me a full second to reach him.

I know because the paper said five bullets were fired.

And all of them found targets.

Two struck the boy—one in the gut, one in the chest.

Two found the girl—one in the left arm, one in the neck.

One hit the mom just below her left eye. Death was instant.

The paper said the boy and girl bled out before the ambulance arrived.

It also said the dad, a bigwig with one of the studios, was putting out a reward for any information concerning the "Bel-Air Bomber," and that he blamed me for everything that happened that night.

The paper didn't mention his teenage girl and wife were half-naked and about to be raped before I came along. It also didn't mention dear old dad was handcuffed to the treadmill with his son and they were going to be forced to watch the rape in helplessness.

At least the paper didn't mention the autograph thing.

That day, I became the villain, the guy everybody hated. I was deemed rash, foolhardy, careless. New caricatures were drawn: a guy with a mask, an evil grin, and boxing gloves covered with blood. One even had a Swastika on my enlarged forehead.

The Bel-Air Brute.

That was the moment I turned my back on the world and its so-called needs. Screw everybody else. They didn't need me? I sure as hell didn't need them.

Gordon and I moved back to Greensboro and a life of tranquil anonymity. I was done. Done caring and done saving the world. Gordon never tried to counsel me—he knew better.

"The good ones cost at least a hundred."

"Huh?" I looked up, yanked back to the present.

Sam repeated herself from the doorway. "I said the good nurse's uniforms, the ones with the lacy garters, cost at least a hundred bucks. More if you want fishnets."

"Oh yeah?" I raised my eyebrows.

She grinned. "How are you feeling?"

I shrugged. "As well as can be expected."

"Good."

"So ... you heard all that?"

"Enough," she said, shifting her feet.

"You think I'm an ass now? For quitting?"

She thought for a second, then said, "I think you almost died yesterday."

She stood there, unspoken words passing between us like electrical currents.

"Listen," I said. "Thanks for helping me. Really."

"No problem. You need anything? Hungry? You should probably eat something."

I shook my head. "Nah. Just tired."

She motioned to the bed. "Get some more rest. I'll make you some food when you wake up."

"You don't have to stay."

"Where else am I gonna go?" She turned and said, "Yell out if you need me."

I rolled over and closed my eyes until Sam woke me eight hours later. Someone was at the door.

Chapter 35

Someone shook me awake. I sat up in bed, the pain less now. It took a second for the disorientation to lift. "Huh?" I grunted.

"Somebody's at the door." Sam frowned. "He's wearing a hood."

I smiled. "It's called a cowl, and it's a she."

Sam helped me up, and I hobbled to the door. I opened it and nodded at Connie, inviting her inside. She shuffled in, and I closed the door behind her, introducing Sam.

Connie slid her cowl back. Her eyes were puffy and swollen. Her face looked waxy. "Are you okay?" she asked.

"Right as rain," I told her, waving my hand like it was nothing. "See. Watch this trick. I can breathe." I took a few exaggerated breaths.

"Please," she said, stepping forward, her expression pleading. "You've got to leave this alone. It's too big for you."

"Want a beer?" I asked.

"Barry, please. You don't know who you're dealing with."

"I feel like a beer." I turned to Sam. "You feel like a beer?"

"Barry," Connie pleaded.

I nodded toward the couch. "Grab a seat. We need to talk."

"I can't stay."

"Oh yes you can. I'm forty-three years old, and for the first time in my life, I've found someone who can answer the biggest questions of my life." My voice hardened. "Make the time."

Connie flicked her eyes at Sam.

"Don't worry about her," I said. "She knows more about me than I know myself."

A few seconds passed before Connie's shoulders slumped. I motioned toward the couch again and asked Sam to grab a few beers for everyone.

Connie sat and rested her hands in her lap. "I don't know where to start."

"How about the beginning?" I said. I sipped my beer and leaned back, hoping I wouldn't fall asleep again. "Like how do I have powers?"

Connie sighed and took her first sip of beer. It turned into a gulp, and then three full swallows before she put the beer down.

"Have you ever read the Bible?" she asked.

"Big leather thing"—I formed a rectangle with my fingers—"about yay size? Stars God and begins with the creation of everything?" I nodded. "I've heard of it."

"Do you remember mention of the Nephilim?"

I shook my head. "What was it?"

"It's not a *what*," Sam broke in. "It's a *who*."

I drank my beer, not excited about the upcoming sermon.

"The Nephilim," Connie continued, "were discussed in Genesis and several other books in the Old Testament."

Sam cleared her throat and added, "'The Nephilim were on the earth in those days,' and also later, 'when the sons of God went to the daughters of man and had children by them. They were the heroes of old, men of renown.'"

Connie nodded. "That's right, loosely translated." Then Connie looked at me.

I glanced from Sam to Connie and raised my eyebrows. "And?"

"And so ... the Nephilim were the offspring of the first humans and the Anunnaki, or Elohim as we're called in the Bible."

"Elohim?" Sam said. "Doesn't that mean God? Yahweh himself?"

Connie scrunched her brow. "That's the usual translation, but it's wrong. The Elohim were the designation humans gave the 'Sons of God.'"

"Okay," I butted in, holding my hands up. "What the hell? Elohim? God? Anunnaki? Nephilim? This doesn't make any sense. You're talking in circles."

"Barry," Connie said. "The Nephilim were *half-breeds*."

And there it was. That word again.

I turned my beer up and finished it.

"So you're saying I'm one of these Nephilim?"

"Your mother was an Anunnaki. As am I."

I leaned toward her and sniffed. "Are you high? Is that wacky weed I smell?"

Connie frowned. "I come from a race of people not from Earth, and when we arrived, we were ... treated special. Worshiped. Revered."

"Uh-huh."

"We have certain abilities that humans don't have. So we appeared to be ... Godly."

"Uh-huh."

"There were only two hundred Anunnaki in the beginning, and so there were some who took humans as mates. And then the Nephilim were born. The half-breeds."

I glanced at Sam. "You buying this?"

Sam's mouth was open, her beer nowhere near it.

Connie said, "Barry. I'm not human. We're not from Earth. I mean, *I* was born here, but our race didn't originate on Earth."

I laughed and turned my beer up, but I'd already finished it earlier. I pulled myself up and hobbled toward the fridge. "So you're saying you're an alien, Connie?"

"Yes. Sort of."

"And I'm half alien?" I grabbed two beers.

"Yes."

I made my way back to my chair and lowered myself gently into it. I popped the top off one of the beers and said, "Bullshit."

"I know what this sounds like," Connie said. "But can you explain the things you can do?"

She had a point, but my life wasn't some B-movie script. Blame Superpowers on being an alien? That was a little overused. Like blaming radiation for the ability to climb walls.

Weak.

"It's still bullshit."

"We were forbidden from having relations with humans"—she hesitated—"because there were unforeseen consequences."

I thought a second, then squinted my eyes. "Like flying?"

"Yes." Connie lowered her head, like my ability was leprosy.

"Why is that such a bad thing?" Sam asked.

When Connie didn't answer her immediately, I said, "Because I'm more powerful than them."

"Yes," Connie whispered.

I shook my head, taking a swig of beer. "I still don't buy it."

Connie exhaled a huge breath. She looked exhausted.

"Why have you never contacted me until now?" I asked. "You say you've known about me all along, and yet, you let me dangle for thirty years trying to figure out who and what I am. That's pretty fucked up, if

I do say so myself."

"Barry—"

"Like that TV show, *The Greatest American Hero*?" I turned to Sam. "The dude got this special suit from aliens and lost the instruction book; had to keep running into walls until some kid showed him how Superman could fly."

I chugged my beer, trying to calm down.

"You know how many walls I hit?" I said, my voice rising.

I was sixteen when I first flew. I was at the roller skating rink for the video games and chicks, and had just beaten the crap out of some guy in Pacman. We were playing for twenty bucks, and back in the mid-eighties, that was a chunk of change to a teen. Twenty dollars could fill up a car and still leave you enough to eat.

The kid claimed I cheated, and I said he needed to pay me my twenty bucks. I was already a big guy, and with my X-Ray-Vision, I was pretty cocky. He said he didn't owe me a dime, and I said, "I know. You owe me twenty bucks. Pay up."

His three friends surrounded me, and they said he didn't owe me anything because I'd cheated.

Such is teenage logic.

I thought if I wasn't going to get the twenty bucks, I was going to get twenty bucks worth of fun. So I cold-cocked the guy in the face and took off running.

I made it out the door and halfway across the parking lot before the four of them caught up to me. I was too big to outrun them, and this was before my Super-Speed. Just as they got close enough for me to hear their breathing, I wished I was fifty feet ahead.

Bam. All of a sudden, I was flying—no, careening—through the air barely two inches off the ground, still "running" with my feet, arms flailing everywhere.

I hit a wall and did a Wile E. Coyote—freezing for a second with my arms and legs splayed out awkwardly—then dropped to the ground.

The guys stopped chasing me and stared. Then, one by one, each of them took off.

I guess I freaked them out pretty bad.

Because I knew how freaked out I was ...

Connie set her beer down and said, "You've got to believe me, Barry. I couldn't take the chance of contacting you. They were watching me."

"Who was watching you?"

"The Council of Lords. Cathy had disappeared, and they knew how close we were. They knew Cathy might contact me." She paused. "So we made a pact never to talk again, for her safety."

"Just how close were you and my mom?" I wiggled my eyebrows.

Connie said, "We were sisters."

And then I dropped my beer in my lap.

Chapter 36

I righted the bottle before too much glugged out, because beer is a terrible thing to waste. "You're my aunt?"

Connie nodded, eyes misting. "Then one day, years after she'd left, Cathy risked everything and found me. She told me she was pregnant, and the father was human. We both knew what that meant. If they got hold of you, you'd never see your first birthday."

I let this all sink in. It was a lot of information at once.

I'm half-alien. I have an aunt. I have beer soaking my crotch.

"But why did my mom run away to begin with?" I asked.

"She didn't agree with the Lord's politics."

I really laughed now, hard, picturing alien politics.

"What politics were those? Unfair trade relations with the Ferengis? You gotta be careful with them; they'll cheat you every chance they get."

"Barry. Please. I'm trying to tell you."

I glanced at Sam. She was giving me the eye. I took a swig and leaned back, sighed. "Go ahead."

Connie sucked in a deep breath, and began again. "You know the Neanderthals?"

Inside, I was rolling my eyes, but outside I nodded with a thin smile.

"We ... the Anunnaki ... created them. They were to be a subservient race. Kind of like mules were for humans. Mules are a cross-breed between horses and donkeys, bred for working farms and long journeys. Humans got the idea from us, because we bred Neanderthals for the same reason."

Connie set her beer down. "But they were a failed experiment. They didn't take direction well."

"You mean they were stupid," I said.

"No, not that."

"Sure. Just like those insurance commercials. 'So easy a caveman can do it.' They were stupid."

"Well ... "

"You're talking about the Neanderthal, right? Big forehead, low jaw, club in one hand? Yeah, Connie, they even *look* like they're stupid."

Connie shook her head. "No, actually, they were very intelligent. They just lacked creativity needed to solve problems."

"Excuse me?" Sam said.

Connie fidgeted. "I know this sounds crazy to you. But we tinkered some more, and created the Homo Sapien."

I raised my eyebrows. "Are you trying to tell me you ... the Anunnaki ... created the human race?"

"Yes."

"Okay." I drank some beer, swished it around in my mouth, swallowed. "I call bullshit again. Major bullshit. Like, the kind of bullshit that drops out shaped like a bull who's taking a shit himself."

"Wait, Barry," Sam interrupted, then looked at Connie. "Are you serious?"

Connie nodded. "The Adama was our first success."

"So," Sam continued, "you're saying the Bible is factually correct?"

"To a point, yes."

"Yeah," I said. "And Moses lived to be nine hundred years old." I scoffed. "Right."

"Actually," Connie said. "That's close. Humans really did live that long back then. But the more they bred, the less their life span became. And more diseases popped up. In the beginning, there wasn't even cancer."

I snorted. "There weren't deep fat fryers and drive-thrus either."

Connie and Sam shot me hard stares.

What?

Connie said, "You know in the Bible where they mention the chariots of fire?"

I wanted to say something about the song but held back.

Connie continued, "Those were our aircraft. And the tower of Babel, remember that?"

"The one that leans?" I said.

The women ignored me, Connie now talking directly to Sam. "Humans are very resourceful and intelligent, and like I said before, creative. They reverse-engineered some of our technology and built a tower ... a rocket tower ... the tower of Babel ... so they could—"

"Reach the heavens," Sam finished Connie's thought. "And God was angry with them so he destroyed the tower and sent the builders to the different parts of the world and confused their languages so they couldn't communicate."

Connie nodded. "Yes, although you guys did the language confusion all on your own. But the tower of Babel was the first sign we'd gone too far."

I threw my hands up. "Whoa, whoa. Enough of this crap. When I said to start at the beginning, I didn't mean literally. I want to know why my mom ran off."

"I'm getting to that," Connie said. "The Lords decided their little experiment needed to be ended. They'd created a race almost equal to theirs. So when the polar caps melted the first time, the Lords orbited the Earth, leaving the humans to be drowned."

"The Great Deluge," Sam said, mouth agape.

"Exactly."

"Huh?" I said. "De-what?"

"The Great Flood. The polar caps melted and the land flooded," Sam said.

Connie continued. "Most of the humans died because like now, most of them lived near major bodies of water."

"You're still not answering me about my mom," I said. "Get to the point."

"Yes I have. You're just not listening," Connie replied. "The politics of the Council of Lords is the complete extinction of the human race."

Silence hung in the air a few moments gathering dust.

"They want to kill us?" Sam asked.

"In a way, yes. You see, they consider Earth their domain. Humans were created to serve them."

"And we don't any more."

"No."

"You've met the current Lord over the Earth, Barry. His name is Rex. And he's ruthless."

I laughed and slapped my knee. "Great campaign slogan! Ruthless Rex Ruther." I bowled over and laughed until my side hurt, which didn't take long.

No one joined me.

Sam spoke up, "Why don't they just drop nukes on us?"

"Because then the Earth would be uninhabitable for them also."

"Wait, wait, wait," I said. "So you guys created a slave race that eventually took over?"

Connie nodded.

I rolled my eyes. "Well, your first mistake was that whole nine hundred year lifespan. I mean, I can understand it from an economics standpoint, but if you're going to give us intelligence and let us outlive you too ..."

Connie shot me an amused look.

I said, "You're kidding." I paused. "How old are you?"

"How old do you think I am?"

I sipped my beer and studied her. Minor crow's feet, graying hair, a few wrinkles. My mom's sister. "Mid-sixties?"

Connie smiled.

"Early seventies?"

Connie shook her head. "Not even close." She straightened her pants leg. "Let's just say that I'm mentioned in the Bible and leave it at that."

My eyes widened, and Sam gasped.

"New Testament, of course," she added.

I shook my head. "Now I really call bullshit. With icing on top."

Connie continued spinning more tales about the Nephilim and Anunnaki and humans and Bible. She warned me again to "leave everything alone," that I "couldn't stop what was already in motion," and "it was bigger" than me.

She said she would petition the Council to release Andrew and Kimmy and reassured me they'd be returned after this week. She wouldn't go into specifics, only that she was "on the inside" and warned me again to leave it all alone, to let her and the other *Sympathetics* work their channels.

I told her I was done with trying to save anything but leftover pizza. I was out of the Superhero business. Someone always wanted to kill me.

No sir. Not any more. I was content drinking beer, scarfing pizza, and using my X-Ray-Vision on hot chicks.

Finally, I'd heard enough and asked her the one question I'd been dying to ask since she confessed she was my aunt. "What was my mom like?"

Connie smiled and leaned forward. She grabbed my hand and said, "Your mother was a wonderful, selfless woman. She was beautiful and smart and strong-willed and—"

"Yeah, yeah, yeah. That's the stuff people always say. I mean, *what was she like*? Was she the type to drink a glass of wine and read a book on a Friday night, or play football with kids in the neighborhood, or never leave a dish in the sink? You know, real stuff."

Connie took a deep breath and looked into my eyes. "She preferred liquor to wine or beer, could drink your father under the table any day. Me too, for whatever that's worth."

"Well, Dad's been practicing."

"And she liked basketball much more than football, although neither has been around very long. She was partial to traditional sports where skill and endurance mattered more than strength. Archery. Golf. Running."

"Boring."

"And she generally kept her kitchen in good condition." She studied me a second. "She would be proud of the way you've used your powers."

Sam broke in, "I don't think you know how he uses them."

Connie raised an eyebrow at Sam, but turned back to me. "Your mother was strong and caring and the kind of woman who made everyone around her better."

I huffed. "Didn't work on my dad."

Connie squeezed my hand. "Have patience with him. Your father was an amazing man when he was younger. So vibrant and full of life. He treated your mother like she was the center of the galaxy. And she loved him very much."

I shook my head. "I don't see it. He's been an ass my whole life. And he'll be an ass the next time I see him."

Sam said, "What's that about apples falling from trees?"

I glanced at Sam, but Connie pulled my attention back toward her. "Farley used to be a very different man. Losing your mother broke him in ways a man should never be broken."

I glared at her. "Broken? How about that time he broke my nose for missing curfew by twenty minutes? That broken enough for you?"

Connie frowned. "I wish you could've gotten to know the man your mother fell in love with." She paused. "One night, your father came home from work with a box full of kittens. They were undernourished, their little ribs poking out so far you could count them. He'd heard them meowing in the bushes outside his work and realized the mother cat abandoned them.

"So he stuffed a towel in a box and spirited them home. Catherine wanted to take them to the pound the next day, but Farley said no, he'd take care of them. Each morning he carried that box of kittens to work, and each night he brought it home.

"He nursed every single one of those babies to health, starting with an eyedropper, and then a tiny hamster bottle, before graduating them to real food. Eventually, when they were big enough, he gave them away. All but one."

Boomer. My cat growing up. He was an awesome tabby—not as awesome as Little Man, but he was pretty cool.

Boomer had always been around. I hadn't known when we'd gotten him. He was just there. As long as I could remember.

And he always seemed to like my dad. I don't know why I never thought that odd, my dad patting a cat in his lap while he watched baseball on television and got shit-faced drunk. It didn't make sense if you stepped back and thought about it.

But there it was. And now I knew why.

Boomer was the last link to his old life. The life that disappeared. The life of happiness and warmth. The life with my mom.

Connie left an hour later after sharing more stories of my dad. I didn't want to hear about this guy I never knew. I wanted to hate him, not pity him. It was hard to feel for a man who'd called you a sissy-boy half your teenage life because you couldn't throw a strike.

Sam offered to stay another day to take care of me.

I winked. "Okay, but be gentle. I'm still an injured man."

"I'll be sleeping in the guest room," she said.

"Cool with me. I haven't done it in there in a long time."

She glared at me.

"Fine. We could just take a shower together."

"Or we couldn't."

"There are places I can't really reach."

"So take a bath and have a long soak."

I shrugged. "How about you take a shower, and I'll watch through the wall."

"You wouldn't."

"You're kidding, right? How well do you know me? I've been enjoying your undergarment choice all night. Black is my favorite."

Sam turned pink. I told her that was cute, her being embarrassed and all. I offered to take my clothes off so we'd be even, but she passed, saying something about losing her dinner.

Whatever.

I fell asleep the moment my head hit the pillow.

Chapter 37

Tuesday morning came, and I figured I'd call Gordon to apologize for being so short the night before. Surely now that some time had passed, he'd understand my decision. I turned the phone on and had a voice mail waiting from Hannah. She said to call her back, it was urgent.

I dialed her, and she answered on the third ring. She sounded like I'd woken her up. It was ten in the morning.

"Late night?" I said.

"Just, uh ... working on your stuff."

"It's not my stuff any more. I quit."

A pause, then she said, "I found out Argyle owns First Burlington, the bank."

"Excellent," I said. "Tell Gordon I just said I quit."

"Gordon knows. I already told him."

"Great. Well, my work is done here. Hey, I've been meaning to tell you, one of my satellite channels is scrambled again."

"One of the porn stations?"

"What else? You got a fix for me?"

She sighed. "Bring it by sometime this week."

"You're the bomb."

Hannah sighed. "So you're really not going to save Kimmy?"

"Don't worry about it. I have it from a good source she's put up at a spa somewhere, and she'll be back in a week or so."

"It's just that, I found all this stuff out—"

"Really. Tell Gordon. It's not on me any more. Gotta go, see you later this week."

I hung up. I'd felt a speech coming, and I didn't want to hear it. If Hannah had almost died, maybe she'd feel different about all this stuff, too.

I know I did. I'd be damned if I was going to risk my life again.

My phone rang ten seconds after I hung up from Hannah. It was Gordon. Now that he was calling me, I didn't feel like talking to him. I knew the conversation would be the guilt trip from hell.

So I didn't answer. I let it go through to voice mail.

He called back again. Damn it. It was morning, and I didn't want a fight first thing.

I answered.

"Good morning, sunshine," I said. "How'd you sleep? Me, I slept pretty good. Woke up a few times when I tried to turn over and forgot my ribs had been beaten like tribal drums. But other than that, not bad."

"You're not quitting."

"You slept good too, huh? That's nice. It's important to get a good night's sleep."

"You can't quit with Kimmy being kidnapped."

"So I was thinking about taking a vacation. Maybe go to the beach. Do some girl-watching. And when I say girl-watching, I mean—"

"I won't let you quit." Gordon had been raising his voice with each sentence. Now he was almost yelling.

I took a breath. "Gordon, I can quit any time I want. That's the beauty of living in a free country. I have the freedom to not do any damn thing I don't want to."

Gordon's voice softened. "It's Kimmy, Barry. It's Kimmy."

I said nothing. He continued, "You practically grew up in our house. You're like a brother to her. You can't give up on her."

"Gordon, I want to save her. I really do. But they almost killed me the other day. Do you understand that? There's one of me, and lots of them. I can't win. Do you grasp the math here?"

"I do, Barry. But—"

"No, Gordon. You're not listening to me. I can barely walk. I was pronounced legally dead almost 24 hours ago. I'm done. I'm sorry you can't accept it, but that's the way it's gonna be. I like breathing oxygen without a tube. Besides, Connie said Rex will let Kimmy go in a week. She promised. So Kimmy's not in any real danger. There's no reason—"

"Connie? Who's Connie?"

"I told you about her. The cowl? My mystery visitor?"

"You never mentioned her. Who is she?"

"You'll never believe this. She's my aunt."

"What?"

"My mom's sister ... and you don't even want to know the stuff she told me and Sam."

"Sam?"

"Oh yeah. Remember that reporter chick, Samantha Gerber? She's the one that found me half-dead the other morning. Anyway, she's been taking care of me since—"

"Reporter? You've not told me about a reporter."

"I didn't tell you about her either? Are you sure?"

"Wait, start over. Your aunt stopped by, and said Kimmy would be alright?"

"Yeah, she's on the inside with the aliens. She's one of them."

"Aliens? Barry, you're not making any sense at all. Are you on pain medication?"

"I wish. Can you write me a prescription?" I paused. "Look, I'll tell you more about it later. Sam's up and about. See you."

I hung up.

Sam appeared at my door wearing one of my big t-shirts and nothing else. I think I drooled.

"I heard you talking," she said. "Thought I'd check on you."

"Yeah, I was on the phone with Gordon." I patted the bed beside me. "You can check me out better over here."

She smiled. "Yeah, you're fine. Just wanted to see if you were up."

I grinned. "By the time you get over here, I will be."

"I'm sure you would. Are you hungry for some breakfast?"

"You could call it that."

Sam rolled her eyes. "Do you ever stop?"

"Not until you beg me to."

She shook her head and left the doorway. I yelled after her, "No need to put on any clothes just for me. I can see it anyway!"

I think she ignored me.

Chapter 38

I hobbled into the bathroom while Sam was taking a shower. She popped her head around the curtain and asked me what I was doing. I told her that if she already had the water just right, why waste it on only one person? She pointed to the door and said, "Out."

"If you didn't want me in here, you should've locked the door," I said.

"I did."

"But you never said to stay out."

She glowered at me. Her hair was soaked with shampoo suds and stuck to the side of her head. Her skin was clear and clean and pale with freckles, like most redheads. The hand pointing at the door was dripping soap and water on the bath rug. I wanted to smell her.

Every woman has her own scent, a mixture of soap, shampoo, deodorant, perfume, and pheromones. At least that's what this article said in a magazine I was reading at the Jiffy Lube once. I wanted to know what Sam's aroma smelled like, to have it close to me. To have it stuck to me all day like a badge of honor.

"I said leave," Sam said.

I threw my hands up and backed out of the bathroom, not even peeking at her *through* the curtain. I trudged to the living room, collapsed onto the couch, grabbed the remote, and clicked until I reached the food channel. Paula Deen was stuffing pork chops with a mixture she'd already made. Her southern drawl seemed fake for some reason.

Sam finished her shower, got ready, and walked into the living room. She sat on the couch beside me and slipped on tennis shoes. She wore khaki shorts and a plain shirt.

She said, "So what do you want to do today?"

I looked at her. "Why are you still here?"

"Huh?"

"You saved me, and I'm very thankful. Don't think I'm not. But I'm all better now. Why are you still here?"

She shrugged. "What else am I going to do?"

I looked at her a second. "I don't buy it."

She pursed her lips together and puffed up a cheek, then said, "I'm a freelance reporter who's found the story of her life, but I can't write it because I'd lose all credibility. You were right. No one would believe me. That's what I was coming to tell you the other morning."

"And?"

"And now I have nothing to do. Actually, I'm kind of lost. You were right about something else. I spent my whole life chasing this, and now that I got it, I have no idea what to do."

"And?"

"*Aaaand,*" she said, elongating the word. "I figure stories would probably happen around you, whether you like it or not. You say you're done with saving the world, but I don't believe it. I'm great at reading people; that's why I'm good at my job. A reporter has to have the ability of figuring out what makes people tick." She paused. "And I don't think you're done."

"I am."

She smiled, "I think you believe that but—"

I leaned over and kissed Sam. Mouth to mouth. It was soft and warm and felt right. Lips parted and tongues met, twirling in exploration, then she pulled away and pushed me.

"That wasn't nice," she said.

"Actually, it was."

"That's because you're horny."

"You didn't seem to mind."

"You caught me off guard." Sam turned toward the TV and tried to ignore me.

I looked at her profile for a bit. Her nose was longer than a button nose, but it fit her face perfectly. Her lips were full and eyes clear. And I had my answer; she smelled of cucumbers and flowers and lime and something earthy I couldn't quite place.

"Well," I said. "I'm coming in for another and this time you know it."

I leaned toward her and she remained still, not facing me but not pulling away either. Lips met again and they parted again and tongues played like wild badgers, rough and yet gentle at the same time.

Her phone rang and she jumped for it.

She talked for a few moments, apologizing and telling the caller she'd definitely have something by the end of this weekend. She hung up and stayed standing.

"That was my editor," she said, answering me before I asked her.

"What did he want?" The asshole.

"The other day I told him I had a big story. Pulitzer material. Now, I'm sort of screwed. I have to give him something by Monday morning. And I've built it up so much there's nothing I can do but deliver."

"That sucks." I patted the couch. "Come back over here."

"Nope."

"Why not?"

"Because I don't want to."

"Could have fooled me."

"Let's go get something to eat." She headed for the door. "I'm starving."

"I need a moment."

Sam looked at me, frowning.

"Got a big problem here," I said, motioning to my crotch.

She looked and grinned. "Looks like a small problem."

"Wanna bet?" I went to undo my shorts, and she was out the door before I got to the zipper. Women, I'll never figure them out.

We ate at a Waffle House since I was in the mood for lunch, and she wanted breakfast, and it was ten o'clock. On our way back, I had Sam detour to my dad's place—she was driving because I let her think she could boss me around, and really, I just wanted to look at her.

She sensed me staring several times and told me to stop it. I said it was a free country, and she told me she didn't care.

I needed to stop by Dad's because I wanted to find out if he knew Connie was Mom's sister and why he'd never mentioned her before. We walked up to the house and rang the doorbell. Nothing. Rang it again, and this time I laid on it. His car was here, and he was probably passed out from another all-night drinking session. Some things never change.

After another minute, I scanned the place and didn't like what I saw. Furniture was askew, stuff was broken on the floor, food was out in the kitchen, and the fridge was left open.

I tried the door. It was locked, so I put my shoulder into it. Sam yipped when the doorframe splintered and burst inward.

The living room was in its normal disarray, plus extra. Beer bottles and cans were everywhere but many were turned over, lying on the floor. Dad didn't do that. He always set them on furniture and never, ever left them turned over. Of all the things in the world, he was weird about that.

Food was out on the kitchen counter, like he'd been making himself a sandwich. Mayo, mustard, ham, cheese, pickles. The mayo was warm. That was when I saw the bloody finger on the kitchen table. A pinkie.

Sam dry-heaved and ran toward the sink.

I went straight to his room, Sam in tow, and checked the top of his dresser where he put his pocket contents every night. His keys were there but his wallet was gone. There were a few slips of paper with writing on them. I picked them up.

Mets over Yankees - $1k. The date on it was two days ago. I remembered the score of the game when I clicked through channels yesterday. The Yankees had won 8-4.

There were other tickets lying around that totaled to more than five grand. If I knew my dad, he'd picked the losing team three quarters of the time.

I knew Rex Ruther didn't have him. For one thing his goons wouldn't need to trash the place; they could just take him. And my guess was that Rex didn't take bets—he was more into controlling outcomes than guessing at them.

"I'll bet he didn't even have foreclosure proceedings," I said.

"What?" Sam said behind me.

I explained what I'd found and how I gave him the money the other day. It was probably used to cover a losing bet so he could place more bets. I wondered if Dad still used the same guy. I knew his old bookie and didn't remember him being like this, but it had been a while.

I turned to Sam, "We gotta go see Steve."

Chapter 39

Steve the Bookie, aka Big Boy Steve, aka Steven Huntley, was still running his front business of a deli. In the back, customers placed bets on everything from horse racing to college basketball to American Idol. Steve had been running the deli and bookie business ever since I remembered.

Big Boy Steve was as big around as I was tall, with thinning, jet black hair slicked back like a 50s greaser. He looked like the cliché Italian, but everyone knew he was originally from Savannah and didn't have a drop of Italian blood in his oversized body.

Steve had always been nice to everyone who came in his deli, giving kids a slice of capicola or salami while their parents chose their selections—meats, cheeses, *and* bets.

We walked in, and Steve's face lit up.

"Mr. Barry, how they hanging?"

Big Boy Steve's accent was deep South, the kind that made you double-take and wonder if he was forcing it. It totally mismatched his Yankee Italian appearance.

"Lower than ever," I answered.

I introduced Sam as my future wife, and she said, "Not in a million years," and shook Steve's sweaty hand.

Steve looked at me and laughed. "She's got spunk. I like her."

"You have no idea, Steve, no idea."

"So, business or pleasure?"

"How about both?" I said. "Let's start with a pound of Muenster and a pound of your finest spicy prosciutto." I pulled the betting slips out of my pocket and tossed them onto the counter. "And can you tell me if these are yours?"

Steve glanced at the papers as he reached for the Muenster, saying, "Yep, they're mine. Your daddy took them out a few days ago."

"He pay you yet?"

"Nope, but I ain't worried. He always comes through. Might take him a week or two, but he'll come in. Paid me eight grand just last week."

"What?!"

Steve shrugged as he ran the cheese through the deli slicer. "He's had a run of bad luck lately."

"Steve, you're what's called an enabler"—Gordon teaches me things—"You gotta stop taking his bets."

"Barry, my man," Steve said, changing the cheese out for the meat. "You know as well as I do if I don't take his bets, somebody else will. You think that next bookie will be as nice as me and give him a week or two to pay up?" He held his hands out to his side, palms up.

"Yeah, yeah, you're right," I conceded.

"You know where he could have come up with eight grand?" Sam asked.

Big Boy Steve raised his eyebrows. "That's a good question, and now that you ask, I just might. When people need cash in a hurry around here, they sometimes to go JJ Tyson." Steve wrote an address on the back of one of the betting slips, then looked up, quizzically.

"What do you wanna know all this for?"

I hesitated, then said, "Dad's disappeared. His place is messed up, and I found a pinkie finger."

Big Boy Steve whistled, and he looked genuinely concerned, his face appearing darker with more wrinkles. He handed me the address without a word. I paid for the food and we left.

Chapter 40

On the way home, Sam looked over at me and said, "I thought you didn't care about anything any more. You quit, remember?"

"You're exactly right," I replied. "That's why I'm not going to do anything." I paused. "Dad's always gambled, he's always drank, and that'll never change. He'll continue to get himself into jams like this. If he wants my help, he can ask, and we'll see then."

That's when I remembered him showing up at my apartment asking for money. That had taken a lot of guts, but he'd lied to me. Dad lying was par for the course, but maybe, just maybe, if he'd told me the truth, I would have helped him.

Instead, he tried to play the "Mom" card, how the bank was taking *her* house, *her* tree, etc.

"It's hard for parents to ask their children for help," Sam said. "It's the opposite role than they're used to. They've always taken care of their children, and to reverse that is anathema to their existence."

I held a hand up. "Look, I already got one therapist in my life. I don't need another, no matter how good you smell. So drop it."

"How good I smell?"

We rode in silence for a moment, then I said, "And next time you criticize me, use English."

I caught her grin out the side of my eye.

Gordon was waiting at the apartment when we got back. "Speak of the devil," I said as I opened the door. He looked up from the couch but didn't say anything.

I introduced Gordon and Sam. Sam said, "Hi," but Gordon grunted and turned back to the TV.

I headed for the fridge, asking if anyone needed a beer. Sam looked at her watch, shrugged, and said, "Why not?"

I popped the top on a cold one and downed half before taking one to her. She'd sat in a chair beside the couch.

"Let me start by warning you," I said as I plopped down beside Gordon. "I'm not in the mood to fight."

He flicked his eyes at me, then back to C-SPAN.

On-screen, a bunch of congressmen were standing around and chatting, and I said, "How can you watch this stuff?"

I grabbed the remote and clicked around for a bit. Gordon still hadn't said a peep, so I told him Sam kissed me.

"I did not!" she said.

"Yeah you did. You sat there"—pointing to Gordon's place—"and I sat here, and you kissed me."

"You kissed me!"

I shrugged. "You liked it."

She gave me a mean face, but I noticed she didn't contradict me.

I said to Gordon. "We used tongues."

"Barry!"

"Twice."

Sam huffed and chugged half her beer. How sexy!

I flipped through the channels some more, looking for something good, but it was the middle of the day. I passed ESPN and a baseball highlight was on. Some guy in the stands reached out and caught a fly ball right out of the left fielder's glove. The player was really pissed. They replayed it slow a few times, then back and forth, showing the ball entering the fan's glove—popping out—entering—popping out.

It made me think of my dad and the mess he was in. I shook my head mentally. That was his problem, not mine.

Little Man slunk into the room, looked around, then hopped in the chair with Sam. She rubbed his belly, and I could hear his purr from where I was. Lucky bastard.

My phone rang. I didn't recognize the number. I answered anyway.

"Mr. Glick? This is Lanny Lancaster."

"Well hello there, Lanny."

I saw Gordon perk up.

"You told me to call you if I found out anything."

"Yep, sure did."

"Well, I found something alright. You remember we print tickets for seventeen states?"

"I do now." I think I mentioned already I'm not good with details.

"I checked the programming on each state's run, and they were fine. I scrunched my face. "And you called me why?"

"Well, we have a software update due to run this week, and I thought I'd check that too. It was wrong. The update changes the payout algorithm and more than quadruples the winning tickets."

"Hmm. Would that have worked? Seems to me as soon as they saw it was screwed up, they'd yank the tickets."

"That's the beauty of it," Lanny said, getting excited like Gordon does when he talks about the brain's inner workings or civil war reenactments—Gordon is one of those guys who gets "shot" each year at the Battle of Guilford Courthouse. "The algorithm is set to increase the payout slowly over half a year. That makes it almost unnoticeable. You know what this could do?"

"What?"

"If nobody caught it, those seventeen states would almost go bankrupt."

Now that's interesting. Didn't see that coming. I thanked Lanny and told him I'd call him back soon.

"What about my door?" he asked.

"Huh?"

"You said you'd fix my door if I called you with something."

"You haven't fixed that thing yet?"

"No."

"Well, yeah, okay. I'll get to it this week or something."

I hung up, and Gordon looked like he wanted to ask what Lanny said. He didn't.

I grabbed the last few beers for Sam and me, and we drank and made small talk and glanced at the TV. Sam rubbed on Little Man, and I wiggled my eyebrows at her. She ignored me.

Gordon even joined in a little conversation about weather and sports, but not much else.

I finished my beer and announced I was going to Shoffner's to get more brews. Sam asked me to get some potato chips while I was at it. Gordon barely glanced in my direction.

On the way to the store, I noticed my ribs—and the rest of my body for that matter—were feeling much better. I was healing pretty fast. Then I thought about Gordon sulking on the couch. I wanted to save Kimmy, but I couldn't. I'd already cheated death once, and a man has to draw the line somewhere.

For me, it's that "ceasing to breathe" thing I have a problem with.

Rafi's dad, Chandra, was working the register. He lit up when I walked in, smiling and chattering away in clipped gibberish. I chose three different kinds of beers from the back coolers; a pale lager called Duck Duck Goose, a mandarin citrus wheat named Orange Cull, and some more Dirty Monk.

I set them on the checkout counter and asked for two Bingo Blasts and four Double Diamonds; that would net me almost forty bucks. Then I scanned the five-dollar tickets and one of the Stock Market Stacks stood out. It was a ten grand winner only three tickets away.

Nah. I didn't need that much. Let some lucky fool win it who lives in a double-wide with a buck-toothed wife, four screaming kids, and a mangy mutt named Buster.

Chandra handed me the tickets and said in broken English, "I never thank you for what you do for my son."

"What? Oh, that was nothing."

"Yes it was something. You save his life. That is everything."

"Really, Chandra. It was nothing."

His eyes widened. "You see the new pizzas?"

"New pizzas?"

He ran to the back of the store and returned with two pizzas by Mama Mia. One had a crust filled with mozzarella cheese and the other had a crust coated with garlic and herbs. He shoved them into my hands.

"On my house," he said.

"Chandra, you really don't need to do this. I have money." Well, the state does.

Chandra touched my hand and looked into my eyes. "You save Rafi's life. I repay you. Take pizzas. Take beer. Forever."

"Chandra, I really—"

He squeezed, and I felt his warmth. "You save Rafi. You save me."

I hesitated. "At least let me pay for the lottery tickets, Chandra."

He smiled so hard I saw his molars. "Yes," he said. "You buy winning tickets. I buy pizza and beer. You good man!"

I grunted. "I don't know about that, Chandra."

Chandra squeezed my arm. "Most people in store getting robbed, they do nothing. They hide. They pretend it not their problem." He paused. "But you save my Rafi. You stand up to bad guy. You no hide. You no run away."

I bit my lip. "Chandra, I was just—"

"You are hero, Mr. Barry. True hero. From now on, I call you Super Barry like in movie. I can never thank you enough."

His words hung there for a frozen moment, echoing around my mind. I smelled the metallic aroma of his aftershave, felt the strength of his trembling hands, absorbed the sincerity in his voice. Chandra was truly grateful. And his words transcended their intended meaning more than he could ever know.

They spoke to me at the basest level.

Maybe the beers I'd had earlier made me emotional. Maybe it was Chandra's eyes misting up. Or maybe I was tired. I don't know what it was, but I felt something give way inside me.

I was cowering behind weak excuses like everyone else, too afraid or apathetic to do the right thing. But unlike everyone else, I had the ability to set the world straight, to stand up for the wronged when they couldn't. I had the gifts.

I had the power.

The world suddenly came into focus, and time once again trudged forward. I needed to use my head for more than a drywall tester. I needed to step up and be a man. No, I needed to be more than a man.

I needed to be a hero.

I smiled at Chandra, and pointed at the lottery rack. "Gimme three of those Stock Market tickets while you're at it."

Chapter 41

I opened the door to my apartment and displayed my pizza and beer for Gordon and Sam to see. They barely looked up from the TV.

"Look, guys. This one's got cheese in the crust."

Nothing.

"Cheese. In the crust."

Not even a glimmer of appreciation.

"This one's got garlic and herbs caked all over it."

They stayed silent, just watched CNN and sat there. Incredible.

I put the groceries up, saving a Dirty Monk to drink. I popped it open and returned to my seat on the couch. I looked at Gordon, saying "You got that foreclosure list of First Burlington's?"

He shot me a look of disdain. "You looking to buy a house?"

I shook my head. "I figure Kimmy's going to be held in a house that was just taken off the market. You know? Seems like that would be the thing to do."

Gordon turned to me. "I hadn't thought of that."

"How current is that list?"

"We got it off their internal servers."

"Are any of the houses not listed on the market yet?"

He stood and said, "I've got it in the car. I can compare it to the MLS online database."

I grabbed his hand as he tried to scoot by me. "Gordon. You know I suck at this apology stuff. I've been an ass ... more of an ass than normal ... but I'm over it. We're going to get Kimmy and her partner back if it's the last thing I do. I figure if I have the element of surprise, the outcome could be different this time."

Gordon smiled, and I swear I could see his eyes welling up through his thick glasses. That or I was squeezing him too hard.

Sam was fully alert too, sitting up in her seat, a big grin plastered across her face.

"I also suck at speeches," I said. "But there you go."

"It was perfect," Gordon said.

I stood as Gordon went to his car, and said to Sam, "And now, I've got an appointment with a scumbag named JJ Tyson."

"Can I come?"

I thought about it and nodded with a grin. Might impress her to see me in action.

She hopped up and scampered to the door. As I watched her curvy little body bounce outside, I thought maybe I was making a mistake. How was I going to keep my mind on things with her around me? Already, I wanted to shove her against the wall and—

"Where are you going?" Gordon asked, coming back through the door, his eyes narrowing.

"To save Dad. Have that list whittled down by the time I get back." I paused and winked at him. "You know, gotta save the girl, too."

Chapter 42

JJ Tyson's place was set up as one of those payday lenders. A crooked lending business nestled inside a legitimate lending business. Pretty slick. Customer needs the *really* hard cash, send them to the back room. No paperwork, no qualifying, no problem.

Sam and I walked in and right up to the first desk. I towered over the little, old woman sitting there. Her white hair was pulled back in a tight bun, and she greeted me with a non-intimidated, practiced smile.

"How may I help you?" she said.

"I need to see JJ," I answered. I lowered my voice and winked. "It's personal."

She smiled and said, "Not here right now. What can I do for you?"

"I need to see JJ himself. It's personal." I smiled and winked again, glancing at Sam.

"I'm JJ," she said with her eyes tightened, voice harder. "Now what do you want?"

This threw a wrench into things. I had JJ pictured as a thirty or forty-something punk with gold teeth and a few bodyguards, somebody I could beat the hell out of for intimidation. I'd never hit a woman before, let alone a crabby old biddy less than half my size.

"You've got something of mine, and I'm here to get it back," I said, the fake happy stuff abandoned.

"Oh yeah? What's that?"

"My dad."

She waved her hand. "Not helping me. What's his name?"

"Farley Glick."

"Ah. Farley. He's not been a very good customer. He doesn't understand you have to pay back what you borrow."

"Plus a little more," I added.

JJ's scowl melted into a smile. "Plus a little more. You got the idea. Maybe you could explain it to him."

I grinned. "I would if I could find him."

"I see your dilemma." She stood. "Let's see what we can do to remedy that. Follow me."

We walked through a door in the back of the office, down a short hall, then through a thicker door into a room that smelled of sweat and shit. Sam gagged as the aroma enveloped us.

Against the far wall was my dad, handcuffed to a metal railing that ran the length of the room. It was a barren brick wall except for the railing and the thick bolts that held it firmly in place.

He sat on the floor, left arm raised to the railing because of the handcuffs. A bucket sat just out of his reach. From the hefty aroma, I suspected that's where he had to relieve himself. Bruises covered his face and a few fingers on his free hand were bent at awkward angles. And of course, one of them was missing.

The other walls sported motivational posters like you'd see in a corporate office. Integrity—The Building Blocks of Trust. Honesty—The Currency of Business. Hard Work—The Basis of a Good Life. The pictures above the words showed rock climbers and men in hard hats.

I walked over to my dad, and he stood. I said, "Foreclosure?"

"I used *some* of it to pay the mortgage."

"Because you'd gambled away the mortgage money."

He feigned indifference. "It's all money."

I stepped back and regarded him. He was in the most pathetic position I'd ever seen, this man whom I'd feared for so long as a child was chained to a wall, smelling like a sewer.

"You could have asked me for help," I said.

"I did."

"No, you lied. I mean you could have told me the truth."

He shrugged like it was no big deal. "Did you bring money?"

"Would it matter? You'll be right back here in a few weeks."

"I had a run of bad luck."

"Have you ever had a run of good luck?"

"Are you gonna get me out of here or not?" He got snippy. Probably hadn't had a beer in a few days.

Sam turned to JJ and said, "How much does he owe?"

She studied Sam's crisp clothes and million dollar attitude. "Fifteen grand."

I stared at JJ. "How much did he borrow?"

"Doesn't matter. He owes fifteen now."

I looked at Dad. "How much did you borrow?"

He glanced at JJ, but I slapped his forehead. "Don't look at her. Look at me." Stunned, his eyes darted to mine. "How much?"

I'd come to save my dad, but his attitude made me want to kick his ungrateful ass myself.

"Eight thousand."

I nodded. "To pay off Big Boy Steve."

I turned to JJ and said, "I got ten. That's all you're getting."

"Fifteen, or he doesn't leave."

"Ten."

"Sixteen. For arguing."

I laughed. "Lady, I eat your weight in food every day. You'll take ten, and you'll be happy to get it. Maybe you could spend the extra to put in some plumbing. You've heard of that, right? Running water, moves through pipes?"

Her eyes hardened, and she snapped her fingers. A big guy appeared in the doorway, followed by another and another. The last one had more fat than muscle and carried a stun gun.

I laughed. "This the best you got?"

The first two guys picked up bats that were leaning against the wall. Sam moved behind me, and I said, "Alright, who's first?"

They narrowed their eyes and studied me. I studied them back.

One of the bat-wielders lunged at me with a wild swing. I side-stepped him and said, "Strike one."

He swung and missed again—I ducked that one. "Strike two."

A scowl covered his face as he swung again. I backed up with Super-Speed and then forward again. It happened so fast it probably looked like the bat had passed through me. "Strike three."

Bewildered and angrier now, he took another swing, and this time I grabbed the bat and wrenched it out of his hand. I shook my head, *tsk-tsking* as I handed the bat to Sam, and said, "Don't you know how the game is played? Three strikes and you're out."

I lunged at him and delivered a jab hard enough to snap his head back like a broken Pez dispenser. He crumpled to the floor.

I turned to the other two guys, their mouths open a little, and said, "Next batter."

They gathered themselves and spread out around me. Sam backed over and stood beside my dad, holding her nose because the bucket was right below her.

The guys circled me, trying to keep me off-guard. The one with the bat didn't want a repeat performance of the previous batter, and the fat one had to get close to use the stun gun. He'd seen my speed and was probably going to wait for the bat guy to hurt me before he tried anything.

They circled me for another thirty seconds, fake lunging at me until JJ said, "Somebody get him, or I'll cut your damn balls off!"

Bat Guy jumped at me, and I met him head on, literally. I head-butted him before he could bring the bat around. He collapsed backwards, and his head hit the concrete floor with a crack louder than the one my head gave him. He didn't move.

Sam yelled, and I turned to find Stun Guy inches from me. I closed my hand over his and winked at him, then turned his arm down and forced the arcing weapon into his crotch.

He yelped and stuttered as I held him up with my grip, electrifying his boys continuously. When I let him go, he melted into a mound of quivering flesh.

I turned to JJ and she darted out the room and slammed the door shut. I heard a deadbolt turn.

I walked over to dad and pinched the handcuffs off him. He rubbed his wrists as I positioned the thugs in the center of the room, sitting down, backs against each other with their legs splayed out like a six-point star.

Next I yanked the metal railing out of the brick wall and began wrapping it around them. I stopped and looked up, smiling. "I've always wanted to do this."

I finished and surveyed my handiwork. They could get it off themselves with a little effort, pushing it up over their heads. But they'd have to wait until they were all awake first. It was too heavy for just one or two of them.

I laughed as I thought about their reaction once they regained consciousness.

The locked door was metal and solid and opened outward. The frame was metal too, but it was still child's play. I delivered a swift kick to the door's middle, and it flew out into the small hallway, frame and all. I led Sam and Dad into the front office and there was JJ, pulling a gun out of an open desk drawer.

She leveled it at me, and I didn't give her a chance to speak. I reached down and grabbed a stapler off another desk and pitched it at her.

It crashed through the glass door behind her.

"You missed," she said, her voice warbling a little. She still had her gun aimed at me.

"He always threw like a girl," Dad said.

"Now," JJ said, gaining confidence. "My Colt here is telling me we should all head back down the hall."

If it was just me, I would have rushed JJ and grabbed the gun. But with Sam and Dad there, she could squeeze off a bullet before I got to her, and somebody could get shot. Just like Los Angeles.

I had to wait until I had the right angle.

JJ waved the gun. "You first, big boy."

I nodded at the gun. "Long barrel. You over-compensating for something?"

She fired a warning shot to the left of Sam, and Sam yelped.

"Get moving," JJ said.

I trudged down the hall trying to figure out my next move. Somehow I had to get Dad and Sam clear before I could take care of JJ. Damn it. Why did I allow Sam to come with me?

It wouldn't have been a bad idea for Dad to get winged by a bullet. Might have scared some sense into him. But I couldn't take a chance with Sam.

We stepped into the back room, and JJ's eyes almost fell out of her head when she saw my bad-guy-pretzel.

"I've always wanted to do that," I said to her.

JJ was speechless. I briefly thought of throwing Dad at the woman but my aim was really bad—I'd probably still miss, maybe even hit Sam.

JJ poked Sam's chest with the gun, nudging her forward.

"Hey, careful where you point that thing," I said to JJ. "I haven't had a chance to play with those yet."

Sam gave me a look.

JJ nodded at my Dad. "You. Pick up the stun gun."

If only she'd lowered the gun or pointed it elsewhere, I could have bum-rushed her and sent her flying through the open doorway. But she was being careful, keeping the weapon pointed at Sam.

My dad picked up the stun gun, and JJ told him to stun me. Before I could protest, he stuck it in my side and squeezed the trigger. The world shook and pain shot across my body in lightning speed. I collapsed to my knees.

He pulled the gun back, and the pain subsided.

I looked at him and said, "No argument?"

He shrugged. "She told me to."

"You could have said no. She hadn't threatened anybody yet. That's a rule. She has to threaten to shoot you before you *have* to do what she says." I looked at JJ. "Right?"

She smirked. "I didn't expect him to do it so quickly."

"I know, right? That's a little screwed up, if you ask me."

"Can I stun him again?" Dad asked.

"What?" I said. JJ nodded, and he stuck it in my side and squeezed. This time I lost control of my bladder before he pulled it away.

"Don't tase me bro," I said, raising a shaking hand.

JJ laughed, and I added, "Glad to see you're enjoying this."

Then Sam spun and knocked the gun away from JJ, clipping the woman's arm with her balled fist. JJ squealed in surprise, and I watched in shocked amazement as Sam shoved her other fist deep into JJ's midsection.

JJ *oophed* and doubled over.

Sam cupped her hands behind the woman's head and thrust her knee up, cracking into JJ's skull with an audible pop. The old woman collapsed, her face a bloody mess—Sam had broken her nose.

I tried to stand, and my dad reached out for me. I flinched, but he didn't have the stun gun any more. I took his hand, and he helped me up. My knees were having trouble adjusting.

"Sorry about all that," he said.

"Yeah, right."

"I told him to distract her," Sam said.

I looked at him. "You didn't have to enjoy it."

He shrugged. "Had to be distracting."

"There's a difference."

I shot him the Super-Stare, then walked over to where JJ was writhing on the floor.

"You broke my nothe, you ath-hole," JJ said.

I leaned down and picked the woman up by her throat, feet dangling, allowing her just enough room to breathe—barely—and said, "Since you didn't play nice, you don't even get your ten grand. And if I ever so much as smell your cheap perfume anywhere again, I'll be back." I paused and nodded toward the bad-guy-pretzel. "And next time I won't be so nice."

I dropped her, and she oozed to the floor, gasping.

I picked her Colt up, bent the barrel into a U, and tossed it in her lap.

"Just a little reminder," I taunted with a wink. The fear in her eyes spoke volumes.

Chapter 43

The ride back to Dad's was relatively silent. Dad was probably feeling humiliated, and Sam was probably hating that she couldn't write about the incident, having seen my awesomeness up close and personal for the first time.

We dropped Dad off, and he went inside without a word, not even a thank you or head nod.

"Strange relationship you two have," Sam said.

"It's always been that way." I wanted to tell her how he blamed me for Mom dying when I was born, and all the Freudian bullshit surrounding that, but I didn't want to get into it right then. Although, I might have gained some sympathy points that could lead to ...

No, I needed to stay focused.

We rode for a minute before I said "Nice moves back there."

"Oh that? Brown belt in jujitsu. It was nothing."

"I'll bet you never did it with a real gun pointed at you."

She grinned. "Yeah, that changes things a little."

"I wouldn't mind showing you *my* moves."

She glared at me. "I'll bet you wouldn't."

We pulled into my parking spot at the apartment. Christine was just returning from the pool. She waved and smiled at me.

"Hi, Barry," she said.

I waved. "Hey. Good sun today?"

She pulled the strap of her neon green bikini bottoms down a little and glanced up at me. "How's it look to you?"

I smiled. "Looking good."

She replaced the strap and bounded up the steps to her apartment. I enjoyed the show until Sam punched me in the arm.

"What?"

"Who is that slut?" Sam asked as I opened the door. "Does she even have a job?"

"That's Christine, and she's no slut. She's a MILF. That's totally different."

"Hmph."

"You're just jealous. You'd kill to look that good after a few kids."

She glared at me and stomped into the apartment.

Gordon was standing in the middle of the living room with a sheet of paper in his hand, grinning like he'd just seen Christine's backside too.

"I've got it!" he exclaimed. "There's only one of their homes that's not on the market at the moment. And it's in Burlington."

I snatched the paper from him and read the address. Webb Ave.

"I need to eat," I said, giving him the paper back.

His smile dissolved. "Eat? This is where Kimmy's being held. I'm sure of it."

"But I haven't eaten lunch, and it's almost two. I've got to keep my energy up. You know that."

That's one thing about having all these Superpowers; my metabolism is a bitch. When I was saving the world every day, I expended so much energy I could down three large pizzas a night. Buffet places hated me.

Comedian John Pinette used to do a bit about going to a Chinese buffet. The owner would eventually visit his table and say, "You go home now. You been here four hour. You go home!"

I dealt with that on a regular basis.

Gordon knew I was right about eating, so instead of arguing, he flipped the oven on and set it to 400.

"Garlic-encrusted or cheese-stuffed?" I said, opening the freezer. Getting no answer, I took both out and got them both ready to put in the oven. While we waited for them to cook, we drank beers and I told Gordon all about what happened with my dad.

Sam was modest about her part, and I did my best to dramatize her flying drop-kick.

"It wasn't a drop-kick," she said. "It was a spin move. And I didn't even use my feet. It was my fist."

"Seemed like it to me. Of course, I had a million volts flowing through me. I saw two of everybody."

Gordon was taken with Sam's Kung Fu.

"Hey," I said, waving my hand. "I did that thing where you wrap the bad guys into a steel bar pretzel."

Gordon wasn't impressed. He asked Sam to demonstrate the knee jerk move.

"Hey," I said. "I stopped a bat with my bare hands."

Sam did the knee jerk thing, showing how she cupped her hands behind JJ's head.

"I made a guy tase his own balls."

Gordon laughed at Sam and did the knee jerk thing himself, asking her if that was right.

"Sam gave me a handjob on the way back."

Sam showed Gordon the spin-fist move, twice, the second time in slow-mo.

Fine. I saw how it was. I checked on the pizzas, pulled some parmesan cheese out of the fridge, and popped open another beer.

After we ate, Gordon said to me, "I've got you something."

"The porn version of Guitar Hero?"

He pulled a bag out of nowhere and opened it for me to look inside.

"No way!" I exclaimed.

"Way."

"How did you ... I thought it was gone."

He grinned. "I got it out after you threw it in."

"And you've kept it this whole time?"

He nodded.

Sam had been watching us like a match at center court and finally said, "What? What's in the bag?"

Gordon held the bag while I reached in and pulled out my Superhero suit his mom made me, the capital "B" still sewn onto the front. It looked as cool as ever. This was the first suit I ever owned, and I thought it was buried under twenty years of New York trash.

Sam studied it and said, "Looks kind of cheap now, doesn't it?"

"Huh?"

"Well, I'm just saying. With all the Superhero movies that have come out, and all their cool form-fitting suits ... what is that, cotton?"

"Cotton-nylon blend. And it breathes."

"It also stains." She pointed to the suit's armpits.

"Just needs to be washed."

"Soaked and bleached is more like it."

I held a hand up. "Just wait until you see it on." I looked at Gordon, "I can't believe you kept this all that time."

"I knew the right moment would come," he said, "when you'd change your mind."

If I had a movie made about my life, I'd want my theme song written by the Star Wars guy, John Williams. And it would play as I slowly walked back to my room to don the suit, growing in rhythm and crescendo with each close-up of me sliding pieces on, culminating in the big climax when I revealed my suited self to the camera.

Real life isn't so dramatic. I trotted down the hall to the soundtrack of C-SPAN's congressional murmuring.

Five minutes later ...

"Do you have it on yet?" Sam yelled from the kitchen.

"Yeah," I yelled back.

"Well, let's see it."

"There's a problem," I shouted.

The door rattled and opened. Sam and Gordon walked in. Gordon brought a hand to his mouth, but Sam wasn't as kind—she fell to her knees in laughter.

"It's not funny," I said.

She looked up from the floor, pointing, and burst into more laughter.

"Gordon," I pleaded.

He shook his head, hand still in front of his mouth. He looked like he would explode at any moment, like a contestant at a pickled-egg eating competition.

It wasn't that bad. Sure I'd gained a few pounds in the last twenty-something years. Everybody did. Right?

I turned to my mirror.

There were Velcro strips that attached the shirt to the pants part, but if I got them attached in the back, they snapped out in the front, which was how it currently was. My gut hung out of the costume.

The armpits were, of course, stained all to hell. The "B" that was supposed to be centered on my chest was just under my neck. The fabric was stretched so tight over my body I felt like I couldn't take a deep breath without ripping a seam.

Sam nodded at my crotch, giggling. "Nice bulge."

I grinned, rapping it with my knuckles. "Cup."

"A cup?" She bowled over.

"Yeah. You try hurtling yourself at breakneck speeds without protection there." I looked at Gordon. "Even the cup's small."

Sam laughed so hard she beat her arm on the floor. Gordon still hovered his hand over his mouth, saying nothing, eyes wide.

"Sorry, buddy," I told him. "I can't wear this to save Kimmy."

He nodded, hand still in place.

I exhaled an exasperated sigh. "Go ahead," I said.

Gordon dropped his hand, doubled over, and laughed harder than I'd ever heard him laugh in the forty years I'd known him. I didn't know he had that in him. His laugh was infectious and soon, I joined them.

I guess I could see the humor in it. In theory.

Chapter 44

I changed back into my shorts, t-shirt, and tennis shoes, then went to the living room and grabbed the paper with the address. "I'll call you guys when I've got her."

They looked at each other. Sam said, "We're coming."

"Oh no you're not."

"Yes we are."

"Hell no."

"Look what I did to JJ," Sam said. "I can take care of myself."

"If I didn't have to worry about her shooting you and Dad, I could've taken her out in less than a second when she first pulled the gun."

Sam crossed her arms. "We're going with you."

"You don't understand. These guys I'll be facing? They beat the hell out of me. *Me*."

Gordon held up two fingers. "Twice."

I frowned at him. "They got in a few lucky punches the first time. I'm not sure that counts as beating me up."

"That's why you need us," Sam said. "To cover your back."

"You don't get it. They're as fast and strong as I am, maybe more so.

You wouldn't stand a chance."

"I'm a brown belt."

Words weren't explaining the situation. Sometimes a demonstration says more. I leapt forward with Super-Speed, grabbed Sam's hands, yanked them up, and suspended her in the air about a foot. She cried out and I pinned her to the wall, my body against hers, so she couldn't move her legs. I moved my face within inches. Her eyes were wide and still trying to focus. I felt her warm breath on my face.

"Do you understand now?" I said.

She struggled to move. "Let go of me."

"You think they would? You think your bedroom eyes would mean something to them?"

"You're hurting me."

"No, I'm not." I let her down and backed up a few inches, keeping my eyes on her. "But *they* would, and I'd hate for you to get killed before we slept together. Major downer."

I let her hands go, and she pushed me with rage. I didn't budge; she only pushed herself back into the wall.

I said, "Stay here where you'll be safe, okay?"

She wouldn't look at me.

I walked to the door, saying to Gordon, "Keep an eye on her. I'll call you when I can."

The traffic to Burlington was light, and I found the address without a problem. It was a two-story Tudor with a decent back yard and a double garage.

I scanned the house and didn't see Kimmy or Andrew. But I did see my two favorite goons. Maybe I could pay them a surprise visit. How does that old saying go? Revenge is sweetest when you beat the shit out of them?

I parked the car down the block and returned to the house. Then a thought occurred to me. I scanned below the house with my X-Ray-Vision.

Yes! An unfinished basement. Kimmy and Andrew were handcuffed to each other, back-to-back, with a pole between them.

I scanned the first floor again. The goons were snacking on chips in the kitchen. I needed to split them up so I could handle each one by himself.

After a few minutes of heavy thinking on some elaborate plans, I decided that sometimes the simplest idea was the best. I strode to the front door and rang the bell.

The door was solid wood without a keyhole, and that's where I had the advantage. I scanned through the door, watching as one of the goons, the smaller one who wore a bandage over the broken nose I'd give him, came walking through the foyer.

Right when he reached for the door handle, I kicked the door in with everything I had. It blasted into the goon, and he yelled something garbled. The door, more solid than I thought, slammed into his face, crumpling his hand along the way.

He fell backwards and the door traveled past him into the hall. I jumped on him and delivered two quick jabs to his stomach and a roundhouse to his jaw. It cracked as it gave way.

He lay motionless, and I stood to find the bigger goon already rushing me. He tackled me with Super-Speed, and we flew into the front yard, rolling over each other once we hit the front porch.

Before I could recover my senses, he stood, grabbed my left hand, and flung me through the air into the side of the house. The vinyl siding cushioned my impact a little, but it hurt—my ribs were still a little sore from our last meeting.

I landed in a rose bush, and by the time I righted myself, I was scratched and bloodied head to toe. I felt the rose thorns still embedded in me, but I was so full of adrenaline, I didn't care. I stepped onto the lawn and said, "You throw like a girl."

He smiled and rushed forward.

Right before he reached me, he threw a punch. I was ready.

I grabbed his fist and used his speed against him, twisting and catapulting him into the house. He crashed through the front bay window, twirling and landing in the living room.

I flew into the room through the open window area, but he'd already recovered and was waiting. He kicked out at me before I could slow and caught me full on the chest, knocking me back out the window.

I landed flat on my back on a sprinkler head.

I rolled over to a crouch, the breath knocked out of me a little, and waited for him to show himself in the window. He appeared and I flew at my fastest toward him. I tackled him, shoving my right shoulder into his gut. All the air left him in a whoosh.

I grabbed him by the throat and crotch, and threw him into the ceiling head-first. That's something else I've always wanted to do. They make it look easy in the movies, but it's a hell of a lot harder than it looks. Partly because I had to grab his junk to do it.

Ewww.

He crushed through the ceiling, creating a hole, and fell back to the floor. I picked him up by an arm and a leg, then flung him spinning through the open window onto the lawn.

As I was surveying his limp body from the window, I saw two heads peek around a huge oak tree. Sam and Gordon. Damn it. They came anyway.

At least they stayed hidden until the fighting was over.

I waved at them, and they stepped out, straightening their clothes. Gordon gripped his trusty three wood and wore a half-scowl. Sam smiled and waved back. Her eyes grew wide, and she pointed at me.

I gave her the a-okay sign and winked, but before she could yell, I realized she was really pointing *behind* me!

I spun just as the first goon swung a roundhouse at my face. He connected, but I'd reacted fast enough that it was only a glancing blow.

It knocked me off balance, and I fell sideways.

I recovered and kicked him swiftly in the nuts. He went down for the count. I don't like to do that to guys, but he should've stayed down to begin with.

I walked in front of the window, and yelled outside that I'd be right back. I searched for the door to the basement and found Kimmy and Andrew alert and standing. Kimmy smiled and exhaled a sigh of relief when our eyes met.

"I knew it was you. I knew it!" she said.

"Was it my cologne that gave it away? I'm told I wear too much sometimes."

Kimmy laughed her amazing laugh as I bent their handcuffs off.

Andrew rubbed his wrists and said, "So, you're Barry?"

Agent Andrew Busbee didn't look as impressive as he did in pictures. He was kind of thin, his hairline was starting to recede, and I'll bet he couldn't bend a crowbar into a pretzel. "And you're Andrew."

Kimmy stepped between us. "Boys. Don't you think we should get out of here before you see whose is biggest?"

I glanced down at her with a smirk. "I already know."

Andrew frowned and puffed his chest out.

"Come on," I said to Kimmy. "Your brother's waiting outside. And you know how he gets when he doesn't know everything that's happening."

I led the way upstairs and diverted to the kitchen, opening the fridge.

"What are you doing?" Kimmy asked.

I rummaged around and stuffed some candy bars into my pockets.

"Getting some food. What else do you do in a fridge?"

Kimmy stared at me like I was stealing from a baby. "What?" I said. "They don't need it."

She rolled her eyes. "I'm going to find Gordon." She and Andrew headed toward the front of the house.

I grabbed a pint of Rocky Road out of the freezer and when I joined them on the front porch, I almost dropped my ice cream.

Rex Ruther stood in front of his Mercedes, gripping Sam's arm, a gun to her temple. He locked eyes with mine and smiled.

No!

I sped down the front steps, and he yelled, "Stop!" as he cocked the gun. "You know I could get a round off before you got here."

I froze no more than twenty feet from them. Gordon was leaning against the oak tree, rubbing his head, the three wood broken in two at his feet.

I gritted my teeth, but held my ground.

"Now, Mr. Glick," Rex said. "I warned you not to interfere." He looked around. "I must say, however, I find it very commendable you found my little hideout. I thought it was a good place, but you have proven to be more formidable than I originally thought."

I took a mini-bow. "I had help," I said.

"Still, I will have to reassess my procedures in the future."

I reacted without thinking—it's kind of a signature move of mine—and hurled the pint of ice cream at Rex Ruther with all the Super-Strength I had.

The Rocky Road sailed far right, clearing Sam and Rex by more than three feet, and exploded into the windshield of his big expensive Mercedes. His driver stared at me as he flicked on the windshield wipers.

Rex frowned. "That was pathetic, Mr. Glick."

"Yeah, well, your mama wears Army boots."

Rex squinted and backed toward the car. The driver got out, shooting me more mean looks, and opened the door for them. Rex shoved Sam inside and turned to me. "You should take your friend to the hospital." Nodding toward Gordon.

Gordon was standing upright now and looked surprised for everyone to be staring at him.

"He looks fine to me," I said.

Rex raised his gun and fired. Gordon collapsed.

Kimmy screamed and ran for him. Rex sneered at me and hopped inside his car. The driver gunned it, and I watched them speed off, I zoomed in on the license plate.

When I joined everyone else at Gordon's side, Kimmy was holding a hand over the bullet wound. It had entered the upper part of his thigh.

"Whew," I said. "It's just his leg."

Andrew shook his head. "There's too much blood. I think it hit his femoral artery."

I watched enough *House* to know that was the big one, and you could bleed to death in no time if it wasn't stopped soon. I shored up the wound with my shirt and wrapped my belt around it.

Kimmy grabbed my hand, saying, "Where's your car?"

But my mind was racing. "We're too far to drive," I said. I looked at Andrew, then Kimmy. I tossed her my keys and picked up Gordon's limp body. "Meet me at Alamance Regional."

Kimmy nodded.

I rose into the air and flew straight for the hospital.

Chapter 45

It was rush hour, and the hospital parking lot was just as busy as the roads I flew over to get there. I don't know how many people reported seeing a large shirtless man in beige shorts flying through the air carrying a bleeding accountant, and I don't care. Gordon was not going to die on my watch.

I landed a few feet from the emergency room doors, scaring the bejesus out of an old man being wheeled out by his daughter. He shouted a curse word as I dropped down in front of them, and they both stared at me.

"Smile," I said. "You're on Candid Camera." I nodded to a van with tinted windows.

The old man shook his head and smiled, waving his finger at the van.

I scooted through the huge revolving door and yelled for help. A startled nurse ran up to me, and I told her I had a gunshot victim who was losing a lot of blood.

I think she already knew about the blood loss. It looked like half of Gordon's blood supply was on me. How could a guy that little have so much blood?

The nurse shouted orders I didn't understand, and I laid Gordon on the nearest gurney. Two other nurses converged, and they began working on him. I backed off, then headed to the bathroom to clean up. I looked pretty scary and my shorts were falling off my ass.

Yes, even Superheroes lose their ass as they get older.

I finished and sat in the waiting room, returning stares until one of the nurses brought me a t-shirt bearing the hospital's logo.

"It's all we have," she said, looking me over.

I thanked her and slipped it on. Just a tad small.

She read my face and said, "We've got our trauma team on him." She squinted. "How long ago was he shot?"

I thought a second. "Five minutes? Maybe ten."

"Were you close?"

I grinned and said, "I flew."

She put her hand on mine. "Well, I think you got him here just in time." She told me she needed some information and she'd be back in a minute.

A guy sitting beside me introduced himself as Larry and said his wife was here with pregnancy complications. I nodded at him and turned away.

Kimmy and Andrew arrived twenty minutes later. She saw me when she came through the door. I stood and we hugged.

"How is he?"

"I don't know anything yet."

I waved the same nurse over—her name tag read *Martha*—and introduced Kimmy as Gordon's twin sister. "She can probably answer all the questions I couldn't," I said.

While Kimmy and Martha buzzed through the double doors to the back, Andrew motioned for me to follow him outside. *Here it comes*, I thought. *The inevitable barrage of questions.*

We went over to the side, and he said, "So, Kimmy explained a few things, but I'm finding them hard to believe."

"Really? I'd think once you saw a three-hundred-pound man flying through the air for yourself, you'd accept any explanation you were given."

He looked away, then back at me, confusion filling his face.

"Look, pal," I said. "Just accept it without trying to figure out how it's possible."

He shook his head. "But it doesn't make sense."

"And yet, here I am." I put my arm around his shoulder and turned him, partly because it was fun making him feel small. I walked him back into the hospital. "Welcome to the matrix. You can't unswallow the pill now that you know."

"But—"

I squeezed his shoulder until I saw him cringe. "And I'm sure it goes without saying that nothing you saw today will go into any of your spook reports."

He hesitated, and I squeezed until he grunted out a yes.

"Good. The easiest thing you can do is forget you ever saw anything. There are people like me in the world, and there's nothing you can do about it."

And then the biggest revelation of my life hit me. Superman wasn't a fictional character. He was a real person. And just like me, he was a half-breed. I could do everything he could, with some exceptions.

Of course, the guy who "created" Superman had fictionalized a character and origin story around the real man, but his core powers were the same as mine.

He could have been my cousin!

Kimmy was waiting when we entered, tears in her eyes.

I felt the blood leave my face, and I grabbed her shoulders.

Kimmy said, "He's fine."

"Fine?" I exploded. "Geez, why the hell are you crying?"

"I'm happy."

I threw my hands up. "God. I will never understand women."

Kimmy bear-hugged me. "You saved his life."

I *had* saved his life. And I had saved Kimmy's and Andrew's too. And Dad's. That had me feeling pretty good, and then I remembered I had one more life to save. Sam.

And maybe I'd save the world while I was at it.

Chapter 46

As soon as I could go back to see Gordon, I did. He was lying in bed hooked up to a couple of beeping machines. He opened his eyes when I stopped beside him. He had an oxygen tube attached to his nose, and he smiled while his eyes adjusted on me.

"Hey buddy," I said. "How you feeling?"

"I wonder what you would look like with short hair?"

I grinned at him and noticed the pain meds button in his hand. The machine probably let him take a hit of morphine every few minutes.

"Do you remember what happened?" I asked.

"My nurse is hot. Have you seen my nurse?"

"Alright buddy." I patted his hand. "I can tell you're feeling pretty good right now."

"I asked her how much her nurse uniform cost." He motioned for me to come closer. He whispered, "She wouldn't tell me."

I decided I liked Gordon on pain meds.

Kimmy walked into the room and said, "Have you met the new Gordon?"

"Yes." I turned to her and raised my eyebrows.

"I know," she said. "He gets some good drugs in him, and he turns into you."

I smirked. "Once you go Barry ..."

"Oh no. Don't get used to it. He's coming off the meds as soon as possible. I can't have two of you in my life. One's more than enough."

"Hey, have you checked in at Homeland yet?"

Kimmy motioned me away from Gordon. He was humming the theme song to the original *Batman and Robin*, pressing the pain button on every beat.

"I have," she said. "Andrew and I both have. We told our stories, and they won't do anything. They're acting like we're rogue agents or something. We're to be debriefed fully tonight." She held me with her eyes. "Something's wrong."

"You think the mole is high up?"

"I think strings are being pulled I didn't know existed."

"Okay, well that kills the next thing I was going to ask you."

"What?"

"I wanted you to use your resources to get me a location on a car."

"Rex?"

"Yeah, Rex. But don't worry about it. Stay here with Gordy. I've got another resource I can tap."

I started to leave, and Kimmy grabbed my arm. She kissed me.

On. The. Lips.

"Be careful," she said.

I hesitated.

"Could we try that one more time with tongue?" I said.

"What?"

"Humor me."

She pushed me toward the door. Once I had the air conditioning going in the Aztek, I called Hannah. We did the hello stuff, and I said, "I need you to track a car for me."

"On-Star again?"

"No. This one's a BMW, an expensive one. I'm hoping it has lo-jack in it."

Silence. "What do you have for me?"

I gave the license plate number to Hannah.

While she was doing her thing, I said, "How are your sisters?"

"Ha ha. Never heard that one."

"Sorry. I've got a little nervous energy."

"I told you to bring your satellite box by this week, I'd get it."

"No. Not that kind of nervous energy." And then I realized I hadn't told her about Gordon. "Hannah? I need to tell you something. Gordon's been shot."

The clicking of keys stopped on the other side of the phone. "What?"

"He's at Alamance Regional. Do you know where that is?"

"Off 40 at the old Elon exit?"

"Yeah. But look, here's the deal. This car I'm looking for is the guy who shot him."

"Is Gordon okay?"

"Yeah. He's fine. He's got some meds in him, so he's a little loopy right now, but he's actually more fun this way."

"He was fun before."

My brow itched. "I'm sorry, I think you have my Gordon mixed up with some other Gordon."

More clicking, then Hannah said, "Uhh ... there's a problem. Either the car's lo-jack is broken, or it's been disabled."

My heart sank. I knew Rex wouldn't take Sam back to Argyle Industries; he probably wouldn't go back there himself. I didn't know what to do next. I thanked Hannah and told her I'd see her in a little while."

I needed to brainstorm, but my sidekick, the one person I always turned to when I worked through problems, was out of commission. He'd probably tell me about the Radiologist's ass. I'd already checked it out anyway. Not bad. Deserved better than the granny panties she was wearing.

I turned the Aztek off and went back into the hospital until Hannah showed up, and then told Kimmy I was heading home for the night. She and Andrew rode with me. Her car was still at my place, and they had the debriefing appointment later. They wanted to get fresh clothes and take showers first.

So we left Gordon in Hannah's capable, spastic hands.

Chapter 47

On the way to my apartment, I filled Kimmy and Andrew in on the last few days. Kimmy still had clothes there so she came inside when we arrived. Andrew took Kimmy's car to get showered and changed at his place, saying he'd pick her back up before they went into Homeland.

Kimmy hopped in the shower while I threw a couple pizzas in the oven. I almost fell asleep on the couch waiting for the timer to ding.

My mind kept wandering to Sam. She was an enigma, and I liked those. But Sam was just a new toy, right?

Kimmy bounded into the kitchen, the shower having totally refreshed her. Her hair was still damp, and she wore a light gray business suit. "Is the pizza ready yet?" she chirped.

I shook my head no and rubbed my eyes.

She walked down the hall and returned with something in her hand.

"Is this what I think it is?

I focused my eyes. "Yep."

She held my old Superhero suit up. "Gordon gave it back?"

"You knew?"

She grinned. "The whole time."

I wagged my finger at her and she laughed. She held the suit out, looked at me, then at the suit, and back to me. "Didn't fit did it?"

I grunted. "Hell no."

"Shame."

The timer dinged, and we ate. It was just what I needed, but my body was worn out. I needed to rest.

I wiped my mouth and apologized for being so tired, but I couldn't stay up another minute. Kimmy hugged me good night, thanked me again, and said she'd lock up on the way out.

As she gathered the dishes, I realized she would always be like a sister to me. No matter how much I wanted more, it would never happen. I came up behind her, hugged her again, and kissed the top of her head.

"What are you doing?" she asked.

I hugged her a little more, then trudged off to my room. I don't remember getting under the covers.

Chapter 48

Maybe it was the Meat Lover's smorgasbord right before bed or maybe it was the craziness of the last few days, but my dreams were nutty. I woke in a sweat, the covers on the floor. It was late at night, and it was still dark outside.

I sat up straight.

Something had woken me.

I didn't know what it was. I tried to replay the moment just before waking and couldn't.

I listened with my Super-Hearing. There was someone outside my window—I could hear them breathing.

I stood and scanned through the blinds to find a familiar cowl outside. I yanked the blinds up, and Connie jumped. Then she covered her eyes.

Opening the window, I said, "You know, in the twenty-first century, that cowl actually makes you stand out." I stopped. "Why are you covering your eyes?"

"You're naked."

I looked down. "So I am."

Not only was I without clothing, I had the addition of the traditional morning surprise. "Come around to the front," I told her.

"Someone might see me," she said, hands still covering her eyes.

I slipped some shorts on and told her she could open her eyes now.

Connie dropped her hands and climbed through the window. She was pretty agile for a woman a couple thousand years old.

"You want some coffee or something?" I offered once she'd straightened herself.

"There's no time."

My neck flinched. "What's happening?"

"I think Rex is going to kill your friend out of retribution."

"So why are you coming to me, to tell me I'm in over my head again?"

Connie slumped and sank into the chair by the window. "I just didn't want you to get hurt. I owe it to your mother to make sure you stay safe."

"Then why don't you help me instead of pulling all this cloak and dagger bullshit?"

She sat up. "That's why I'm here now."

I stepped toward her. "Well?"

Connie took a breath, then said, "Rex has her at Argyle's compound north of Burlington."

"What compound?" I hadn't seen a *compound* north of Burlington in the addresses we'd found. In fact, I'd plugged all the addresses into Google to see where they were, and they didn't own a thing north of Burlington.

"It's near Altamahaw. All the Lords are there. It's their command bunker, where they plan to ride out the coming months. Years if need be."

"So they're really going to try and ruin the world's financial systems?"

Connie stared at me. "You've figured it out?"

"Sure. I'm big, not dumb. I mean, it's obvious if you step back from it. They've got their hands in every major financial area: mortgages, state budgets, Wall Street, currency conversions. And those are just the ones I know about." I paused. "You think they can really crash the world's economy?"

"You've heard of Black Friday?"

"The Will Smith movie marathon on TBS?"

"No, it was—"

"Connie, I know what Black Friday was. What of it?"

"Rex collapsed the stock market and sent the country into one of its darkest times ever."

"Rex brought about the Great Depression?"

Connie nodded. "He also assassinated John Kennedy and tried with Ronald Reagan."

"Really?"

She nodded again.

"Did he invent Disco too?"

Connie didn't laugh. "No, but he assassinated an Archduke named Ferdinand about a hundred years ago, and later, he was the personal assistant to Adolph Hitler."

"Alright, I'm gonna call bullshit again. There's no way he did all that. No way. What is he, the Forrest Gump of the Anunnaki?"

Connie threw her hands up. "Have you not been listening to me at all? For over ten thousand years, the Anunnaki have been trying to eradicate the human race in one way or another. The Bubonic Plague, civil conflicts, worldwide wars, A.I.D.S.!"

"Whoa ... calm down. Kind of seems to me like economic collapse is a letdown compared to the stuff you've just mentioned. I mean, didn't the plague kill a third of the world? That seems a little bigger than some schmuck having to eat mac-n-cheese for a year."

"Barry, think about it a second. For the first time in history, the entire world's economy is tied together and based upon a single currency, the U.S. dollar. If the United States were to collapse, the rest of the world would follow. Complete civilizations would crumble into anarchy. Health systems would fail to function."

She paused. "You saw what happened when just the stock market imploded. The Great Depression was a test run. Back then, the world's economies weren't linked together like they are now. After World War II, the Allied nations met at the Bretton Woods Conference and created the IMF and World Bank."

She fixed me with a stare. "Guess whose idea it was to tie all the economies together?" She let that sink in. "Can you begin to imagine what would happen if every single market of trade collapsed into disarray and chaos?"

I thought about it. I had a hard time imagining such turmoil in today's world of political correctness and unity. The internet, banking, ATMs. If the economy disappeared, paper money and credit would go with it. Utilities. Sanitation.

Disease would run rampant.

The world as I knew it would cease to exist. We'd be thrown back into the Biblical ages, but with a hundred times the population, and weapons a hell of a lot more powerful than a chariot and sword.

Forget high gas prices, try no gas at all. Food couldn't be distributed. The U.S. would drop to less than a third world country. Chaos wasn't the word.

"You've sold me," I said. "Where's this compound?"

Connie drew me a map and wrote some notes on security and buildings and where she thought Sam was being held.

"I'm going back there now," she said.

"Why?"

"Because I'm supposed to be there. We all have to be. I snuck out to warn you." She grabbed my hand. "Barry, the Council of Lords is about to set something into motion that will destroy the human race."

She paused. "They're going to begin the Apocalypse."

Chapter 49

Connie left through the window, and I paced around for a moment. I decided to make a pot of coffee before I did anything. Couldn't go charging into the enemy's lair with a muddled head and no plan, now could I?

I walked into the kitchen and straight to the coffee station. I started a pot of the darkest, strongest stuff I had. Kimmy had left my suit in the middle of the kitchen table, folded.

There was a note on it.

I plucked it off and it read: KICK ASS.

There was a smiley face after the message. How Kimmy.

I stared at the suit. I was going to need a lot of luck to take on an entire compound of Anunnaki, each one having my speed and strength. I didn't like my chances.

Something looked different about the suit. I picked it up and let it unfold. I shook my head. That Kimmy.

I put the suit on right there in the kitchen. Like her mother, Kimmy had learned to be a whiz with a needle. She had added another swath of cloth along the belly, extending the shirt. From the looks of it she had cannibalized one of my plain t-shirts and created a belt-like section.

She had even taken the time to move the "B" down to the center of my chest and resew each velcro piece to the ends of the new fabric. It would have taken me hours, and I would have done it crooked, but she probably finished in twenty minutes.

The armpit stains were still there.

Oh well, it fit and that's what was most important.

I sat there in my suit, the mask raised above my eyes, drinking coffee and thinking. I needed more than a full frontal assault. That wouldn't work this time. Then I knew what I needed to do.

I scarfed down the candy bars I'd taken from the goons' house and went outside. It was still dark. I pulled the mask over my face and flew straight to Alamance Regional.

There's nothing like night time flying under moonlight. The air was thick with humidity and sticky to the touch. Gordon had a room with an outside window, and I didn't think it would be too hard to find.

I hovered around the hospital peeping in third floor windows. The rooms were dark so it took me a while to locate him. It also involved seeing a lot of stuff I didn't care to see, like an old man struggling to poop in his bedpan. One should never see that unless they're getting paid very well.

I had one problem though. Hannah was in Gordy's room, and she didn't know my secret. But there was no time for stealth. I forced open the window and hovered inside. Took off my mask and flicked on the wall light.

Hannah woke in her chair. It was reclined most of the way back. She sat up and smiled, then frowned.

"Is it Halloween already?" she asked.

"More than you know," I replied.

Gordon stirred, and I laid a hand on his shoulder.

"Barry?"

"Yeah, buddy. It's me. How you feeling?"

"Quite numb."

"Good, you don't want to feel all the pain your body's in."

"Heading somewhere?" His eyes moved up and down my suit.

"Yeah, I'm going to get Sam and end all this nonsense." I slid the map out of the only pocket I had and unfolded it. "This is their compound."

He squinted at it. "Where is it, Iran?"

I looked at him. "Was that another joke?"

Gordon grinned.

"Is that tapioca pudding," I asked, pointing at his food tray. "You mind?"

"What are you looking at?" Hannah said, peering around me.

"A strategy game me and Gordon always play," I said.

"At four in the morning?"

"We're diehards."

Hannah met my eyes. "Do I honestly look that stupid?"

"Okay, fine." I glanced at Gordon, then back at her. "I could use your help too. I'm a Superhero, and this is the bad guy's compound. They have a hostage, and I'm going to save her, and as a side note, prevent the destruction of the world as we know it. Got any ideas?"

She opened her mouth.

"And no questions," I added. "Gordon can answer those after I've left. Right now, I need a strategy"—tapping the map—"oh, and one other thing to know, everyone at this camp has Super-Speed and Super-Strength just like me."

Hannah stared at me like I'd just told her I had a 14-inch penile implant.

I shook her. "Fight your sanity and pretend it's all true. Now put that amazing brain to work."

It took us thirty minutes to come up with something that had a chance. If hell froze over.

But knowing what I knew about the world now, it might already be frozen.

Chapter 50

A half moon is great for flying, but it's not the greatest for infiltrating a Supervillain's secret compound. I flew north of Burlington keeping an eye out for landmarks to follow because one thing I didn't have with me was a GPS.

I had forgotten how much fun flying could be. Other than the bugs, it was a very enjoyable and freeing experience. And once you got to a certain altitude, the bugs weren't that bad. Even in the summer time.

The temperature had begun to drop, and clouds were gathering. Flickers erupted in the distance. I landed twice to check out road signs to get my bearings, but I finally made it to my destination twenty minutes after beginning.

Connie's drawing of the compound was pretty good; I planned to stick it on my fridge after everything was over.

The place was split into two distinct sections. In a circular area were the admin building, the medical facility, two dorms, the main house, two more dorms, the garage/maintenance building, and the commissary, all surrounding the chow hall and water tower. Then off to the side were the storage building, armory, and power plant. And of course, if I was entering by vehicle, I'd have to pass the guardhouse at the entrance.

Connie had told me there would be ten guards on duty: two at the guardhouse, two at the armory, two at the admin building, two patrolling the outer perimeter, and two wandering the interior. And they would be on high alert now that their plan was coming to fruition.

I flew in from the west side of the compound and perched myself high in a tree behind the main house. From there I could see most of the grounds including the dorms and living area buildings.

Thunder rumbled closer and lightning spidered across the sky as I watched the camp activity for thirty minutes, trying to find patterns. I studied the two sets of perimeter guards and two sets of interior guards. It looked like they'd doubled the security now that "D-Day" was getting close.

Or maybe they were expecting me.

I saw something I didn't like: the guards carried submachine guns, and that made me nervous—even more reason to be stealthy.

I flew around the outer part of the compound just below the top of the tree line until I reached the power plant. According to Connie, the whole place ran on a combination of fuel cells and advanced solar cells—they weren't connected to the grid—so when all hell broke loose, it wouldn't matter to the Anunnaki.

I landed on a limb near the top of a tree just behind the building. The plan called for me to disable the power plant for two reasons: to create confusion, and to quiet any alarms I might set off when I broke into the admin building to free Sam from the underground jail cells.

If I waited long enough, this storm would give me the perfect cover. They might think a lightning strike took out their power, and I'd have another advantage I hadn't counted on: the element of surprise.

Lightning lit up the sky a short ways to the south giving me a flash picture of the power plant. Perfect! It was coming together better than the plan we'd drawn out. The storm was almost on top of us. As soon as it started raining and the guards ran for cover, I'd make my move.

Wait. Something was off. I ran the memory of the power plant flash through my head again.

Something was missing … something important …

Wires!? There were no wires or cables leaving the power plant? What the hell? They must have run their power lines underground.

That wasn't good. The plan called for me to knock a tree down over the power lines to disconnect them, but now that was shot. Everything depended on the electricity being knocked out.

I could always rescue Sam without disabling the power, but that was risky.

And if I went inside the power plant to search for a way to cut the electricity, I wouldn't know what I was doing. Unless there was a big throw switch labeled "Main Power." I didn't think I'd be that lucky.

I crumpled the map up and threw it, watching it hit a few branches before falling below my eyesight.

Time for plan—my world lit up like a thousand flash bulbs went off as a lightning bolt hit the tree I was in! My ears exploded and sweet gum branches began hitting me in the face and chest. Then my left leg, my right arm.

Must control—left leg hit again. Face. *Slow*—chest. *Must slow*—my entire body crashed against the ground, belly down, face to the side.

I breathed, slowly. The world smelled of burnt hair.

Smoke everywhere. Scorched curtains. Burnt popcorn. Burnt fingernails.

Time for a nap. Close eyes. Just for a little bit. Small nap. Tiny. Ten seconds. Maybe fifteen. Twenty?

Sam. She needed me. Locked in a cage.

Water. Rain. Hitting my face. Small drops. Bigger. More.

Open eyes. Blink. Feel fingers. Toes. Pain.

Cough. Think. Sam.

Wake up! Building. Power plant. Sam.

I laid there for a few minutes, gathering my thoughts, slowly putting them together like an A.D.D. kid might put together a puzzle of an all-white picture. A blank canvas.

The balled-up map was lying a few feet in front of my face, taunting me.

I drew my world out again, filling the canvas with the important stuff.

Sam, compound, guards, machine guns …

A few minutes more and I sat up, soaked, everything coming into focus. Reality returned.

Another few minutes and I stood. My balance back. My wits restored. My mission clear.

I hovered into the air and looked for guards. They'd disappeared like I thought they would.

This was now going to have to be a smash-and-grab whether I liked it or not.

And honestly, I kind of liked it that way.

I flew toward the admin building where Connie said Sam would be held. I scanned the place as I swooped around to the back.

It was a two-story brick building, about fifty feet wide. I hovered to the second floor, busted a hole in a darkened window, opened it, and entered. I wiped the water from my eyes and looked around.

The room contained a desk with a computer, a credenza, a captain's chair, two side chairs, and a lateral filing cabinet. The computer's screen saver was an animated Scooby and Shaggy creeping from right side to the left, then left to right, each time at different zooms.

Damn, I wanted that. I'd have to see if Hannah could get it for me.

I crept out of the office and found the stairs to the first floor.

I needed to split the guards up, so I decided to do something similar to what I did at the kidnap house. I went back to the office and grabbed a baseball I'd seen on the credenza. It was autographed by Randy Johnson. Hmm ... made me wonder.

I stood just off the side of the steps and rolled the ball down. I heard voices, then footsteps. One set.

Perfect.

He stopped at the bottom of the steps—I was scanning him through the walls—and picked up the ball. He lifted his gaze and shined his flashlight up the steps.

"You smell burnt popcorn?" he asked his partner.

The response was mumbled.

He raised his gun and crept up the stairs.

This guy must have never been to the movies. Either that or he was a complete idiot.

I waited, listening for him to reach the top. I pressed myself close to the wall. Halfway up, he stopped.

Then, he took a step. Another. Another.

I braced myself.

As soon as I saw his foot on the top step, I turned and threw a punch where I thought his face would be. He sidestepped my fist and yelled in surprise. I swung through and around and fell headlong down the stairs. He got tangled up and fell with me. We reached the bottom a jumbled mess of arms and legs and charred Superhero suit.

The gun came clattering down behind us.

He reached for it, and I slapped his hand. He pulled away, shaking his hand, then tried for the gun a second time.

I slapped it again, harder. He pulled back, waving his hand back and forth, this time saying, "Ow."

"Stop doing it."

His eyes widened, and he went to strangle me.

Sometimes I have this effect on people.

I blocked him and popped him in the forehead.

"Stop!" he said.

"You stop."

"Both of you stop," the other guard said, standing over us with his gun pointed at me.

"He started it," I said.

"Get up," the second guard said, waving his gun.

"Does it look like I can do that?" I nodded my head toward my midsection. "His knee's in my crotch, and I think my spleen is still somewhere back up there." I pointed up the stairs.

When the guard looked for my spleen, I reached out and yanked his gun away. I rammed the butt end into his crotch, and he doubled over, exhaling in a shrill whine that sounded like the air being slowly let out of a balloon.

He stood for a moment, me and the whiny guard watching, until he fell backwards, his hands belatedly guarding his crotch.

The guard I was tangled with looked at me. I looked at him.

"Sorry about this," I said.

Before he could react, I shot my foot out and banged his head against the bottom step. It bounced twice and his eyes closed.

I untangled myself from his limp body and found the staircase to the basement. I descended, flipping on the lights as I went.

The basement was way bigger than the above-ground floors, which threw me off a little. It made me wonder just how big the compound was. Connie had told me all the buildings were connected underground, but I figured they had narrow tunnels with bare bulbs, not an underground system reminiscent of Area 51. I wandered for a bit until I found the sign for prisoner cells—they actually had a sign—pointing down a barren hallway.

I followed the maze of hallways until I turned a corner to find a locked metal door with the sign "Prisoner Cells" stuck on it. No problem. I gave it a strong shoulder and the door blasted inward.

Sam was in the first cell, and she woke with a start. I smiled at her. "Somebody order room service?"

"Barry!"

The cells looked kind of Mayberry-ish: vertical bars with horizontal supports every three feet, and a cell door to match. It was going to be a piece of cake. I strode right up to it and—

"Wait!"

It was too late.

I gripped the bars on the cell door, and my eyes crossed. My heart sped up, and I saw stars. Everything blurred, and I shook like a 60s fat machine. The jolt from the electricity coursing through the bars threw me backwards out of the cell room and into the opposite wall.

The world darkened, again, and the last thing I remembered was Sam screaming, "Nooooo!"

Chapter 51

I woke in a sputter, like I'd been underwater for an hour and had just come up for air. I sucked in and flinched. Something wasn't right.

The first thing I saw was Rex Ruther reclining, his feet propped on a desk. I was strapped to a swiveling table with the top rotated back just a little from a fully upright position. My feet rested on a ledge attached to the edge of the table, and my ankles were bound to the corners. My arms were splayed out and bound to the top corners so that I looked like DaVinci's drawing of Man.

With a beer gut.

"Look who's awake," Rex said, dropping his feet and sitting up.

I tried to say something witty. It came out, "Wuhh."

My mask was off, and Rex said, "You've been a bad boy, Mr. Glick."

I lolled my head to one side. There was Whiny Guard and his partner, Nut-Shot Guard. He had an icepack on his balls. Does that really help? It seems like it would compound the problem.

"I have two new friends of yours that would like to say something to you."

Whiny Guard approached first, spit at me, and delivered a

roundhouse to my face that spun my head to the other side. I instantly tasted blood.

He backed up, flexing and shaking his hand. I wanted to say something about Gordon always insisting I had a hard head. I said, "Wuhh uhh oggg."

Nut-Shot Guard stepped forward and spit at me—what's with the spitting? He reared back and threw an uppercut at my boys.

There was a loud "tock" as his knuckles connected with my twenty-year old cup. He grimaced and collapsed with a strange mewl, holding his hand out as it pulsed and swelled.

"Wuhh uhh guhh," I said.

His eyes teared up, and he replied, "Ahheeeiiee aoooo."

"Wuhh huh."

"Aaaaaaooooh."

"Alright," Rex blurted. "Enough of this."

He flipped a switch and a hum filled the air. My fingers twitched and my ankles vibrated.

"You might want to stretch out a little more, Mr. Glick."

I did as he said and the tingling stopped.

"Your restraints are highly durable and unique. Not even you can break them, but if you should feel the need to try, you will feel several thousand volts shoot through your body."

"Wuhh?"

"The harder you pull, the more the electric current. Would you care for a demonstration?"

"No thank uhh."

Rex smiled and said, "Good." He nodded to Whiny Guard.

The guard looked at him.

Rex nodded again, then nodded toward the door.

The guard squinted and tilted his head.

Raising his eyebrows, Rex said, "Get the girl."

The guard formed an "O" with his mouth. He opened the door and motioned with his hand. Sam was pushed into the room, and she stumbled forward until Whiny Guard caught her. He pointed her toward me.

"Barry!" she exclaimed. "I tried to tell you."

"I ohhh."

"I'm so sorry."

"Is okahh."

My mouth still wasn't forming words right. I could finally think straight, but the combination of the electrocution and the shot to the jaw made expressing the thoughts difficult.

"Did you really think you could waltz in here," Rex said, "rescue the girl, and save the world?"

Damn, he must have found the plan.

"Yeth?" I said.

Rex sniffed. "Does anyone smell burnt popcorn?"

Whiny Guard sniffed. "Smells more like burnt dog hair."

Rex shook his head. "No, burnt popcorn." He shook his head and turned to me. "You really don't know who we are, do you?"

"Anunnaki."

Rex smiled. "So you do." He paced. "I'm curious. How were you planning to stop me? What did you think you would actually do? Find a red button with a countdown and disable it?"

"That would make it easier," I said, my words coming out normal now.

Rex sneered and slid behind his desk. He reached down and pulled out a metal three-foot rod. He held it out and clicked. The end erupted in blue sparks.

"Do you know what this is?"

I nodded. I'd seen specials on National Geographic.

"Tell me, Mr. Glick," he said, strutting up to me, clicking the cattle prod on and off for effect. "How did you find my hideout?"

"It was thirteen down on the Sunday crossw—"

He stuck the prod into my chest and clicked it on. I flexed inward and felt the current double through my extremities. I screamed like a Wes Craven film until he pulled the prod away an hour later.

Maybe it was more like ten seconds.

"Change your answer yet?" he said.

I stretched my arms and legs out until the current subsided. I looked Rex in the eyes. "It might have been eleven down."

More cattle prod. More electricity. More screaming.

"The clue was: The Villain's Hideout."

Cattle prod. I felt my insides liquefying.

"Stop!" Sam yelled.

The prodding stopped. Rex turned to Sam. "Ms. Gerber, that's a grand idea. Since Mr. Glick is unwilling to get serious when his own body is in jeopardy, maybe he'll be more willing in your case."

Nut-Shot Guard grabbed her wrists and held them above her. She struggled as he lashed them together with a rope in Super-Speed. Then he looped the rope through a ring in the ceiling, stood back, and pulled the rope taut. Sam's arms were stretched above her and she stood on her tippy-toes.

Rex turned to me and winked as he stuck the cattle prod into Sam's side. He clicked it on and Sam jerked back and forth violently. An eerie sound oozed from her mouth, and when Rex stopped, she sagged and drooled on her shirt, breathing hard.

Not once did he look at her. He kept his eyes on me the entire time, and his crooked mouth broke into a wide grin. Sam groaned.

"Let's try setting two," he said and adjusted a dial on the rod.

"Wait," I said.

He looked at me and stuck the prod into Sam's side again. "What was that?" he said.

"Please don't—"

He clicked the prod on, and Sam flailed about. Rex pushed the prod in so deep it never lost contact with her, despite the violence of her movements.

"Wait! Stop!"

Rex held the prod in another three seconds before he pulled it away and turned it off.

"You have something good to say or are you still wasting your words?"

"What do you want to know?"

Sam's head lolled forward, drool seeping from her parted mouth. She mumbled, "No, don't say anything."

Rex stuck the prod in again.

"Wait! I'll tell you whatever you want." I flinched so hard that my restraints shocked me until I could relax and stretch again. And let me tell you, relaxing is very, very difficult with a million volts flowing through every muscle in your body. And your balls. Especially your balls.

"So?" Rex said.

I frowned. "What was the question?"

He clicked the prod on, and Sam jerked up in agony.

"Wait! I was being serious! I don't remember the question!"

The prod clicked off.

Rex pursed his lips, then relaxed. "I asked how you found me."

I let out a deep breath. How could I betray Connie, my aunt? But I couldn't allow Sam to take any more pain. I was conflicted.

"You have a mole," I said, hanging my head.

"A mole?"

"Someone came to me. They told me where you were. They told me about my Mom. They told me about the Nephilim, the Anunnaki, and your plans."

Rex smiled, amused. He crossed his arms. "You didn't know your mother?"

I shook my head. "She died when I was born." I looked at Sam's limp body hanging from the thick rope, twirling in place. "I killed her."

Rex grunted. "And she was Anunnaki."

"Yes."

He grunted again. "It was a fit punishment for breaking our laws."

I held back my emotions. Rex moved close and lifted my chin with the cattle prod. "Even though you're a half-breed, you could join us, you know."

"I'm a pacifist," I said, staring into his beady eyes.

He studied me a second, then smirked. "Another joke. You fancy yourself a funny one, don't you Mr. Glick?" He paused, then narrowed his eyes. "You joke to hide your pain. The pain of killing the traitorous bitch who birthed you."

I lunged at him. Electricity filled my body, pulsing in rhythms. I bit through the pain, trying to break the bonds. My jaw clamped shut, my scream muffled by my constricting throat muscles. And I think my balls went to hide somewhere near my kidneys.

When I came to a few seconds later, Rex was in my face, still smiling. He said in a low voice, "I could teach you what it is to be Anunnaki. I could show you wonders you've never dreamed of." A pause. "Tell me who the mole is. You and your human will be freed."

Me and my human. Sam. An innocent bystander drawn into this by her curiosity. A woman who intrigued me by her ambition and her heart. She didn't give me up when she could have. I couldn't abandon her now.

But then there was Connie. My mom's sister. An Anunnaki. A link to my past. She warned me to leave everything alone. She told me I was in over my head. She tried to help me, to steer me in the right direction. How could I betray her? She risked her life to tell me Sam was here. She helped me to save Sam.

Ha. *Save Sam.* Here I was strapped to an electric table, Sam held captive no more than ten feet in front of me, and I was powerless. I couldn't save myself, let alone her.

"You are beset with a quandary, are you, Mr. Glick?" Rex said.

I looked down.

"I will give you some advice. Save yourself. From what I have learned about you, that seems to be what you are good at. So take my counsel. Save yourself. Save the girl."—waving at Sam—"Tell me who my traitor is. What do you care who this person is?"

I looked up and opened my mouth. The door to our right opened and in stepped Connie. "It was me," she said, her eyes hard and unmoving.

Rex turned to her, his face one of surprise and horror. It contorted like he'd bitten a bad grapefruit. "You?!" Anger crept into his voice as it rose. "You?!" He shook and his hands clenched into fists. "How could you?"

"I don't agree with you." Connie's face remained a mask of stone. "What you're doing is wrong."

"Wrong? It's our planet and these ... these ..."—Rex spat and sputtered, his face turning red—"*vermin* have overrun it, wasting its natural resources. They're destroying our Eden!"

"But you are wrong."

"Wrong? We created these beings, and we have the right to exterminate them before they destroy everything we've built."

Connie stepped closer. "They've already destroyed everything we built. And look what they've constructed in its place. Look how far they've come in ten thousand years. Anunnaki have forgotten their meager beginnings, and how long it took them to become a civilization."

"Humans had our help."

"They are our children. It was our responsibility to help them."

"Bah." Rex spun away and stomped to his desk. He slammed the cattle prod into it and stood there shaking his head. He turned on his heels and pointed the prod at Connie. "How could you do this to me? How could you betray everything I've worked for?"

Connie lowered her eyes. "My only regret is that I didn't leave with Catherine."

Rex leapt toward Connie. "Don't ever mention her name again."

Connie looked at me, her face drawn.

Rex followed her gaze and when his eyes landed on me, they narrowed. He backed up into his desk and sat on it, slumping, but keeping eye contact with me.

Slowly, I let the realization creep over me. The way Rex and Connie looked at each other. And the way they looked at me.

Then it was there, in big bold letters I couldn't ignore. Rex Ruther was my grandfather, and he was trying to destroy the world. And I was the only one who could stop him.

My life was a bad country song.

Rex pushed himself off the desk. "This changes nothing."

"What do you mean?" Connie said.

He turned to her. "This half-breed won't join us, and therefore, he is against us. He must be dealt with."

"He's your own flesh and blood!"

Rex shook his head. "My Catherine has been dead to me a long time. Therefore, this one means nothing to me."

He motioned to Whiny Guard. "Kill them both."

Suddenly, Sam straightened and twisted around. Her knee shot out at the guard who held her captive. For the second time in the last hour, Nut-Shot Guard had his balls rammed back into his intestines.

He dropped the rope that restrained her arms and keeled over sideways, hands gripping his boys. She wriggled out of her bonds and jumped on him. She wrestled his gun away and turned.

Whiny Guard appeared at her side in a blur and swung the butt of his gun toward her face. Connie reacted at the same time and tackled the guard.

Or rather, tried to. He outweighed her by about a hundred pounds, all of it muscle. Her tackle succeeded in upsetting his swing enough to deflect it to Sam's shoulder.

Sam cried out, and her gun fired several times as it swept left. Two bullets found Whiny Guard's chest.

He jerked backwards and fell flat, his own gun clattering to the side.

With an inhuman growl, Rex sped into Sam's midsection. The impact flung her backwards into the wall. She hit her head and sank to the floor.

He picked her gun up, saying, "If you want something done right—"

Connie slapped him, hard.

Rex recovered and stared at his daughter. His eyes burned fire, and I could tell she had never openly disobeyed him, much less touched him in anger. He backhanded her so hard she spun completely around, blood flying from her mouth. He raised the gun toward Sam.

"No!!!" I screamed.

And then I felt a rage boil up inside me like never before. My entire body fluxed and convulsed, and I felt an intense heat build and surge through me. I thought my eyes would explode. I remember staring at Rex's gun, and then my world turned red and faded.

The next thing I remember was my restraints being loosened. I lolled my head to the left and saw Connie's smiling face. She released me from the electrocution table, and my body slithered to the floor.

Rex was gone.

I looked over at Sam; she was still dazed. But alive. I crawled to her and tried to wrap my arms around her. Not enough strength. I got an arm across her legs and rested my head on her lap. So soft. So warm.

Sleep called, and I wanted to answer.

I closed my eyes.

Chapter 52

Somebody shook me. Voices. Shook me some more.

"Barry, get up. Get up!"

I opened my eyes. Sam was there, upside-down. "Get off me," she said.

"But you're so soft."

"We've got to go. Security will be here any moment."

"I'll confuse them while you two get away," Connie said.

I frowned. "You'll make them do Sudoku?"

She looked at me. "Get her out of here."

"Rex?" I said, struggling to sit up but not making much headway.

"He's gone. Hurry, you've got to go."

"But I have to stop him."

Sam pushed my head. "Get off me, Barry! I can't move."

I tried to roll off her, but I was weak. Connie grabbed my hand and pulled me to a standing wobble. Damn, she was strong. She shook my shoulders, and I focused on her.

"Can you fly?" she said, pointing toward an open window.

I blinked a few times, trying to gather myself.

"Barry. Listen to me. Take Samantha and fly out of here, now."

"What about you?"

"I'll be fine. He wouldn't dare hurt me."

The memory of Rex's backhand knocking Connie off her rocker popped into my mind. I tried to walk and stumbled over something. A hunk of molten metal. Huh?

Then it came flooding back to me, what I'd done. I'd melted Rex's gun. With my eyes! I grabbed Connie. "I've got Heat-Vision!"

Connie slapped me and pointed. "Go. Now."

We heard frantic shouting coming from the other side of the door. Distant, muffled.

"Hold on!" I said. I steadied my hands in front of me, looking at Sam. "Heat-Vision? It doesn't sound right. I don't like it. No marketing value. How about ... Laser-Vision?" I glanced at Connie. "Did it look like lasers? Did lasers shoot from my eyes?"

Connie pulled me toward the window. "Get the hell out of here. You can name it later."

The shouting came closer. Louder. More frantic.

I smiled at my aunt. "Thank you," I said.

I opened my arms to give her a hug. She shook her head and tried to push me toward the window. I snatched her close with my left arm, wrapped Sam into our hug-burrito with my right arm, and shot out the window. Thank God it was a big window.

Tucked close with the women screaming into both of my ears—in different frequencies—we rocketed into the damp night air.

My mind began to clear, and I knew what to do next.

I made a pass by the armory, focusing my new Heat-Ray-Laser-Vision-Thing through a window. I ignited something and started a chain reaction that created a fireball large enough to knock us sideways.

With that one cool move, I destroyed the Villain's hideout in a massive explosion that Bruce Willis would have been jealous of, and yet, all I could think of at that moment was how I could cut the time of cooking a pizza in half.

And I wouldn't have to leave the couch.

Chapter 53

We landed behind my apartment building. Flying always takes it out of me. But flying with an extra three hundred pounds really takes a toll. I needed to eat and regain my strength, but I needed to sleep too. I felt pretty woozy. We went inside and I headed straight for the couch.

"Barry?" Sam said.

I grunted as I spread out and got comfy.

"You're bleeding."

I tried to sit up, and when I couldn't, gave up and laid there. "Where?"

"Your leg."

I felt her pressing on my calf and then pain shot up my leg to my spine.

"Yow!"

"I think you've been shot."

Connie said, "You've definitely been shot."

They were both kneeling at my lower right leg. Connie disappeared and came back a minute later. Meanwhile, I had successfully pulled myself up, and Sam jammed a pillow behind me. I could see the blood.

"What are you doing?" I said as Connie began cutting my uniform from the bottom up.

"I need to get a better look at the wound."

I wondered if Kimmy could fix the suit.

Connie gave Sam a list of things to go get: gauze, knife, tweezers, towels, athletic tape, etc. If I had half that stuff, it was because Gordon had bought them for me. I'm such a bachelor I keep cookies in the bathroom drawers, just in case I get hungry while I'm in there.

Sam brought back an armload of stuff and dumped it on the coffee table. "This is all I could find."

"Hey, you mind getting me a beer while you're up?" I asked her.

She frowned until Connie said, "Yes. I need alcohol too. Liquor or rubbing alcohol. Something clear."

Sam headed to the kitchen. "Get me two," I said. "And some cookies."

I looked at Connie. "You know what you're doing, right?"

"Just settle back and don't think about the pain."

"I mean, you've gotten a bullet out before? You're not just gonna do some stuff you saw in a movie?"

She positioned towels under my leg, smiling at me. I didn't know her well enough to read her. Was she saying "I was a surgeon in a former life; you're in good hands" or "I saw this once on an episode of CSI, and I've always wanted to try it?"

Connie poured the alcohol over my leg, and I almost jumped off the couch. I bit back a girly yell and gave my aunt the meanest look in my repertoire. She never looked up to receive it. Instead, she grabbed the knife and tweezers. I covered my eyes before I saw what she did with them.

I'll tell you what it felt like, though. She jammed the knife into me all the way up to the Ginsu hilt, wiggled it around for about an hour, then flayed my skin open so she could shove a thick pair of pliers in and squeeze my bone. Once she found that my bone wouldn't come out so easily, she grabbed the bullet instead. Then she poured acid into the open wound, wiped it a few times with 40-grit sandpaper, applied a burlap sack, and said, "All done."

I wiped the sweat from my forehead and stopped screaming.

"Piece of cake," I said. "Somebody wanna get me breakfast so I can throw it up?"

Sam handed me one of my beers, and I chugged it. I said to Connie, "You invented that electro-table didn't you? You can tell me. I won't judge."

Connie looked at Sam. "Is he always this way?"

"I think so."

"Well, he needs to rest. Make sure he gets it."

Sam put her hand over mine. "Not a problem."

Connie patted my knee and stood up.

"Where are you going?" I asked.

"To find a way to stop my father. Those explosions tonight won't change a thing. The Apocalypse is still set to begin tomorrow, the thirteenth."

It was Thursday morning already.

The explosions would look good on the big screen when my movie came out, but she was right, they didn't affect the plan that was already in motion.

"About that," I said. "I have a few ideas how to stop Rex."

I told them the plan I'd dreamed up on the flight home.

"That just might work," Connie said. "But you two shouldn't stay here. He'll come for you."

"I've been meaning to take a vacation." I looked at Sam. "What do you think? You up for the beach? How about a mountain lake?" To

Connie, I said, "Where's the best place to ride out the Apocalypse, the beach or the mountains?"

Sam raised her eyebrows.

I waved my hand and struggled up. "Don't worry about it. Since I thought of the plan, I vote for a cozy lake cabin in the mountains."

"What are you doing? You need to rest," Sam said.

"Cleaning up and packing. You want me to go on vacation in a charred, bloody Superhero uniform? Not very sexy if you ask me." Sam didn't move. "Go ahead and get what you need from Connie. I'll call Kimmy and Gordon and tell them to lay low for a week while everything sorts itself out."

I started toward my room. "And then I'll search the net for a cabin with a Jacuzzi tub."

Chapter 54

We grabbed Little Man and headed to Smith Mountain Lake just over the Virginia state line. My plan was simple—exploit our opponent's weakness. That's Sports Psychology 101. Rex Ruther had done it by grabbing the people closest to me and kicking me while I was down. Literally.

It would have worked, but he hadn't counted on a simple Pakistani shop owner reigniting my capacity to care. Hell, I hadn't seen that one coming myself.

For us, exploiting the Anunnaki's weakness meant exposing their plan to everyone, because its very success depended on its secrecy. We'd use Sam's contacts in the news industry and Hannah's hacking expertise to get the story out there on every level, and if we did it right, we could stop the dominoes before they started to fall.

Sam pulled out her laptop and mobile phone and worked the whole drive up. I got us some Sausage and Egg McMuffins at a McDonald's drive-thru and stopped at a few gas stations to rack up more lottery money. Then we dropped by a Walmart to pick up a week's worth of supplies. We each had our own idea of what defined "supplies."

Me: beer, chips, frozen pizzas, beef jerky, cookies, cat food, etc.

Sam: regular food, flashlights, batteries, radio, medicine, bandages, bottled water, feminine products, etc.

By eleven, we'd pulled into a secluded cove at the lake. Sam found the wifi and continued working while I unpacked the Aztek. The cabin was smaller than I would have liked, but it had a washer and dryer, a full kitchen, and a huge Jacuzzi—you thought I was kidding about that?

And it also had a gorgeous view of the lake, the mountains rising majestically in the distance. It was the perfect spot to ride out the Apocalypse, although I was pretty sure we would turn it into more of a drunken weekend at Disney World than a real Apocalypse.

I made us a couple of ham and cheese sandwiches while Sam finished up her story.

At noon, she clicked a button with a flourish, closed the laptop, and stood. She stretched and worked out the kinks in her back, then looked at me and said, "Done."

"Everyone?"

"Everyone I know. My boss was stunned. Didn't know what to say at first. He wanted the exclusive and wasn't too happy about me contacting all the competition, but he'll get over it."

"Connie's names panned out?"

Sam grinned. "Oh yeah. They were some Anunnaki bigwigs that were highly placed in the government and financial sectors. Of course, I didn't say they were aliens, just members of a vast financial consortium with plans to make billions of dollars each.

"And when you add all the people you gave me that wanted to go on the record officially with the anomalies they found, the evidence is overwhelming." She nodded at the laptop. "Now it's out there and up to the people in charge to do what they do. You can't force them to take it seriously, but I think we have enough documentation to get their attention."

"Good. I checked in with Gordy while you were busy. He said Kimmy and Andrew were called to the home office in D.C. for debriefing. Sent a private jet for them and everything. Looks like Homeland Security is taking it seriously."

"That's promising."

"Yep. And I heard Hannah in the background telling him to get off the phone and pay attention to her."

Sam raised her eyebrows, and I said, "I know. Scary, right?"

We ate our sandwiches on the covered porch and enjoyed the birds chirping. There's nothing so relaxing as a cold beer on a mild summer afternoon.

Sam changed my bandages after lunch. The bullet wound had almost healed.

I convinced her to drive to the harbor a few miles east. I rented us a pontoon boat and drove it back to the cabin while she returned in the Aztek. She flipped on the TV as soon as we got back.

The story was everywhere.

CNN, NBC, ABC, CBS, FOX, MSNBC. You name it, every station we turned to was covering the "financial anomalies" Sam had alerted them to. Even C-SPAN had a low-level Senator giving a speech on the Senate floor to three attendees about how easily stocks could be manipulated.

Wall Street and other major international financial markets had already been suspended from trading. As of that moment, the world's economies had ground to an almost complete halt as the high muckety-mucks assessed the situation. Every major government enacted a temporary "price gouge moratorium" to stave off any panic of inflation or rising prices. The recurrent "expert opinion" was that the markets would remain closed through the weekend and reopen on Monday.

Every news anchor had a different theory about what could have happened if the information had not come to light as soon as it did. But they all seemed to agree on a single point: a crisis of epic proportions had been narrowly averted. And since every major government would have been affected, speculation was sporadic about who was behind the plot and what they'd hoped to accomplish. Of course, the buzz term of the day was "terrorist plot."

And maybe that wasn't too far off.

I logged into the Naked News to see what they were saying. Sam closed the laptop on my hands. I told her she'd never experienced real news unless it was reported by a topless woman, but she gave me the Super-Stare.

We settled on the porch again, fresh brews in hand, the scent of honeysuckles thick in the air.

As we were enjoying the fresh mountain air, Kimmy and Andrew were probably getting a medal and a pay raise. Gordy was probably sharing his hard drive with Hannah. And Lanny Lancaster was probably figuring out I was never going to fix his door.

Life was pretty good.

I nodded toward the water. "There's nothing like a sunset over a mountain lake, is it?"

Sam narrowed her eyes at me.

"What?"

"I wouldn't have figured it."

"Figured what?"

"You talk a big game, but you're really just a romantic at heart."

I shrugged. "I used to be. When I was young and naïve."

She hugged me and kissed my lips. "You're still a softie."

I gave it a few seconds, then said, "No. Right now, I'm definitely not soft."

Her mouth formed a crooked smile, then she jumped up and skipped back inside.

"Where are you—" But she was gone. *Damn, and it was just getting good.*

I leaned back in the love seat rocker and sipped my beer. A warm breeze rustled the trees and tickled the wind chime hanging from the eave. In the distance, a jet ski vroomed.

The porch door creaked open. I glanced over and spit my beer out.

"So what do you think?" Sam asked. She twirled and placed her hands on her hips. "I went all out for it. Fishnets and everything. Even got some spiky shoes."

I drooled onto my chest.

"You like?" She ran her hands down the uniform and over her thighs, tilting her head like a sixties pin-up model.

"Uh-huh."

"Should Nurse Gerber check on her patient now? See what that awful hard thing is and recommend a course of action to bring the swelling down?"

I nodded, still in shock.

"Well then. Let's see what we can do to get those restricting clothes off."

She pranced toward me, and I couldn't take my eyes off her. Not only did she have the little hat and garters and fishnets, she had a stethoscope.

I hadn't thought of that.

Cue badass theme music ...

Written by

Ross Cavins

Cover Concept and Design by

Ross Cavins & Joe Dodd

Illustrations by

The Amazing Joe Dodd

Published by

RCG Publishing

Please review this book on:

Amazon.com, Goodreads.com, and BN.com.

Your reviews help small publishers and
independent authors thrive!

About The Author

Ross Cavins is a web developer and author of the award-winning book, "Follow The Money." A self-appointed disciple of Elmore Leonard, he writes from his home in North Carolina where he pretends people pay him to do what he loves. His sense of humor is sort of like Disco: you dance to it even if you don't admit it.

He has also edited and published the award-winning humor book, *Thing Go Wrong For Me*, by Rodney LaCroix. And in 2014, this book, *Barry vs The Apocalypse*, became a Claymore Award Finalist. You can find him toiling away on the web at [RossCavins.com] and [dumbEcards.com].

And of course, keep up on the latest in Barry Glick's adventures: [BARRYvs.com].